THE COMPLETE ADVENTURES OF
SECRETS, INC., VOLUME 1

Frederick C. Davis

FREDERICK C. DAVIS

THE COMPLETE CASES OF

SECRETS, INC.

VOLUME 1

FREDERICK C. DAVIS

ILLUSTRATIONS BY
JOHN FLEMING GOULD

INTRODUCTION BY
WILL MURRAY

ALTUS

PRESS

BOSTON • 2015

TABLE OF CONTENTS

WILL MURRAY

FREDERICK CLYDE DAVIS was one of those prolific pulpsters who made his mark with the series character. His first pulp sale was to *Action Stories* while he was still in high school. "Grip of the Green" appeared in the magazine's third issue, dated November, 1921. "The Smoke Devil" in *The Detective Magazine* August 3, 1923, began his first series. It featured a criminal protagonist.

For a period after high school, Davis toiled as a cub reporter for the *St. Joseph News-Press*. He wrote pulp on the side.

Entering Dartmouth College in 1924, he wrote a short story every week while maintaining a grade point average of 3.8 to supplement a scholarship. Davis dropped out in his sophomore year to get married.

Davis soon became prolific for Fiction House and Street & Smith under his own name and a pseudonym of Art Buckley. When author Hal Dunning died, Davis was picked to continue his popular stories of Jim-Twin Allen, The White Wolf. But with the start of the Great Depression, Fiction House began foundering and S&S folded many of their magazines, including *Complete Stories* and *High Spot*, to which Davis contributed regularly.

He found a welcome in Harry Steeger's new outfit, Popular Publications. Steeger recalled that Davis was a friend of Rogers Terrill and that Terrill brought him on board. No doubt they knew one another from Terrill's editorial stint at the failing Fiction House. Terrill jumped over to Popular circa 1933.

"Fred Davis was a nose-to-the-grindstone type of author who was quite businesslike in his transactions and did not commit any of the pranks indulged in by Norvell Page," Steeger remembered. "As I told you, Norvell had a complete Spider outfit made for himself and flitted about the office in much the same manner as his hero. For Fred, such lighthearted doings would not have been part of his 'thing.'"

Davis did not dispute this assessment, telling *Detective Fiction Weekly* in '33:

> Writers are supposed to be interesting fellows who lead exciting lives. Some are and do. Unfortunately I'm not and don't.
>
> I've been told that I'm disgustingly normal.
>
> I think hard, plot carefully, and write fast, 6,000 words or more a day when I'm at the machine—which is, by the way, an electric one. (No one has ever invented an attachment to think up story ideas.) I work systematically and produce on schedule. To me writing magazine stories is a business and a study, but also it's fun.
>
> I've written almost every type of story—but it's most fun to write detective and mystery stories. And I try to write 'em so the reader will have as much fun reading them.

Frederick Davis was at the height of his pulp career during the first half of the Depression. He was by temperament a construction-ist.

"In 1930 or thereabouts," Davis once recounted, "I found myself back in Manhattan and it was then that I began to develop a full head of steam. Before long my output was 125,000 words a month. I kept up this pace month after month for years, with hardly a vacation. A day's stint at the typewriter was 30 pages. But I didn't work at the typewriter every day. I took time for research and for plotting. I have never written a story on a make-it-up-as-you-go-along basis. Every story I ever wrote was carefully plotted before the writing."

Davis was well established as a solid pulp professional by the time *Dime Detective* was launched in 1931, although he did not make his first appearance in its pages until '33, the year he was banging out his popular Moon Man stories over in rival *Ten Detective Aces,* published by A.A. Wyn's Magazine Publishers, another house that took him in after the Street & Smith implosion. For their *Western Trails,* he produced the Duke Buckland and Jingling Kid series. He had two series running in the back of *Secret Agent "X,"* Ravenwood and Paul Kirk. His "Show-Me" McGee was a *Detective Fiction Weekly* regular during this same period. Davis was a serious writing machine.

Davis paid the usual price for pulping them out.

> "One day in a pulp editor's office another writer asked me, 'Do you know that you have, on the stands right now, seven different magazines

with your name on the covers?' No, I hadn't known it. Another writer warned me, 'Sooner or later you'll have to cut down or you'll find yourself staggering around on your heels.' I shrugged this off; I wasn't feeling any strain. Yet this very thing came to pass. I had to pull myself back from the verge of a nervous crack-up. I didn't stop writing, but I did drastically reduce my output. Later, when I started doing books, my output went still lower mostly because I took greater care. If I had gone on to produce detective books at half the rate I had done pulp fiction, I would have been another John Creasy before Creasy was.

"I suppose it's fair to say I was one of the most prolific pulp writers. But not *the* most prolific. I don't know who was except probably the writer best known as Max Brand, who certainly made a bigger success of it than anyone else."

The nine stories starring Hollywood investigator Clay "Oke" Oakley of Secrets, Inc., began with "Blood on the Block," in the December 15, 1933 issue. It marked Davis's only third *DD* story, but the speed with which a sequel appeared suggests both Secrets, Inc., and Davis had already been tapped as regulars.

Assisted by the lovely Charmaine "Cherry" Morris and the rather effete Archibald Brixey, "Oke" Oakley investigated some of the most weird and ingenious crimes in the long history of *Dime Detective Magazine*—all centering around the film industry. They appeared during the period after Harry Steeger relinquished editorial control to Rogers Terrill, but before the legendary Ken White took over the magazine.

"Rogers Terrill was probably the hardest-working editor in the business," Davis noted. *"Dime Detective* did run stories with a horror touch in its beginning. Later, when Terrill took over the field for Pop Pubs, it began running stories of a higher grade, including those of Cornell Woolrich and Raymond Chandler."

This mix of hardboiled P.I.s and incipient weird menace story that would by year's end infiltrate *Dime Mystery Magazine* was first brewing in these pages. And Fred Davis, along with Norvell Page, was one of its earliest practitioners. It's difficult to imagine that at the same time these two men were turning out reams of wild yarns for other magazines, they were pseudonymously writing the monthly adventures of *Operator #5* and *The Spider,* in their own titles. On *Operator #5,* Davis wrote as "Curtis Steele."

He never commented on Secrets, Inc., except to reveal that its background was authentic.

"The Hollywood background of some of my stories came from a six-month sojourn in Los Angeles," he once explained. "I went there hoping to make a connection with one of the movie studios, but I never did."

Davis soon abandoned Oke Oakley for a fresh character and series. He produced several successive sleuths during his long association with *Dime Detective*, among them Carter Cole, M.D. Keyhole Kerry, Bill Brent and the Hackett series. When the magazine finally folded in 1949, he had a story in the penultimate issue.

In 1942, well into a transition from pulp magazines to slicks and hardcovers, Davis updated readers of *Writer's Digest* on his career to date:

> Since selling my first short story in 1921, I have published some 700 stories, more or less, in the magazines, the great majority of them long novelettes. They have ranged from the purely literary magazines, through *Collier's* and *The American* (a mystery novel in the February, 1942 issue) but most of them have been in the pulps.
>
> The Crime Club will bring out my eighth mystery book, *Deep Lay the Dead,* later this year. Most of my books have also been published in England. The last previous one is about to be released as a movie by Twentieth Century Fox under the title of *Who is Hope Schuyler?*
>
> I live in Bucks County, Pennsylvania, on a twenty-acre farm, where I'm busy at my writing job every day, day in and day out, from eight in the morning until about four in the afternoon, and where my wife is equally busy bringing up our son Ricky, who has just celebrated his first birthday.

Bucks County was popular with pulp writers. Paul Ernst lived there at the same time and Art Burks also took up residence there. So did Ted Tinsley. No doubt there were others.

During the 1940s, Davis established himself as a successful hardcover novelist under his own name and those of "Stephen Ransome" and "Murdo Coombs." He continued writing into the early 1970s, his final books as Ransome. He died in 1977.

BLOOD ON THE BLOCK

LIKE LEAVES FROM
A TREE IN FALL
THEY FLUTTERED
OFF—THE HEADS OF
THOSE MURDERED
MEN—WITHOUT THE
SLIGHTEST WARNING
THAT DEATH WAS
NEAR, FOR GHASTLY
HORROR STALKED
THE SETS OF SUPER-
CLASSICS STUDIO—THE
HEADLESS HEADSMAN'S
GHOST HAD COME TO
LIFE AND NO ONE KNEW
HIS WEAPON OR HIS
MOTIVE.

CHAPTER ONE

THE HEADLESS HEADSMAN

S OUND STAGE SEVEN of the great Super-Classics Studio was bustling with preparations for a climactic scene in Hollywood's latest horror picture.

Activity centered on a huge set constructed at one end of the vast room. A battery of hot, blinding lights concentrated upon a reproduction of a castle dungeon. Black electric cables snaked across the floor. Half a dozen "blimps"—sound-proofed recording cameras—were gazing upon the scene with crystal eyes. The place was alive with actors, technicians, gaffers—all of them waiting for the final word from Vladimir Kostov, the renowned director who was making the picture.

Kostov, a pudgy, cherub-faced little man whose hands were continually fluttering, strode on the set. His nervous gray eyes came to rest upon three men who were busy beside a wooden bench built against one of the set walls.

One of them was an actor garbed in full evening dress. The other two were minor assistants of Kostov's, and they were industriously binding the hands and ankles of the actor with strands of old rope. That done, they tied a handkerchief across his face, lifted him, and laid him on the bench.

Kostov's two assistants turned their attention to a young woman at the opposite side of the set. She was wearing a clinging evening gown of red velvet which was torn and stained. In spite of her fallen hair and the disarray of her dress, she was beautiful—the star of the picture, Elyse Seymore. Kostov stood by until her hands were bound behind her to a heavy iron ring in the wall.

"Remember, Elyse," the great director warned her in thick accents,

The head of the bound man dropped off the chopping block!

"one scream only. When you see the ax go up, only one scream. Then we cut."

"Yes, Mr. Kostov," said Miss Seymore.

The director's assistant, Arthur Driscoll, was at his elbow.

"To your place, Arthur," Kostov directed. "You begin lowering the hidden trap as soon as the victim is placed on the block. By the time we cut, the trap should be entirely open. Are we ready?"

"All set," declared Driscoll briskly.

Kostov shouted an order which sent the men scurrying off the set. He walked majestically to the chair, which bore his name, and surveyed the scene through his fingers, formed into a frame. The sound cameramen waited for his word. The monitor in the double-glass-windowed

booth high up on one wall bent to his dials and knobs. The gaffers kept their hands on the light switches. An assistant bawled out: "Quiet!"

Utter silence filled the cavernous room.

"Lights!"

Some of the lights blinked out. Others flashed on, completely changing the aspect of the scene. Beyond the walls of the set lay darkness; within them hovered a weird glow.

The dungeon of a castle. In the eery light the walls seemed to be of moldering stone, age-old, crusted with strange growths. In its depths a door could be seen dimly—a door that was heavy and stout, bound by rusted iron bands, held shut by a tremendous wrought-iron latch. On the stone floor were two patterned patches of light which shafted obliquely down from high, square windows criss-crossed with black bars. In the dim light and the silence it all looked uncannily real.

Kostov's voice came quietly. "Camera."

The big scene of Hollywood's latest horror feature, *The Headless Headsman,* had begun.

FOR A MOMENT the silence continued. In the glow of the shafts of light, the man on the bench could be seen vaguely, bound hand and foot, his mouth covered by a tightly drawn handkerchief. He was lying still, as if exhausted. Across the black dungeon, her shadow cast against the wall to which she was fastened, stood the woman. Her head was lowered in abject despair, her lustrous hair falling across her bare shoulders. For long seconds the man and the woman did not move.

Then a soft metallic sound echoed. The woman's head came up; she peered through the gloom in terror; and her gaze came to rest on the tremendous oaken door in the rear wall. Metal clanked again; and the heavy door began to open. Slowly it swung, while a ghostly glow came through it, spreading a fan of flickering light across the stone floor. And in the doorway appeared a figure.

It was a man garbed in immaculate evening dress. His gloved hands moved slowly as they dropped from the latch; his polished shoes glistened as he stepped into the dungeon; and he stood a moment silhouetted against the glimmering light coming from beyond. He stood erect, dignified—a walking horror.

For, above his white wing collar and tie, his neck was a ghastly red stump. He had no head.

The headless man walked slowly from the open door into the depths of the dungeon. The woman was staring at him, recoiling in speechless terror. The headless one turned as if to regard her—turned toward her a head which did not exist! Then he turned again, toward the man lying bound on the bench.

The man without a head had no eyes with which to see, but he moved with certainty. He lifted the man from the bench. The still form made no response; the bound man was unconscious. Carrying the form in his arms, the headless horror stepped toward the center of the dungeon.

In the middle of the floor stood a black object. It was a stout wooden block, tapering upward from its base; it was eighteen inches high, ancient and stained. The headless man lowered his prisoner carefully to the floor behind it. He propped the unconscious man on his knees, and balanced him so that his neck rested across the narrow top of the chopping block.

Then he turned again, while the terrified woman watched, and walked to the wall beside her. In the shaft of light, as he passed through it, his stump of a neck glistened redly. His gloved hands lifted, from two iron pegs in the wall, an ancient battle-ax.

The headless man returned slowly to the center of the room. He balanced himself on straddled legs beside the chopping block. He lifted the weighty ax and placed its sharp edge against the nape of the neck of the bound man, gauging his mark. Then he began to lift the ax—to swing it upward. Higher and higher it went—its edge glistening, a frightful thing in the shaft of light—poising for a powerful downward swing.

Suddenly a shrill scream of terror rang through the gloomy silence.

In the darkness beyond the set, director Vladimir Kostov rose, on his lips the call to end the scene.

But something happened.

There was no warning. There was no preliminary sound. There was nothing to prepare those who were watching for the ghastly horror they were about to witness.

The head of the bound man dropped from the chopping block.

It struck the floor with a dull thump. It rolled once, while blood streamed down the block and splashed the artificial stones. Then it came to rest on one cheek, staring out into the darkness with widened, popping eyes.

At the same instant the air vibrated with a booming tone—a pulsing note like that of a deep-voiced bell.

For a moment—quiet, while the reverberations of the bell died away.

Then another scream shrilled through the silence—and another and another—while the severed head lay in the patch of ghostly light and grimaced from the center of a slowly widening blackish pool.

VLADIMIR KOSTOV forgot to cry "Cut!" The script girl, who had been seated beside him, sprang from her chair whimpering, and rushed away through the darkness.

Kostov took three quick steps toward the set and stopped short.

"Lights!" he bellowed. "Lights!"

The stunned gaffers threw their switches. A flat glare flooded the sound stage. The weird lighting effect of the set vanished in the brilliance of the powerful globes which blinked on. For an instant there was a stunned, tense silence.

Then Elyse Seymore screamed again.

In the center of the set the headless apparition was still standing. He was erect beside the chopping block, but he lowered the battle-ax to the floor. In the blinding light the horror that was his neck lost its ghastliness. It was revealed as nothing more than a contrivance made of varnished *papier-mâché*.

The headless man dropped the ax, and his gloved hands tore at his shirt-front. A stud went flying as he ripped it open. From inside a pair of horrified eyes peered out as the tall, headless man became a short one with a head hidden below a pair of artificial shoulders.

Vladimir Kostov stood pale and trembling, peering at the chopping block, at the head lying beside it. He strode forward swiftly.

The blood on the block was wet and real. The head was a real head, the face, that of the actor who had played the part of the prisoner in the dungeon. The decapitated body was still braced against the block, bound hand and foot.

This was not part of the script of *The Headless Headsman*. This was something totally unexpected.

Arthur Driscoll rushed onto the set, stopped beside Kostov and stared, pale as death. "Good God, what's happened?" he blurted.

Kostov turned away, shaking from head to foot. He saw that two men were releasing Elyse Seymore from the ring which fastened her to the artificial stone wall; she was babbling hysterically.

"Go back—clear away!" he shouted hoarsely. "Stay off the set. Call the police!"

CHAPTER TWO

CLIENTS FOR OKE

CLAY OAKLEY, private investigator of affairs Hollywood-ian, was sitting at his desk in the *sanctum sanctorum* of Secrets, Inc., listening to a woman client talk.

She was a very beautiful woman, with golden hair and bright blue eyes and ripe red lips; hers were legs which might make Marlene Dietrich blush with envy.

It was Oakley's business to know Hollywood in all its sordid and glamorous phases, and knowing about Valerie Vance was one of the more pleasant elements of his job. Her first part, a year ago, had brought her remarkable notice. She was being groomed for stardom by Super-Classics. It was all the more remarkable because she was thirty and married and a mother. This morning, as she talked with Oakley, she looked unhappy and harassed.

"Why," asked Oakley when she paused, "do you want me to keep an eye on your husband? Are you contemplating a divorce?"

"No—not at all!" Miss Vance exclaimed. "Divorce is farthest from my mind, Mr. Oakley. I love my husband. I want you to watch him—to keep him from doing something rash that might—lead to trouble."

"As for instance?"

"My husband sometimes becomes insanely jealous—without just cause. He knows as well as I do that I love him devotedly—that I would never be guilty of even a slight indiscretion—but at times he loses control of himself and makes threats. Not to me, of course. Maurice is never harsh to me. But to—those he thinks are—interested in me."

"It must keep him busy," Oakley commented dryly.

Miss Vance smiled. "You see," she went on, "it was Arthur Driscoll who started me in films. I was just another Hollywood wife until he induced me to take a part. He is devoting himself to building me up into a star. He is Kostov's assistant now, but he is soon to be made a full-fledged director, and he has arranged a contract whereby I work with him exclusively. You must understand, Mr. Oakley, that between Arthur Driscoll and me it is purely business—nothing more.

"It's absurd for Maurice to be jealous. Arthur—well, Arthur is as happily married as I am, and as devoted to his wife as I am to my husband. But we are together a great deal of the time, talking over my part, and planning new pictures. It has become very difficult for me because Maurice—has threatened to kill Arthur Driscoll. Only last night he gave way to a savage burst of temper—the worst I've ever known."

"And threatened murder?"

VALERIE VANCE paused a moment, caught her breath visibly. Then, "Yes," she said. "Arthur and I were alone in Arthur's office at the studio, working over a new script. Maurice rushed in, without warning. He accused Arthur of—of absurd things—and gave Arthur no chance to defend himself. He shouted, 'If you ever lay a finger on Valerie, by God I'll kill you,' and then he rushed out."

"And you want me to watch your husband to prevent any such thing happening?"

"Yes."

"That means I'll have to keep an eye on him all the time he is not at home with you—when he's in the studio, included. That's a big order, Miss Vance."

"I am ready to pay any fee rather than—have Maurice do something so frightful. In time I'm sure he'll see how silly his suspicions are, but until then I must make sure that he doesn't give way and—kill Arthur."

Oakley eyed Miss Vance keenly. "Are you being absolutely honest with me?" he asked softly. "Your concern is for your husband and not for Arthur Driscoll?"

She lifted her clear eyes to Oakley's and returned his gaze unflinchingly. "My concern is for Maurice alone," she said.

Oakley teetered back in his chair. Bright sunshine splashed on his desk, and through the open window behind him came the noises of Hollywood Boulevard. Mixed with the grinding of a street car were the shrill cries of a newsboy. "Hextra-a! Hextra-a paypah!"

"Very well, Miss Vance," Oakley said quietly. "I'll take the case."

"Thank you," she said. "I—I'll give you a retainer."

Oakley rose as Miss Vance opened her purse and removed a checkbook from it. He stepped to the door of the waiting room and looked through.

Seated at a typewriter in the outer office was Miss Charmaine Morris. She was pretty, pert, red-headed, and could do things in the way of private investigating. She was powdering her patrician nose when Oakley said: "Cherry, darling, hop downstairs and grab one of those extras."

She went out of the door, a trim slender figure with perfectly curved ankles, her red hair sparkling in the sunlight. Oakley, smiling, returned to his desk, and Miss Vance handed him a check.

"Thank you. Where is your husband today?"

"Working at the studio," Miss Vance answered. "I will see that you get passes so that you can go on the set with him. I'm particularly worried because Kostov is making the picture, which means that Maurice and Arthur are working on the same set. I—I am placing full reliance on you, Mr. Oakley, and—"

The door opened swiftly and Cherry Morris's red head appeared.

"Oke!" she exclaimed.

She came in hurriedly, her eyes wide, alarmed. She placed on Oakley's desk, before him, the newspaper, and said not a word. Oakley peered down at the black headlines which screamed across the front page of *The Examiner*.

MAURICE VANCE BEHEADED ON SET!

A low moan came from Valerie Vance. She was leaning forward, peering at the electrifying headline. As she passed one perfect hand across her forehead, Oakley sprang toward her. But even as he moved, her eyes closed, and she slumped down in the chair. She had fainted.

HALF an hour later Oke Oakley was seated at his desk, frowning at the extra, snatching sentences here and there from its column. It had been a bad half hour for him. With Cherry Morris' help he had brought Miss Vance back to consciousness, then called a physician from the adjoining building. The doctor was escorting the actress home now. Cherry sat in the chair which Miss Vance had occupied and watched Oakley's grim face.

"It was a stupid thing for me to do," she said sheepishly. "Only, I'd heard everything she said, and when I saw that headline I came rushing in—"

"Not stupid, Cherry—brilliant," Oakley said. "Even if you didn't know what you were doing. She had to learn it anyhow. It was a shock, the way it came, but at least it provided me with a reaction to observe. She fainted. Interesting."

"She wasn't lying to you, Oke."

"Nope. Not any. She did love her husband and she really was worried about him. Queer. She wanted me to save him from committing murder, and suddenly it's the other way around—her husband gets it."

"No doubt that it was a murder?"

"None whatever. It certainly wasn't suicide—nobody'd choose to bump himself off that way—slice himself, rather. It couldn't be an accident either because, apparently, nobody knows how it happened. Murder, certainly."

Another voice spoke. "Very bloody," it said.

Mr. Archibald Brixey made the remark. He was Oakley's second assistant, a dapper, foppish young man of social lineage, whom hard times had forced into association with Hollywood's chief private investigator. Beneath Brixey's dandyish clothes were hard, lean muscles; behind his placid, aristocratic forehead there was real brain-matter.

"Very bloody," Oakley agreed. "And damned strange. I'd like nothing better than to jump into the middle of this case, but—"

The telephone rang and Cherry Morris reached for it. She announced. "Secrets, Incorporated," listened, said, "He's right here," handed the phone to Oakley and added in a whisper: "I'll bet a dinner against a new lipstick that you've got your wish. It's Kostov."

Oakley's eyes brightened. "Oakley speak—"

"Mr. Oakley, please come to the Super-Classics Studio at once!" came Kostov's thickly accented voice. "It is very important. I will be waiting for you in Mr. Madtz's office."

"I say, what—"

But the line had clicked and gone dead. Oakley smiled, replaced the instrument.

"I am being consulted on the subject of the recent decapitation," he told his assistants. "In fact, I'm commanded to report to Kostov. In this instance I don't mind being ordered about. Archie, stay here and hold down the fort. Cherry, put another dusting of powder on your elegant nose and grab my arm. We're off."

OAKLEY pulled his car up at the gate of the impressive Super-Classics Studio. It looked like a high-walled fortress and he had to talk his way past the gateman and three of the omnipresent studio cops before he got to the executive offices. With Cherry Morris at his side he finally entered a door labeled in gold—Samuel Madtz.

"Wait here, beautiful," he bade the young lady, "while I beard the movie lions in their dens."

Mr. Madtz's secretary, upon hearing Oakley's name, punched a number of buttons and spoke through an inter-office telephone. She conducted Oakley to a connecting door and opened it for him.

A chubby little man was beating his heels back and forth across the rug. A huge, sullen-faced man was slumped behind a desk. Both jerked and stared at Oakley as he came in.

The chubby one jabbed a quivering forefinger at the detective. "You've got to keep them away from me!" he exclaimed hoarsely, in heavy accents. "They're driving me crazy!"

Oakley was accustomed to the eccentric behavior of movie people. The little man, he knew, was the tempestuous Kostov. The larger one behind the desk was one of the principal supervisors of the studio, Sam Madtz, credited with some of its outstanding box-office hits. Kostov looked frantic and Madtz dismal.

"You're Oakley?" asked the supervisor, half rising. "Sit down, Oakley. It is Mr. Kostov who sent for you. Excuse me, please."

The supervisor stepped from the office as Oakley turned to Kostov. The dynamic little Russian was a bundle of nerves. He sputtered as he paced back and forth again.

"You want me to protect you from somebody?" Oakley asked him.

"Those—those police!" Kostov spat out the word. "They follow me around. They ask me questions, questions, questions. They think I am the murderer who chops off actors' heads. They're driving me crazy."

"Naturally, there's an investigation," Oakley commented.

Kostov glared. "Mr. Oakley, since it happened, this has been a madhouse. Everybody has been grilled by the police. Nobody can work any more. Everybody is suspected. Everybody is upset. A big detective talks like he thinks I'm a head-chopper."

"Sounds like McClane's on the job," Oakley said.

"McClane—that's his name!" Kostov blurted. "He hounds me. He thinks because I am the director of the picture, I am a murderer.

Questions—he asks me millions of questions. Probably he will try to arrest me. Oakley, you have got to keep him away from me."

"I can't very well stop a police investigation, you know," Oakley pointed out.

"No—you can't stop that," Kostov answered. "But you can save me from that idiot. You can investigate the case for me, and prove to him that I had nothing to do with it. That's why I want you to help me—to prove I am innocent—so I can go on with my work. Every single minute lost costs us thousands of dollars. You—you must clear this matter up, Oakley."

"A large order," Oakley smiled. "I'll tackle it, but it will cost you money. Are you retaining me personally?"

"Yes, because I am personally responsible for the completion of the picture on schedule. I will pay you anything you want. Oakley, for God's sake do something!"

Oakley rose, briskly. "If each lost minute costs thousands of dollars, let's not waste any," he said. "Take me to the place where this happened. I want to see that spot before—"

Suddenly the door swung open. Sam Madtz lumbered back in, still chewing his cigar, his face beet-red. Following Madtz came a tall, aesthetic-looking young man wearing an artist's smock. He looked gravely frightened and he was talking excitedly.

"Why does he think I should kill Vance?" he was demanding indignantly of Madtz. "I built the set, but does that make me a murderer? Is he crazy—accusing everyone in sight of being a criminal? I've put up with enough of it!"

KOSTOV signaled Oakley from the room, and as they passed through the outer office Cherry Morris joined them. Oakley introduced her to the director, then asked quietly: "Who's the excited chap—the one who built the set?"

"Stephen Devine," Kostov answered. "A true artist—a fine man. He has done marvelous things for me. Everyone is like that now—upset, half crazy. Devine, being questioned! It's senseless."

Kostov led the way rapidly out of the executive offices. As Oakley and Cherry Morris were following him down the steps, a young man rushed up. He was Arthur Driscoll. Oakley knew him by sight. Driscoll spoke to Kostov.

"Chief, the rushes are ready. The police are going to look at them. Will you come?"

"We certainly will come," Oakley spoke at once. "The cameras were running at the time, weren't they, Mr. Kostov?"

"Yes—you will be able to see everything," Kostov said.

"Lead the way," Oakley bade.

Kostov conducted them along one of the studio streets. Oakley glanced back at Arthur Driscoll, and saw that Driscoll was not following. He noted also that Driscoll seemed distrait. Then he lost sight of the young man as Kostov entered the lobby of a small theatre built into one of the studio buildings. In the theatre it was the custom to display the films of rival producers, and also to show the rushes of any shots made during the day of pictures under production. The place, Oakley noticed, was thronged with uniformed police and plainclothesmen.

In the doorway a huge, bull-necked detective stood. He tapped Kostov's arm and grinned at Oakley.

"Dear old McClane," Oakley greeted him. "How are things coming?"

McClane grunted. "Oakley, you're a smart boy, so see what you can make of it." To Kostov he remarked: "Well, we've gone all over the sound stage and we're through with it. You've been howling about losing time on the picture, so you can use it again whenever you like."

"Thank God for that!" Kostov said heartily.

He stepped into the theatre; and Oakley, following him, made an imperceptible signal to Cherry Morris. Cherry paused in the doorway and turned her wide eyes upon McClane. Oakley chuckled as he found a seat beside Kostov. Within a few minutes, he knew, Cherry would be reporting to him facts which McClane would never have told him directly.

CHAPTER THREE

THE SECOND HEAD

THE LITTLE THEATRE was furnished with luxurious seats. In the rear, just under the ports of the projection room, were a desk and several movable chairs on a platform. In front of the platform, the seats were filled with actors and actresses, technicians, executives, and fully a dozen police and plainclothesmen. McClane ambled in and seated himself as Oakley waited.

In a moment Cherry appeared, snuggled beside Oakley, and fluffed her red hair. "Darling, I learned everything McClane knows, but since he doesn't know anything that's not much help. Literally, he's stumped. He doesn't know what did it, or who might have done it, or anything else."

"No instrument of murder?"

"None whatever."

The lights went out. Kostov touched Oakley's arm. "Now you shall see exactly what happened. We have had the sound track trinted in, so you will hear too.

"The story of the picture is laid in an ancient castle in England, which is supposed to be haunted. The ghost is the Headless Headsman. The dungeon you will see is a relic of the past, and the ghost is that of a man who was once beheaded there. He has captured two prisoners and intends to kill them. That is enough so you will understand."

The screen began to flicker. Abruptly the scene appeared, dark, foreboding, sinister. It was immediately blotted out by a young man in shirt-sleeves who stepped into the center of the screen, exhibited a slate bearing cabalistic symbols for the information of the cutter in assembling the master negative, and clapped two sticks together to mark the start of the sound track. He stepped away, and the scene returned.

The dungeon looked dank and ancient. The two shafts of light shone on the floor, illuminating the crusted walls in a dim glow. On the bench at one side, a bound man was lying—Maurice Vance. Against the opposite wall Elyse Seymore was standing in an attitude of silent despair. For a moment there was no change in the scene.

The theatre was silent save for the faint hissing that issued from the loud-speaker.

Now a metallic sound echoed from the screen. The woman on the screen gazed toward the huge door in the rear wall; its latch was lifting and it was opening. It swung wide, and the headless figure appeared in silhouette.

Every person in the theatre knew that the headless man was a clever bit of costuming, but at sight of his stump of a neck they gasped.

The headless man came slowly into the room. He stooped, lifted the still figure of Maurice Vance in his arms, carried it to the chopping block, and placed the man so that his neck rested on its apex. Then, while the woman against the wall watched hypnotically, the headless figure lifted the battle-ax from the wall, and returned to the block.

A horrified tension filled the projection room as the headless figure placed the edge of the battle-ax against Vance's neck. Then the blade rose—higher and higher. When it flashed in the light, a terrific scream rang from the screen—uttered by Elyse Seymore. Then—

The head of Maurice Vance simply dropped to the floor. Those in the theatre gasped again. Dark blood flowed on the screen. The head rolled to a stop, looking out at the audience. At the same time the note of a bell sounded, deep, resonant, donging softly through the darkness.

The scene flickered off.

The lights flashed on.

OAKLEY blinked. Cherry Morris was gripping his arm tightly. Kostov was muttering curses. Those in the audience stared at each other in horrified silence. The quiet was broken by Detective-Lieutenant McClane, who reared out of his seat and shouted toward the projection booth: "Show that again!"

Now there began a long wait while the film was rewound.

Oakley sat back, his eyes grim. "Who played the part of the Headless Headsman? McClane has probably grilled hell out of him?"

"Yes, he has," Kostov answered. "Charles Beck plays the part—because he is short enough to seem headless, in that outfit, without appearing too tall. But he had nothing to do with it. You saw for yourself, the battle-ax never came down on Vance's neck."

"The police have it? Was it stained?"

"They have it, and it was not stained. Not a drop of blood was on it. The ax did not kill Vance."

"That bell—was it part of the scene?"

"That's the strange thing," Kostov answered. "No—it wasn't. I scarcely remembered that sound until I heard it again just now. It was not part of the scene as it was planned. I am positive that there is no bell on the sound stage, either."

"It means something," Oakley declared. "That bell-note sounded the instant Vance's head dropped."

The theatre went dark. The scene began exactly as before, and ran through to its termination in exactly the same manner. Oakley was particularly interested in the sound of the bell. He noted again that the tone rang softly the moment Vance's head dropped off.

Oakley remained in his seat when the lights flashed on. As the others left he asked Kostov: "Was the scene enacted exactly as it was rehearsed?"

"No. One thing went wrong. The trap did not open."

"The trap?" Oakley asked.

"In the side wall there is supposed to be a secret door. It was to begin to lower as the headsman raised the ax. By the time the ax got all the way up, the trap was supposed to be all the way open. The hero of the film was supposed to rush in and shoot the headsman. But the trap didn't open."

"Why didn't it?"

"I don't know. In the excitement I forgot all about it. Arthur Driscoll was supposed to be in charge of that piece of business because it was important. The trap is pulled open by a wire attached to a lever. I put Driscoll in charge of the lever with exact instructions. But for some reason he did not obey orders—and I haven't been able to ask him about it."

"I'll ask the questions," Oakley said rising. "First of all I want to look at the sound stage."

"I will take you."

KOSTOV led the way out of the theatre. It was growing dark. Cherry Morris kept her hand on Oakley's arm. They walked along the studio street toward the heavy sound-proof door of Sound Stage Seven.

Kostov tried it and found it locked. He produced a key from his pocket, used it, and drew the weighty door open. Oakley strode in first. The door thudded shut behind Cherry Morris. Kostov stepped past, to lead the way; but Oakley's hand shot out, gripped his arm and stopped him.

Except for a few bare bulbs burning high against the ceiling, the sound stage was dark. The flat light threw deep shadows, and at the far end of the stage the set of the dungeon was a black, ominous hollow.

"Wait a minute!" Oakley said in a tense whisper. "Somebody's in there!"

Suddenly a dark figure darted out of the set. It was a man, his coat-collar turned up to shield his face, a hat pulled low over his eyes. He moved swiftly, darted behind the set, and disappeared. One moment after he vanished in the darkness, his heels beat upon the floor; then even the sound died away.

"Funny," Kostov said. "Who could it be? The stage was locked."

Oakley was staring into the dungeon set. "Great Lord!" he gasped. "There's somebody—somebody on the chopping block!"

He broke into a swift run toward the set. Cherry Morris hurried after him. As he came closer, he could see the vague form more clearly. It was the figure of a man, kneeling—kneeling beside the ghastly block, his neck across its top! His collar had been torn away, and his head was lolling, his arms dangling limply.

"It's Driscoll!" Kostov exclaimed. "Driscoll! For God's sake—"

Suddenly, without warning, the head of Arthur Driscoll dropped to the floor!

Blood ran down the block. The head rolled and lay still. And in the silence of the stage rang that same vibrant tone that had sounded upon the death of Maurice Vance—the deep-toned ringing that seemed to come from a full-throated bell. Kostov and Oakley and Cherry Morris stood stock still, staring, their ears pulsing with the weird sound.

Then Cherry Morris screamed.

Oke Oakley blurted a curse and sprang forward. He darted past the set, glancing in horror at the body of Arthur Driscoll—a headless body now that had slumped to the floor. He sped into the dark recess into which he had seen the unknown man dart. Utter blackness enveloped him, darkness that baffled his eyes and halted him momentarily.

His hand snatched at the automatic in his arm-pit holster. He crouched, ready to fire. But there was only silence ahead of him—silence and black emptiness.

Suddenly a sound—a dull thump.

Oakley whirled. He dashed into the open again, peering about. Kostov and Cherry Morris were still in the center of the vast room, staring in horror at the dungeon set. Oakley moved fast—guessing at the source of the sound.

A movement in the gloom brought him to a sliding stop. He whirled, and glimpsed a figure against the wall—a black tall figure.

A white face was peering, scarcely visible in a shadow. Oakley leaped toward the man.

He grasped an arm. Instantly a hard fist crashed into his face. He jerked his gun up to fire; and another blow caught him just below the ribs. Gasping, disabled by reflex reactions which he could not control, he was helpless a moment. He scrambled to keep his grasp, but the man snatched his gun away, tore out of the shadows, leaped toward the side wall.

Oakley pulled himself up, gulping in air, and leaped. It was a flying tackle. His shoulder crashed against the legs of the man who was struggling toward the door. The impact tore him down. Oakley wriggled over, received a hard kick, then leaped up and planted a knee in the small of the other man's back. His gun clattered to the floor; he snatched it up and held it ready, panting.

The man beneath him writhed, gasped, struggled to get up. Oakley pushed the gun against his face.

And then over his shoulder he howled: "Get a light!"

Kostov was running toward Oakley. After a moment of fumbling Kostov's hand found a switch. Then a snap, a bright glare. Oakley reached down, grasped the shoulder of his captive, and turned the man face up.

His prisoner was white as paste, terror-stricken. He was garbed in an artist's smock. Kostov peered into the face of the man who was scenic designer for Super-Classics and blurted his name—"Steve Devine!"

CHAPTER FOUR

FIND THE WEAPON

OKE OAKLEY clambered to his feet.

The blow he had received in the solar plexus was still making him gulp. He fastened a fist in Devine's smock and jerked the man erect. The scenic designer's aesthetic features pictured horror. Convulsively he covered his face with his hands and gasped: "Oh, God!"

Oakley kept his automatic leveled.

Kostov was staring at Devine, his hands fluttering nervously. "What—Devine, what are you doing here?" he demanded.

"Well, well!" Oakley said, "we've caught a fish. Kostov, beat it out of here and get McClane. He must be somewhere near. Snap it up!"

Kostov, his hands still fluttering, loped toward the door through which they had entered. Devine backed away in horror, staring past Oakley at the ghastly sight on the set. The brighter light revealed the spectacle in all its gory frightfulness. Devine shuddered violently and tore his eyes away, covering his face.

"Suppose you cut out the acting," Oakley suggested sourly. "It won't go with McClane."

Devine was gripped in a spasm of revulsion. Oakley regarded him puzzledly. If this was acting, it was superb work. The scene designer collapsed into a chair and sobbed while Oakley kept him covered and waited.

A dull thump came from the door. Oakley glanced back to see McClane plodding in. Kostov followed him, and Sam Madtz lumbered after the director. Three plainclothesmen continued the grim parade, and one of them latched the door behind him. The big police detective hurried, stopped beside Oakley, and peered at the set.

"Great Lord!" he gasped. "Who's that? What's happened?"

"It's Driscoll," Oakley answered. "We've had another nice decapitation. Take Devine off my hands, will you?"

Sam Madtz was peering stolidly. "This is horrible—horrible!" he mumbled.

"You should not come, Sam!" Kostov ejaculated. "I told you you should not come."

McClane was looking bewildered. He grumbled an order, and two of the plainclothesmen closed in on Devine. Devine was scarcely aware of what was going on around him; he sat with his head in his cupped hands, shuddering.

"I was just ready to go—stopping in to see Madtz," McClane said confusedly. He glared at Devine. "What's the matter with him?"

"Just as Kostov and Miss Morris and I came in," Oakley explained, "we saw somebody rush off the set. It must have been Devine. Then we saw Driscoll on the chopping block, and the next moment Driscoll's head dropped off like a ripe apple. Devine was trying to beat it out of here when I grabbed him."

Devine heard that. He jerked erect and blurted: "That's not true! I wasn't trying to get away. I wasn't on the set. I—"

"Save your talk until I want it!" McClane snapped at him.

He turned and strode toward the set but Kostov and Madtz remained with the detectives and Devine. Oakley went with McClane, and they stopped on the artificial stones, eyeing the head and the headless body lying at the base of the chopping block.

"One sweet mess!" McClane diagnosed. "Did you see the face of the guy who ran off the set when you came in, Oakley?"

"No. It was dark and he moved fast. He beat it around behind the set. Then we saw Driscoll—and it happened—and Devine must have had time to run out again, along the wall toward the door."

McClane's eyes were searching the set. "No ax in sight this time—no nothing. What the hell did it, anyway? Did you see anything?"

Oakley wagged his head. "Not a thing. I'll swear on a stack of Gideons that Driscoll was alone on the set at the time. There was absolutely no one else in sight—not even the Headless Headsman this time. Just Driscoll, bent over the block, with his neck across the top of it. And suddenly—" Oakley made an eloquent gesture.

"How can a guy get his bean sliced off when there's no weapon and nobody around to use a weapon if there was one?" McClane questioned savagely.

"Then there was the sound of the bell," Oakley continued explaining. "It sounded the instant Driscoll's head dropped. Finding out what it is may mean something."

McClane grimaced and turned away. He called aside one of the plainclothesmen and ordered the medical examiner and fingerprint expert and photographer to be brought back. As the detective hurried away, McClane ordered one of the others: "Look all around the stage, Garson. Hunt for some kind of a bell. Don't let anything slip past you."

"There is no bell," Kostov said softly.

"Hunt for it anyway, Garson," McClane ordered, and plodded back to the set. "Though why in hell a murderer should take the trouble to ring a bell when he kills a guy is more than I can see."

"We'd better check up on doors, McClane," Oakley suggested. "Devine was already in the place when we came in, but he was probably heading for a different way out."

Oakley led the way to the narrow recess between the wall of the set and the wall of the sound stage, into which he had seen the furtive figure dart. It was lighted now. Wooden supports and dangling, snaky cables made a jungle of it. They crept back to the rearmost wall of the set, behind which there was only a narrow space filled with more braces and lights.

"Hello!" Oakley exclaimed. "Another door." This one filled almost half the rear wall of Sound Stage Seven. It was provided for the erection and removal of whole sections of sets; but in it was a smaller, ordinary door. Oakley tried it, and saw that it was fastened shut by a spring catch. McClane opened it and inspected the lock carefully.

"Easy to open from the inside, but locked from the outside," he said. "Probably fifty different people have keys."

Oakley was frowning puzzledly. "This is one way out. Devine could have made it. Then why the devil did he turn back into the stage? If he hadn't done that he could have slipped away clean."

"Maybe he found somebody outside the door and couldn't beat it without being seen."

"Then where was he heading when I grabbed him? He was halfway along the side wall."

Oakley and McClane groped their way back to the edge of the set. Beyond another jungle of lights and cables, they saw another door, in the side wall. It was a small one, heavy and sound-proof. Oakley inspected it and found that it was fastened with a spring lock, too.

"That's it," he said. "Devine was heading for this door when I grabbed him."

McCLANE tramped across the stage to Devine. The scene designer looked up haggardly at the big detective. McClane demanded: "You've got a key to this place, haven't you?"

"Yes, of course," Devine said breathily. "Everybody—most of us have—"

"All right!"

McClane snapped the man short, and trudged back to the dungeon set. Oakley went with him. They walked slowly to the grisly chopping block. Again they looked around, searching for a weapon; but there was none. A glance was enough to show them that death had come to Arthur Driscoll instantly, that whatever had severed the head had done so cleanly.

Oakley stepped close, inspecting the block. He saw that it was of solid wood, treated with acids so that it appeared to be very old. On its tapering sides designs were traced, made by a hot iron. The decoration was a series of concentric circles charred into the grain. Oakley stooped and made a close inspection.

"May mean something," he said. "Two small tacks on the front side."

He pointed them out. They were ordinary tacks imbedded in the wood at opposite sides of the outer circumference of the largest circle of the design, which was about fifteen inches across. They had not been driven home; their heads stood perhaps a sixteenth of an inch above the stained surface.

"Well?" McClane demanded.

"Don't know," Oakley answered. "Here's something else."

He was gazing directly down at the top of the block. With a pencil he probed at what seemed to be a small spot in the exact center. It became a hole, a quarter of an inch in diameter, obviously cut by a drill, and it extended down into the wood—how far, Oakley could not tell. McClane made impatient noises as he examined it.

"The carpenters probably drilled it when they built the block. It can't mean much," he said.

Oakley said nothing. He grasped the block and heaved against it, attempting to shove it aside. It would not yield; it was nailed or bolted to the raised flooring of the dungeon set. McClane pulled him back, mumbling something about not disturbing any evidence, and went plodding out across the stage again.

Oakley followed. Garson, dusty and moist, came from a far corner. He reported to McClane glumly. "I've looked over every square inch of this place, Mac—but there's no bell anywhere."

"There wouldn't be," McClane said sourly.

Oakley paused in thought. He stepped to Cherry Morris's side and spoke quietly. "Skip out to a telephone, beautiful," he said. "Get Archie on the wire. Tell him I want him to begin keeping an eye on Valerie Vance. He's not to let her out of his sight an instant. It's just a stab in the dark. But it seems a bit peculiar to me that the two men Valerie Vance was worried about—her husband and Driscoll—have both literally lost their heads. Run along now, like a good little girl."

McCLANE, his hands in his hip pockets, teetering on his bulldog toes, was regarding Devine grimly. The scene designer was still seated, exhausted, in the chair, trying to compose himself. McClane's gaze shifted to Kostov, then to Madtz.

"What'll this do to the picture?" he asked.

Madtz shrugged. "It's publicity, but what kind? Who knows what will happen? Maybe we won't be able to show the picture."

"Going ahead with it just the same? Who do you think you can get to put his neck across that chopping block now, instead of Vance?"

Kostov's hands fluttered. "If you don't make trouble for us, we can go on with the picture and find an actor to take the part. Plenty of them would be glad of the chance. My God, do you think everybody who takes the part will be killed?"

"What do you think?" McClane demanded, and fixed his glittering eyes on the director.

Kostov colored. "You look at me like you suspect me! Are you crazy? Because I am the director of the picture—"

"Did I say I suspected you?" McClane interrupted. "We've got the guy who ran out of that set just before Driscoll died, haven't we? Well?" He peered at Devine. "You can talk any time."

Devine rose unsteadily. "You're mistaken," he said. "I wasn't on the set before Driscoll was—killed. I wasn't even inside the stage. I—"

"If you're going to try to lie out—"

"I'm not lying!" Devine blurted. "Give me a chance, and I'll tell you exactly what happened. I came in the side door. I saw Kostov and the young lady standing in the middle of the stage, staring at the set. I saw Oakley running behind the set—and Driscoll—Driscoll was already dead."

"In other words," McClane remarked, "you're trying to say you didn't even come in the side door until after Driscoll was beheaded."

"That's true," Devine said, and he ran his tongue over his dry lips. "Kostov and the young lady were so intent on the set that they couldn't have noticed me coming in. Anyway, it was getting dark outside—and it was pretty dark in here. I was so stunned for a moment I didn't know what I was doing. And then Oakley rushed at me. I must have gone crazy, I guess. I tried to get away from him, to get out of here— and that's all there is to it."

"Yeah?" McClane drawled. "And why did you come into the set in the first place?"

"I was told by one of your detectives—this one"—Devine indicated Garson—"that I might. I'd left my hat and coat inside, and I was going home. Just before I opened the door I thought I heard a scream, but the door is sound-proof, and I wasn't sure."

"A scream?" McClane asked.

"Miss Morris screamed," Oakley remarked. "That was just after she saw what happened to Driscoll."

McClane teetered again and his shoes squeaked. "And," he went on, "can you prove that you were outside the sound stage when Driscoll was getting killed?"

"Yes," Devine said.

McClane jumped. "What?"

Devine said: "I certainly can prove it. I wasn't alone when I was outside the door. This detective"—and again Devine indicated Garson—"was with me.

"I met him outside the stage, in the street. I asked him if I could go in, and he said I could. Just as I took out my key to unlock the side door, we heard the scream—both of us—very faint. I said 'Probably it's a rehearsal—Kostov's behind schedule and he must be going right ahead.' He said 'I hope so.' Somebody came along and spoke to him, and I went in. That proves I was outside the stage when it happened, doesn't it?"

"God's sake!" McClane blasted. "Garson, is that right?"

Garson said solemnly: "That's the truth. Devine was with me outside when he heard the scream and thought it was a rehearsal. There's no chance of a mistake about it."

McClane snapped: "What the hell, Oakley—you telling me Devine was the man you saw beat it off the set! What Garson says proves he couldn't've been. It was somebody else. He did get out the rear door—he got away clean! By now he's God knows where!"

"I know, I know," Oakley moaned. "I've pulled a boner. The man I saw must've been the murderer—and he slipped me."

CHAPTER FIVE

THE UNKNOWN

OKE OAKLEY was burning the midnight oil. In the inner sanctum of Secrets, Inc., he was bent over his desk, studying a mass of material taken from the voluminous files of the office. In the big green cabinets in an adjoining room he kept stored every scrap of information it was possible to glean concerning anyone and everyone working in the film industry. Those heaped before him now revolved around Maurice Vance and Arthur Driscoll.

Oakley had come late from the Super-Classics Studio. He had been working at his desk for hours. Archibald Brixey was on the job of shadowing Valerie Vance; Charmaine Morris was dozing in an easy chair. Oakley kept reading assiduously.

On Arthur Driscoll he had been able to find nothing but a few clippings taken from the Film Daily and Variety. They were merely notes about Driscoll's activities in pictures then under production. The latest mentioned that he was soon to become a full-fledged director for Super-Classics. Concerning Maurice Vance there was a great deal more.

Oakley glanced over pages clipped from a motion-picture monthly. The article was headed, "Day By Day With Maurice Vance," and it purported to be excerpts from the actor's diary. It had been published six months past and it consisted of intimate sidelights on other movie personalities.

Oakley put it aside and took up a page of smaller clippings, more recent. There was a series of them.

May 5

Maurice Vance's contract will not be renewed when it expires in two weeks. The reason is said to be waning popularity. Vance is planning a vaudeville tour.

May 14

Maurice Vance has signed a new contract with Super-Classics. The studio reports he is being held because several suitable parts have come along for him.

August 14

Maurice Vance's option was taken up yesterday by Super-Classics and he will handle several prominent roles in forthcoming pictures. He is supposed to have received a sizeable advance in salary because of recent good work.

Oakley sighed and pushed the stuff aside. He found the prosperous shift in Vance's fortunes interesting but unprovocative. He sat a moment, then rose, trudged into the file room, and returned carrying a sheaf of newspaper clippings somewhat yellowed with age. On them Vance's name was ringed with blue pencil. The headline of the first clipping announced—

MRS. SAM MADTZ KILLED AT MALIBU

Oakley remembered the sensational case, and recalled that Maurice Vance's name had entered into it.

Sam Madtz was at his Beverly Hills home when the news reached him. He was conferring with Maurice Vance concerning a new picture about to go into production. Madtz and Vance rushed at once to Malibu Beach.

Later—

Madtz has stated that he is forced to accept the police theory that Mrs. Madtz was shot and killed by a thief whom she discovered in the act of rifling the safe of her beach house. The missing jewels bear out the theory. Maurice Vance, one of Madtz's closest friends, who was with him during the entire evening when the crime occurred, and who accompanied Madtz to Malibu, declared that Madtz had tried to prevail upon his wife not to take her jewels to the beach house, but she insisted.

Oakley sighed and pushed the clippings away. "Cherry," he said, "Oke is buffaloed. Has that bright head of yours been evolving any theories?"

Cherry Morris sighed and opened her eyes at Oakley. "Lady detectives," she yawned, "have got to get some sleep. Seriously, Oke, it's beyond me."

"I'm going to try my damnedest to crack this case," he declared, "because I came such a cropper this afternoon. There's no doubt of it—Devine is perfectly innocent. And I thought I had him cold!"

"I," said Cherry, "would like a hamburger sandwich."

Oakley's fingers drummed. "No weapon," he mused. "No murderer in sight. No bell, even though we heard a bell. No motive hinted. Nobody to suspect, unless you suspect the whole studio full of people. Only one interesting new angle—Driscoll's being knocked unconscious by a blow on the head before said head was lopped off."

"Would you," asked Cherry, "like a hamburger sandwich?"

Oakley kept drumming. "Rotten break—Driscoll's getting it just when he did. Remember what Kostov said about the thing that went wrong with the scene? The trap door didn't open as it should have. Driscoll was in charge of that, and he didn't follow orders to open the trap. Why didn't he?"

"With mustard," Cherry sighed.

"Why did he go back into the sound stage? What was he after?

The man we saw must have followed him in, blipped him on the bean, then put him on the block. I've got a hunch that Driscoll knew something—perhaps suspected who the murderer was—and the murderer got to him before I could. Well, he won't talk now."

"And relish," Cherry added.

The telephone rang. Oakley placed the receiver to his ear and a voice twanged through—the clipped, broad syllables of Archibald Brixey.

"Oke!" gasped Brixey. "Listen. I've been watching Valerie Vance. I'm down at Santa Monica Beach. I followed her down here in a car. She's gone into Stephen Devine's place, Oke—and they're alone there together."

Oakley tightened. "Stick, Archie!" he snapped. "I'm coming down!"

OAKLEY whirled the roadster out of the parking space beside Grauman's Chinese, whipped around corners and swung into Wilshire Boulevard. Straight to the west lay his destination. He whizzed through Beverly Hills, Westwood Village, Sawtelle, and hit Santa Monica at a good clip. When he spun into Ocean Avenue the broad, moonlit Pacific stretched away on his right.

He swung down to the Palisades Beach Road. With the surf beating on his left now, the high earth cliffs rearing on the opposite side of the road, he skirted behind the rows of beach houses. He passed Harold Lloyd's, Norma Shearer's, and began to slow when the immense edifice that was Marion Davies' place loomed into sight. Somewhere in here, Oakley knew, was Stephen Devine's cottage.

The road was usually lined with parked cars, but now there were few about. Oakley pulled onto a slope of sand, locked up, and slid from the seat. In only one of the houses along the beach was a light burning. It was a stucco building with a court in the rear which was separated from the road by an iron-posted gate. Oakley was striding toward it when a shadow emerged from a doorway and fell in step with him.

"You don't waste time getting places, Oke," said Archibald Brixey. "But you're too late. The lady stayed only a few minutes, and went back. I didn't follow her because I knew you'd want information right here. Devine's place is the one with the lights."

"Well?"

"Well, nothing," said Brixey. "They were in one of the rooms off the court and I didn't dare try to get in. Couldn't hear a word. Very sorry."

Oakley started in. "Devine seems to be up. I'll shoot a few question marks at him. Archie, ennoble the place with your presence until I come back. Better keep on the alert."

Oakley stepped toward the recessed door of Stephen Devine's house. As he waited for an answer to his ring, Archibald Brixey melted away into the shadows. Presently a port-hole opened in the door.

Oakley announced his desire to see Devine to the head which appeared, and a moment later the door was open. He was conducted by a maid through beautifully decorated rooms to a small one on the opposite side of the court. It was outfitted for work. Devine was rising from a drafting-board as Oakley entered.

Devine looked pale and wan. His hand was clammy in Oakley's, and he signaled his caller to a chair with a worried jerk. Oakley sat on the far side of a desk; Devine took the chair behind it, and teetered back. The window directly behind him was the one through which Oakley had seen the light shining; it was open a few inches. Devine flicked the ashes of a cigarette through it as he talked.

"I hope," he said, "I convinced you this afternoon."

"Quite," said Oakley. "A major *faux pas* on my part, for which I beg your pardon. I'm quite sure you're not the man who ran off the dungeon set when we came in. However—"

"However?" Devine questioned as Oakley paused.

"Assuming that that man was the murderer is only assuming," Oakley went on. "He may not be. My suspicions center around the set itself—I think some strange engine of death is concealed in it. Since you built the set—"

"Designed it," Devine corrected. "The carpenters built it. I supervised the work, but I did not take part in it. As for some strange machine of death being concealed in that set—I can't imagine what it might be."

"Nor I," Oakley admitted, "but something certainly decapitated two men while their heads were on the chopping block."

Devine turned pale at the mention. "The block is solid wood," he said. "It is nailed to the floor. The floor is quite ordinary, raised a foot or so above the sound-stage floor. I see no possibility—"

"What about the little hole drilled in the top of the block, and the two tacks on the front of it?"

"What?" Devine looked puzzled. "I know nothing about them. What could they mean?"

"What about the visit of Valerie Vance here tonight?" Oakley asked quietly. "What could that mean?"

Devine studied Oakley. He teetered back in his chair, eyes narrowed.

"Miss Vance and I are old friends," he said at last. "Also, Arthur Driscoll was a close friend of mine. She was so upset tonight, after hearing of his death, that she had to talk with someone. And she came here. She naturally wants to see the murderer of her husband and Driscoll punished. She has become obsessed with a suspicion. She has a feeling—no evidence, you understand—only an intuitive feeling that she knows who did it. She came here to talk it over with me."

"Why with you? Why didn't she go to McClane?"

"Because she has no tangible evidence—and to accuse this man mistakenly would be—dangerous."

"Dangerous? Why?"

Devine hesitated. "For many reasons. It's dangerous to accuse anyone of a serious crime mistakenly, isn't it? In this case it's especially so. I listened to Valerie, and sent her home to rest but—" Devine leaned forward. "It is very strange. She named the man whom I suspect myself."

"You too?" Oakley exclaimed. "Why the devil are you keeping so close-mouthed? Are you making this up as you go along, or what?"

Devine studied Oakley's face, teetering back in his chair. For a long moment he was silent. Suddenly he sat up straight, balanced against the window sill.

"Oakley, I'll come clean with you," he stated abruptly. "Valerie's suspicions I can't very well discuss, except to say that she has a strong hunch. To make it all the more terrible, Arthur Driscoll suspected the same man—the same man Valerie and I suspect!"

"What! Driscoll knew who killed Vance?"

"No, he didn't know. But he had a suspicion. I believe he became convinced of it immediately. Vance was killed—but he didn't speak to me about it. He didn't dare—for the same reason that I have hesitated to speak. I believe he began to reason it out, to make an investigation—an investigation of his own—and he must have stumbled upon the truth, because the murderer silenced him!"

OAKLEY pondered this a moment. "You mean he went back into the sound stage while the place was empty—while the rushes were being shown—because he thought he could find evidence—"

"Yes—it must be true. The murderer must have been watching him—or perhaps was hiding in the sound stage for some reason. He attacked Arthur—silenced him—to save himself."

"But what could Driscoll have known that no one else—"

"Listen to me, Oakley. Driscoll and I were working together on the set for *The Headless Headsman.* Kostov was especially fussy about the atmospheric effect of the dungeon. The set was finished the day before Kostov was ready for it—yesterday. Scenes were scheduled for shooting this afternoon. Last night, after checking over details in the script, Driscoll and I went into the sound stage to make sure everything was all right.

"Kostov had cautioned us to see that the trap in the dungeon wall would work properly. I'd helped rig up the lever arrangement. Driscoll was going to operate it, and I wanted to explain it to him. It was really very simple—a pull on the lever would allow a weight to shift, and a counterweight would lower the trap door—yet it had to be done carefully. We went into the sound stage—"

Devine's eyes narrowed as he remembered the scene.

"—and it was dark, except for a single light beside the set. We were alone there. At least we thought we were alone—but as we went toward the set, we heard footfalls. They seemed to be behind the walls of the set. We called, but there was no answer. We thought that was curious, so we walked together behind the set. We were just in time to see the rear door closing—a man stealing outside."

"The rear door!"

"Yes. He was in the dark, but we could see him dimly. The light was in our faces—I fancy he could see us better than we could see him. He hurried out, closing the door. Arthur and I opened it and looked across the lot—but he was gone."

"Did you see his face?"

"No. We came back, wondering what it meant, but it was late and I began to show Arthur the lever arrangement for the trap in the wall of the set. It didn't work. That surprised me, because I'd tested it only a short time before, and it was right. Now it wasn't. I went over the contraption and discovered that someone had twisted a wire off the lever. It was only a few minutes' work to fix it again—but it was strange—"

"Why should anyone have changed that arrangement?"

"I had no idea at the time. I showed Arthur how to work the thing, and he did it several times. We went out and prepared to leave the studio—then I discovered that I'd left my pipe on the set. We went back together. As soon as we opened the door we saw—"

Devine paused, leaning back, eyes narrowed. "We saw someone hurry off the set. This time we got a better glimpse of him. We still couldn't see his face, but both of us thought it was the same man. He hurried out of sight again, and slipped out the back door. Well—it was late, but I took a look at the trap arrangement and found it all right. Arthur and I left. We thought nothing more of it until—until Vance died. Then I began to feel—"

Devine's voice became a tense whisper. "I felt that the man we had seen had, somehow, been preparing to kill. I felt that he had been doing something—what, I don't know—that he had intended to keep an absolute secret. Whatever he did, it was to kill Vance."

Oakley gestured impatiently. "Who the devil was it you saw? You didn't see his face, but both you and Driscoll recognized his build—is that it? You agreed on the man? Good Lord, Devine, what's his name?"

Devine hesitated again. His lips moved to form the name of the man he had seen lurking on Sound Stage Seven. And suddenly—

A terrified gasp came from Devine's mouth. He straightened in his chair as if in a spasm. His hands flew to his throat and a horrible choking sound broke out of it.

Oakley leaped up. "Devine! What's the matter?"

Devine was kicking crazily; he was clawing at his neck. His eyes popped in horror; he gave another gasp which broke off sharply. Oakley sprang around the desk toward him, vaguely conscious that somewhere outside the house the motor of an automobile was roaring. Then Oakley stopped short, staring.

Devine's clawing fingers were wet with blood. Crimson was streaming over the man's collar. His face was twisted into a horrible grimace; his eyes were popping. And then—

Devine collapsed off the chair. As he spilled over, Oakley caught at him. Nausea hit at Oakley's stomach as he stared. The scene designer's body slipped from his numbed hands and spilled onto the floor. And beside it, now, lay—Stephen Devine's severed head!

CHAPTER SIX

SIX CAKES OF SOAP

OAKLEY sprang back. His ears were ringing with a strange reverberation—a sound like a muted bell. It had struck through the air the instant Devine collapsed, headless—now it was gone. But, somewhere outside the house, the rushing of the automobile engine could still be heard, swiftly moving away.

Oakley stood a moment, frozen, staring at the decapitated corpse on the floor. Suddenly he tore away. He leaped from the room, snatching crazily at his automatic. He bounded through two rooms and grabbed at the knob of the outer door. He flung it open and howled: "Archie!"

He whirled as he heard a slow step through the sand which bordered the sidewalk. A tall figure was slouching toward him, arms bent to his lowered head. He stumbled, tottered; and Oakley jumped toward him.

"Archie! God's sake!"

He shook his assistant violently and was immediately sorry for it. Brixey's head lolled. Blood was flowing from a cut in his temple.

"The car—stop the—car!" he gasped.

"What car?" Oakley snapped. He peered along the road. "What about it?"

Archibald Brixey summoned strength. He fumbled a flask from his pocket. Oakley unscrewed its cap and dashed a shot of rye down Brixey's throat. Brixey took in air, steadied himself, and peered at Oakley with brightening eyes.

"He—socked me with a tire iron."

"Who did? What happened? Good Lord, Archie, speak up! Devine's in there now with his head cut off—and it happened right in front of my eyes!"

Brixey gasped. "I didn't notice that car until it—it started up, all of a sudden. It was just parked here, that's all—just as they are all along the road. I didn't know there was anyone in it. But all at once the engine roared and it started up with a jerk. Only it didn't move—"

"Archie, make sense!"

"I'm jolly well telling you what happened, Oke!" Brixey sighed. "The engine raced like mad, and the wheels spun—but it scarcely moved. Just a few inches. I stepped out of the doorway and went toward it. Just trying to be helpful, I poked my head in the door and began to ask what the trouble was. I received a very undeserved blow upon the head."

"Who was in that car, Archie?"

"I don't know. I didn't have time to see. A man, that's all. He made a swing and clipped me with the iron. I staggered back, and at the same time the car went off like a shot. Funny thing—I heard a bell strike—"

"You heard that, too? Out here?"

"It was right out here," Brixey answered. "It seemed to come out of the air all around me. But I was seeing and hearing so many odd things—"

"Come inside, Archie!" Oakley snapped.

He dragged Brixey in through the open entrance. In the room adjoining Devine's study he left Brixey. The connecting door was open. Oakley peered in, half believing the thing he had witnessed was a weird dream; but the reality of the horror on the floor was only too vivid. Devine, like Vance and Driscoll, had suffered swift and terrible death. Oakley closed the door, went to the phone.

"Police headquarters," he said.

THE POLICE came—in swarms. First a detachment from the Santa Monica headquarters swooped down on the beach house of Stephen Devine. While Oakley was subjected to a barrage of questions, a radio squad car from Los Angeles whined down the Palisades Road, and stopped; and another horde of detectives crowded in. Leading them was McClane.

Oakley was again subjected to cross-examination. Then McClane plodded into the death room and viewed the cadaver.

"Whatever does it makes a neat job," he observed. "Sliced off as slick as a whistle, just like the other two."

Oakley sighed. "I was looking right at Devine when it happened, McClane. Suddenly he was choking and his neck was bleeding, and the next moment he collapsed, headless. We were alone in the room, absolutely. I didn't see any weapon. It's the damnedest thing I ever ran up against."

McClane grunted. "Well, there's nothing to do but try to fit it in with the two other killings—but how it's going to be done is beyond me. You heard that bell again—and a car starting up and—aw, hell!"

Oakley asked: "Do you mind if I look around a bit, McClane?"

"Go as far as you like."

He watched glumly as Oakley moved about the room. The investigator paused at the window which looked out into the court. Its curtains were stained with blood, and there were streaks of red across the panes. Oakley covered his hands with a handkerchief and carefully raised the sash.

Peering at the upper edge of the lower frame he remarked: "Here's something, McClane. Two nicks."

McClane came and peered also. Oakley indicated, on the inner edge of the upper cross-piece of the lower sash, two indentations in the wood. They seemed to have been pressed deep; they were about six inches apart and an eighth of an inch wide. McClane said nothing as Oakley stooped and peered again.

On the lower edge of the upper sash he found similar nicks, the same depth and width and the same distance apart.

"Make something of it?" Oakley asked.

"Might be anything," McClane grunted.

Oakley straightened, and pushed the curtains away. He inspected the frame of the window. Suddenly he took a sharp breath, and reached up. He ran his fingertips over something protruding from the wood—a tack. It was quite ordinary, driven within a fraction of an inch of its head. Turning quickly, Oakley found another on the opposite side of the frame.

"Same as on the chopping block!" he exclaimed.

McClane gave another grunt. "Maybe they mean something," he said, "but damned if I can see it."

When the medical examiner and fingerprint expert and police photographer arrived, Oakley was forced to abandon the death room. He had no idea that the experts would discover anything of importance. He, an eye-witness, was completely at a loss. Returning to the forward rooms, where the frightened maid and Archibald Brixey were being bombarded with questions, he relapsed into silent thought.

The investigation came to a bewildered standstill. McClane plodded about morosely, poking aimlessly. The police detectives settled into chairs and smoked. Reporters began coming, crowding the place anew. Cornered, Oakley could not escape them. Hours passed before he succeeded in shaking himself free. At last, grasping Brixey's arm, he negotiated the door.

In Oakley's roadster they started back toward Hollywood, silent, thoughtful.

Dawn was breaking.

IT WAS past noon when Oakley opened the door labeled *Secrets, Inc.*, and strode into his inner sanctum. Cherry Morris was there, her red hair resplendent in the eternal California sunshine shafting through the window. Archibald Brixey was also present, a plaster on his injured temple.

Oakley sighed and asked: "Anything new?"

"Nothing new, Oke," said Cherry brightly. "The rest of the population of God's Country still have their heads. Where've you been, may I ask?"

"Trying to get a little sleep. Hopeless," Oakley sighed. "I'm hungry. Hold down the fort, Cherry, darling, while I grab a bite. Archie, come along if you like."

"I jolly well like," said Archie.

They trod down the steps and walked a short distance along Hollywood Boulevard. Oakley led Brixey into a small lunch room.

They perched on stools at a counter and a comely blonde waitress approached. Brixey ordered coffee; Oakley asked for a sliced-egg sandwich. They lapsed into silence while the girl began to produce the food before their eyes.

The cups of coffee slid before them. The waitress took a hard-boiled egg from a refrigerated glass counter and began peeling it.

"Well named, these waitresses," Brixey observed. "They're all waiting for a director to spot them and hand them five-year contracts in the movies."

Oakley said nothing. The girl peeled the last of the shell from the egg. She deposited the white ovoid on a little patented contraption and brought a lever down upon it. The egg was magically converted into slices. Oakley peered, jerked, came to his feet.

"Good Lord!" he gasped. "Good Lord!"

"I say!" Brixey gasped. "What can be the matter?"

Oakley snatched at his hat. "Archie—come along!"

He slapped a dollar bill on the counter, whirled and dashed from the restaurant. Brixey scurried after him as he darted across the boulevard toward the parking space. Through the restaurant window a goggle-eyed waitress watched in amazement.

OAKLEY shot his roadster into the street and whipped around a corner, whizzed along a broad street, penetrating deep into the studio environs.

At last he swung to the curb beside the tremendous Super-Classics lot and, with Brixey trotting beside him, pushed through the gate into the outer office.

Moments later Oakley was past the guard at the door and climbing the steps of the executive offices. Without a glance at costumed figures walking past him, he pushed through the door labeled *Vladimir Kostov*. To the girl at the desk he said briskly: "I want to see Mr. Kostov—in a hurry."

She recognized Oakley. "Mr. Kostov is in Mr. Madtz's office."

Oakley tramped down the corridor. He pushed through Madtz's door, repulsed the girl at the desk with a glance, and without ceremony trod into the modernistic room beyond. Madtz was at his desk, chewing on a cigar; Kostov was pacing up and down the rug.

"Sorry, to come barging in like this," Oke said quickly. "But I've got it! At least, part of it."

"Part of what?" Kostov demanded.

"I think I know how these men were killed. I want to go to Sound Stage Seven right now. I need your help. Come along, will you?"

Madtz rose, his cigar dangling in his teeth. Kostov's gray eyes widened. Oakley turned and walked out, with Brixey trotting beside him. Kostov and Madtz followed. They strode quickly along the studio street to the door of the sound stage. Trying it, Oakley found it locked.

"You mean to say you know—who did it?" Kostov demanded excitedly as he produced a key and inserted it in a lock.

"No, not who," Oakley said. "How."

The door swung open. Oakley marched into the vast realm of darkness of the sound stage. Kostov snapped switches, and lights appeared. The weird dungeon set emerged from the gloom fantastically. As the door thudded shut, Oakley walked toward it, stopped, and regarded it grimly.

"What have you found out, Oakley?" Madtz demanded. "If you know—"

"I'm not sure yet," Oakley interrupted. "More lights, if you please. Kostov, I want you on that set."

Kostov snapped more switches, and a greater brilliance flooded the dungeon. Oakley trod into the set peering around; and his gaze stopped on the sinister chopping block. Turning to the wall, he perceived a large rectangle faintly marked against the squares of artificial stone.

"The trap?" he asked.

"Yes," Kostov said.

"Open it," bade Oakley.

The director turned away puzzledly. Against the side wall a large metal lever hung. It was mounted on an iron plate bolted to the wall, and a wire was attached to it. Kostov grasped the handle of the lever and slowly moved it. It swung an inch—two inches—then a full foot. And the trap in the side of the set did not move.

"It doesn't work," Kostov said.

"I thought so!"

Oakley strode toward the lever. He pulled it back and forth; it moved without resistance. The wire attached to it ran upward along the wall. Above, under the ceiling, were metal grille platforms, on which a number of lights were arranged. Iron ladders led up to them.

Oakley peered at the bewildering maze above, then turned back. At the edge of the set, he paused, and dropped to his knees. The flooring of artificial stones was raised a foot above the floor of the sound stage. Kostov, Madtz and Brixey looked on in surprise as Oakley went flat and began to wriggle under the set.

Oakley pulled himself completely out of sight beneath the flooring. Brixey, unable to restrain his curiosity, lowered his head and peered under. Oakley was wriggling along, groping through the darkness. "Deuced strange," Brixey muttered as Oakley began to slide out again.

"What the devil are you up to, Oakley?" Kostov demanded.

Oakley's eyes were gleaming. "Listen," he said. "I want you to get me, say, six bars of soap. Any kind of bar soap. Also a bucket of water. Also a screwdriver and a small hammer. Hurry!"

Kostov turned, bewildered, and trudged out of the corner door. Sam Madtz watched Oakley pace back and forth in front of the set.

Oakley's eyes were shining. Suddenly he turned, went to one of the iron ladders fixed to the wall and climbed up.

HE CREPT along one of the elevated platforms, and fumbled along the wall. Presently he found the loose wire which connected with the lever below. Dangling it, he saw that its other end was attached to a heavy weight which was hanging low, on another wire. Oakley gripped the second wire and began drawing the weight upward.

He heaved it to the edge of the metal platform and balanced it there. It was plummet-shaped, and the wire was affixed to a handle on it. Immediately he turned, slipped down the ladder, and hurried back to the set. Again he dropped on all fours. This time face up, he slipped beneath the flooring of the set and wriggled out of sight.

A faint noise came from beneath the flooring. Presently Oakley wriggled himself out again. His eyes were still afire. He was coming to his feet when the outer door opened and Kostov hurried in. Under one of Kostov's arms the screw-driver and hammer were held; in one hand he was carrying a bucket of water, and in the other half a dozen bars of laundry soap.

Oakley took the odd assortment, put the things on the floor next to the chopping block. And as he set to work, silently, the others drew close and watched.

From the hole in the center of the block a loop of wire was protruding. Oakley grasped it, pulled, drew it into a larger loop. Then he carefully loosened the two tacks on the front of the block. He bent the large loop of wire forward—it was steel and springy—then tapped the tacks down on it. When he straightened, the loop of wire lay in the outer circle of the burned-in decoration; it was scarcely visible.

"Notice," said Oakley. "The wire is discolored. The discoloration is blood."

Rapidly he peeled the wrappers from the six cakes of soap. He immersed them one by one in the pail of water. Then he stuck the six cakes together, like bricks; the moisture made them adhere. That done, he placed the cube of soap on the top of the chopping block.

"Soap," he said absently, "is about the same consistency as flesh—offers the same resistance. Ballistic experts fire bullets into big cakes of soap in order to see what effect they will have when entering a human body. That big cake of soap on the block there, represents a man's neck."

"My word!" said Archie Brixey.

"Now, watch!" Oakley warned.

He strode from the set toward the side wall. He placed his hand on the metal lever. One moment he waited, gesturing that the men should not look at him, but at the chopping block. When their eyes were directed to the cake of soap on the top of it, Oakley began slowly to pull the lever.

The thing happened swiftly.

The loop of steel wire, almost invisible, hidden in the burned circle in the wooden block, suddenly disappeared completely. The block of soap jerked. At the same instant a sound filled the great room—the vibrant tone that had seemed to be the single toll of a deep-throated bell!

Oakley sprang toward the set. He lifted the soap from the block and exhibited it. Now it was in two pieces—it had been cut through the center as cleanly as though a knife had slashed downward through it!

"That," said Oakley quietly, "is how it was done."

CHAPTER SEVEN

LOOP OF DEATH

KOSTOV and Madtz stared at Oakley. "But I don't understand!" the director exclaimed. "What did you do? What—"

"It explains a great deal," Oakley said swiftly. "And it is not difficult to understand. That's why the trap door didn't open. The lever arrangement which was to move it had been disconnected, and this other murderous arrangement substituted. Arthur Driscoll didn't fail to follow your directions during the taking of the scene, Kostov. He did as he was told. He pulled that lever. And when he pulled that lever, Vance died—beheaded."

"Great Heavens—you mean Driscoll murdered Vance?" Sam Madtz asked swiftly.

"No—not at all. Driscoll didn't realize what he was doing. He thought he was opening the trap in the wall of the set. In reality, he was setting off the machine of death—but he didn't know it. It's a damned diabolical thing. Driscoll actually committed the murder of

Vance, unintentionally—the machine was arranged by the murderer, and Driscoll was his unwitting tool."

"How do you know—" Kostov began.

"It's perfectly evident, isn't it, that Driscoll himself was not guilty of planning Vance's murder?" Oakley asked quickly. "He died himself, by the same machine. He was killed by the same man who killed Vance—because Driscoll suspected both the identity of the murderer and the means of killing Vance. That's why Driscoll came back to this set alone, after the police investigation was ended—to try to find out what had happened. The murderer surprised him, knocked him unconscious, and killed him on that chopping block."

"But—how?" Madtz demanded.

"Very simple. Beneath the floor of this set a wire is stretched—a strong, fine, steel wire. One end of it is fastened over there, at the far side of the set. The wire runs under the floor, directly beneath the chopping block. It passes from under the floor at the opposite side of the set, and around a pulley, and runs up to the ceiling. There it passes over two more small pulleys; and the other end of it is fastened to that heavy weight you see hanging against the wall.

"When the machine was set to kill, that weight was hoisted high up and balanced on the edge of the platform above. That gave the wire under the set floor some slack. The murderer doubled the wire into a loop, beneath the set floor, and passed it up through the block, through the hole drilled down its center. The hole goes completely through the block and the floor. Then the loop which came out the top of the block was bent over and tacked down loosely, hidden in that large circle of the decoration. It was done just as you saw me do it."

"But—"

"Then the machine was all set. Notice how it worked. Vance's head was on the block. The weight at the other end of the wire was balanced on the edge of the platform above. Another wire leading from the weight was attached to the lever which was supposed to open the trap in the side of the set. Driscoll, at the proper time, began to move the lever to open the trap.

"The moving lever pulled the one wire which tilted the weight off the edge of the high platform. The weight fell instantly. The sharp pull jerked at the loop of wire hidden in the design of the block. Torn from under the heads of the tacks, it sprang to a vertical position—a loop of fine steel. The heavy, falling weight tightened that loop instantly around Vance's neck. The momentum of the weight was enough to draw the wire through Vance's neck.

"Still pulled by the falling weight, the wire loop disappeared down the hole in the block. Beneath the floor it snapped taut. It made the sound we heard—the sound like a bell, or a plucked harp string. Muffled by the floor of the set, it sounded more like a bell. And there you have it—the way Vance was beheaded, the way the weapon of murder vanished, the way a killing was done when the murderer was not near his victim!"

"Great God!" gasped Madtz.

"THE MURDERER killed Driscoll in the same way," Oakley went on. "By setting the machine, after knocking Driscoll unconscious, and putting him on the block. Driscoll was silenced because he learned too much. Almost exactly the same thing happened to Stephen Devine last night.

"In the case of Devine, the loop of wire was hidden behind the curtains of the window of his study, and held in place lightly by two tacks. The wire ran out through the window, through the crack between the upper and lower sashes. There was free passage for it because the window was partly opened. The murderer had stolen into Devine's beach house—probably climbed over the gate into the court and in through the study window while Devine was away. He led the wire out along the wall and tied it to some part of his car, which was parked just outside.

"He waited until Devine sat in his chair and leaned back. Then, like a flash, he started the car up. The pull on the wire snapped the loop down over Devine's head. Imagine all the power of a big car's motor drawing that loop of fine steel wire tight about Devine's neck! The car had a little trouble getting away because the sand, which is always blowing across the road there, made the wheels spin. But when they caught, the loop passed completely through Devine's neck—and it was done. The car rushed away, trailing the wire after it—making the instrument of murder vanish. The murderer must have stopped a short distance away and dragged the wire in."

"Then it was the murderer who bopped me on the head last night!" Brixey gasped.

"It was," Oakley declared solemnly. "And if Devine hadn't died at the very instant he did, I would have heard him speak the murderer's name. He suspected the man, as Driscoll did. We know perfectly well now why Driscoll and Devine died—because the murderer knew he was suspected by them, and feared them. As for a motive for Vance's death—that's still a mystery. And the identity of the man who did it—I'm still in the dark."

"It doesn't seem possible that a wire could behead a man in that way, Oakley," Sam Madtz said in a breath.

"That thin steel wire is as effective as a razor-edged knife, with all the power of that falling weight behind it," Oakley insisted. "Powerful enough to cut through even a man's vertebrae like a falling ax."

"Yes, yes!" Kostov exclaimed. "Oakley, I want you to come to my office at once."

The director was peering at Oakley strangely. Oakley noted the menacing glitter in his eyes—a cold, deep gleam. He said, softly: "Very well."

KOSTOV turned abruptly and marched toward the door. Sam Madtz followed. Oakley trod along beside Archibald Brixey. Without speaking they walked to the entrance of the executive building, and up the stairs. Kostov went into his office with Madtz behind him. Oakley gestured Brixey to wait in the reception room.

The director sat at his desk, jerked open a drawer, withdrew a check book, and scribbled. He ripped the check out and offered it to Oakley.

Oakley took it, puzzled. The check was made out to the amount of three thousand dollars. "What's this?" he asked.

"Your fee. Is it enough?"

"Plenty—but I'm not through with the case, Kostov. Not nearly through."

Kostov's face was white. "You are definitely through, Oakley. I hired you. I've finished with you. It is not necessary for you to handle the case further. You are a private detective, and I am discharging you. You may go."

Oakley's eyes narrowed. "Just like that?" he asked slowly. "Firing me out like some dumb extra, are you? Not quite, Kostov."

Kostov jerked to his feet. "You are not wanted here!" he snapped. "I tell you, you are finished. You are paid off. Now you may go. Leave here at once!"

Oakley began to smile. He leaned across the desk toward the director.

"Kostov," he said, "I don't do that. When I take hold of a case, I keep hold of it. I don't let go—ever."

He tore the check deliberately in two, then quartered it and tossed the fragments on Kostov's desk. Turning, he walked out of the office.

A SINGLE light burned in the inner office of Secrets, Inc., concentrating its brilliance on Oakley's desk. Busy noises came through the open window—swarms of cars leaving Grauman's Chinese following the night's performance. In the office, Oakley paced back and forth. Cherry Morris and Archie Brixey watched him curiously.

"I say," Brixey remarked, breaking the silence, "I am very suspicious of this chap Kostov. His throwing you out of the case so abruptly, Oke—it was very rude."

Oakley scarcely heard. He paused at his desk, fingered through a mass of data taken from his files. With a baffled gesture he pushed them aside; and his heels thumped across the room again. Presently he remarked absently to Cherry: "Try to get Valerie Vance on the wire again, will you? It's damned strange that nobody at all answers her phone. If she—if she suspects the same man Driscoll and Devine suspected—"

His voice trailed off. Cherry reached for the telephone. Before her rosy fingertips touched it, the bell clattered. She picked it up quickly.

"Secrets, Incorporated," she announced. "Oh, yes. He's been trying to get you." And holding the instrument toward Oakley, she said quietly: "It's the lady herself."

"Miss Vance," Oakley said into the transmitter.

"Mr. Oakley," the actress's voice came strainedly, "if you're not busy, will you come to my place at once? I'm worried—very worried. If you—"

"I'll come at once," Oakley told her. "I've been trying to get you on the phone all day."

"I've been at the studio, and the servants are away," Miss Vance answered. "Perhaps I'm—I'm unduly nervous, but I'm alone here now, and I've been hearing strange noises about the place. It sounds as if someone were prowling about. I'm so uneasy—"

Oakley's eyes grew grim. "Lock yourself in," he told her sharply. "You have cause to be worried. You're the only living person who has any sound suspicion of who perpetrated the three murders, Miss Vance. Do you understand—the need for caution?"

"Yes. If you'll come—"

"One thing before I start," Oakley went on. "I've noticed in an old movie magazine an article by your husband called *Day by Day with Maurice Vance.* It was written in diary form. Now, did he choose that form as a convenience, or did he actually take excerpts from a diary he kept?"

"He kept a diary," the actress answered, "and he used it as a basis for the article. Why do you ask that?"

"I want to see that record. I realize it's private, but my reason is important. I'm leaving at once."

Oakley set down the phone. Cherry was already on her feet, powdering her shapely nose. Archibald Brixey eagerly rose. Oakley pulled on his hat and smiled grimly.

"Come along," he said.

He left the office with his assistants at his side, crossed to the parking space and got his roadster. With Cherry between him and Brixey, he pulled into the boulevard and sped away. He turned toward the north. The Vance place, he knew, was located in the hills outside Hollywood, in a comparatively unsettled section.

The cement road soon turned to tar, and the tar to unpaved dirt. Hollywood lay behind, a glow against the sky. The moon was obscured; the open hill country was black, swept by a wind from the ocean. Oakley drove swiftly, silent; Cherry and Archie Brixey said nothing.

At last Oakley turned off the road, toward a high iron gate. A hill lay before him, bordered by a tall iron-spiked fence. It was the Vance place. The house itself was out of sight beyond the crest of the hill. The driveway had been cut through, so that it rose between two steep banks. The gate was closed and locked.

Oakley slipped from the wheel, went to the gate, and rang the bell. He waited thoughtfully, long minutes. Getting no response, he rang again. Oakley peered at Cherry and Brixey, who were still in the car. "I don't like this," he said.

He was reaching for the bell again when his hand froze in midair. He grew rigid, and stared through the darkness blanketing the hillside. On the sighing wind came a sound—a scream!

It was prolonged, shrill—and it disappeared, quavering, in the silence.

"I say!" Brixey exclaimed.

Oakley whipped about. "Archie, stay here with Cherry!" he snapped. "Keep an eye on this gate. I'm going in."

Oakley fastened hands on the iron bars of the gate. He braced against it, pulled up. A sharp heave brought him to its top; there he balanced above the sharp pointed spikes. With a twist he threw himself over. Inside the gate he paused again, listening, his hand stealing toward the automatic in his arm-pit holster.

He started on a run up the driveway. The house over the crest loomed suddenly. It was a sprawling *hacienda,* white-walled; lights were shining through half a score of windows. Oakley trotted on, peering into the darkness intently.

And abruptly another scream, penetrating, bearing a note of terror, carried on the wind!

CHAPTER EIGHT

WIRED FOR MURDER

OAKLEY ran faster. The driveway curved to the broad front of the house and passed a door above which a light was burning. Oakley sprang toward the door, clacked its latch. It yielded against his shoulder.

As he darted into the dimly lighted hallway beyond, he sensed movement ahead. Swiftly he swung toward a door through which shaded light was streaming. He brought up short on the sill, his automatic leveled.

The room was empty. Whatever had caused the rustle of movement was gone now. But someone had been in the room a second before. On the opposite side half of a French door was standing wide open. Near it a large chair was overturned. Against one wall stood an antique Spanish desk, and the cupboard space beneath its leaf was open. Out of it spilled bundles of papers, and a bond box which had been jerked out lay open on the rug.

Oakley started across the room—and stopped. He heard a moan behind him—a low cry of pain. Oakley spun, returned to the hall, went along it swiftly. He passed a dark door, turned back. From inside the sound came again, an anguished groan.

Oakley slipped through. His hand passed the wall near the door jamb, found a switch, and pressed it. Amber lights flooded the room with a dim glow. It was a bedroom. Oakley whirled toward the bed.

Valerie Vance was lying there, sprawled on the spread. Her hair was torn down, as though she had engaged in a struggle. Her dress had been ripped from one shoulder. A red bruise shone on the delicate line of her jaw. Oakley bent over her swiftly. Her eyes fluttered, and she clutched at him.

"He came!" she gasped. "He—" She covered her face with her hands and sobbed.

"Easy! Who came? Who did this to you?"

Her eyes widened in terror. She blurted: "I—I didn't see his face!"

"Stay here," Oakley commanded her grimly. "He can't be far away. My assistants are at the gate. If anything else happens—call!"

HE HURRIED from the room, along the hall, into the library. He glanced swiftly at the disarray as he crossed to the open French door. Quickly he slipped outside into the darkness, his automatic ready for action. He peered across the slope of the hill, alert for any sound or movement—but the darkness was silent.

Oakley skirted off. The estate covered many acres. It had been extensively gardened; the blackness of the trees and bushes made it a bewildering jungle. All around it ran the high iron-spiked fence. Oakley spent precious moments circling the expansive grounds. At last he paused, breathing hard, grimly disgusted.

The prowler was gone.

He hurried back to the French door. The library was still empty; Miss Vance had remained in the bedroom. Oakley went at once to the rifled antique desk. He fumbled through the contents of the bond box, flipped over a packet of papers. He saw correspondence addressed to Maurice Vance, sheafs of personal papers. The prowler had ripped into all of them in a hasty search.

Oakley straightened, looked around. The overturned chair indicated a swift exit. Perhaps the prowler had been in the room when Oakley had reached the front entrance! The chair had been standing in front of the French doors. Oakley peered at it, and half consciously raised it to its legs. He saw that something had lain hidden under it.

The object was a small, black, leather covered book. Oakley snatched it up, flipped through its pages. Maurice Vance's name was stamped in the leather in gold; it was a diary. The entries flicked under Oakley's thumb. His eyes lighted as he paused and read swiftly a score of finely written lines under the date of May 10.

"That's it!" he exclaimed aloud. "That's it!"

He realized that the prowler had been after this diary—searching for it in the desk. Oakley's sudden entrance had surprised him. He had darted toward the French doors, tripped over the chair, and dropped the book in his desperate hurry to get out of the room before he was seen. Oakley looked around swiftly, stepped toward the open door; then he paused, peering again at the open page of the diary.

The lines drew his intent gaze. He did not glimpse a furtive movement beside him. He did not see a thick arm swing from behind the heavy drapes which curtained the closed half of the French door. The arm raised; the hand was gripping an automatic by its butt. It poised—slashed downward.

The weapon cracked against the side of Oakley's head. Oakley groaned as his knees bent. The diary dropped from his numbed fingers as he collapsed.

Swiftly a heavy-set man stepped from behind the curtain. His hat was pulled low to shade his eyes; his coat collar was turned up. He leveled his automatic at the sprawled form of Oakley, his eyes glinting madly in the shadow of his hat brim. Then, swiftly, he snatched the diary of Maurice Vance from the floor and thrust it into his pocket.

He whirled, darted out of the room, then ran quickly through the darkness, across the slope of the hill, toward the fence. The unpaved road circled past the side of the estate, and in the center of the side fence was a gate. The man stopped at the gate, threw it wide. He hastened to a heavy sedan which was waiting outside in the darkness.

Quickly he started the motor. Without turning on the lights, he backed the car through the open gate. Quickly, still backing, he sent the sedan crawling up the slope toward the house.

AT THE MAIN gate Oakley's roadster stood lightless and still. In its front seat Cherry Morris and Archibald Brixey sat and listened. Brixey raised his head alertly. Abruptly he stood, peering into the darkness beyond the fence.

"I hear a car," he said. "It's inside the place. Wait here a moment. Archie is going to investigate."

He slipped out of the roadster and ran along the road with his long legs swinging swiftly. When he reached the corner of the fence he ran still faster. Abruptly he stopped, peering. He saw a gate ahead—open. And from beyond it the sound of an automobile motor was audible.

Brixey sped back toward Oakley's roadster. Cherry Morris had climbed out of the car. Archie exclaimed: "Something's up. I'm going in through the side gate. Stay here, Cherry!"

He bounded off again. Cherry Morris heard his swift footfalls beating in the gravel along the fence. She held tight to her purse and spoke to herself disgustedly. "Stay here," she said, "my foot!"

She went to the locked gate. She could still hear Brixey running, and the motor spinning inside the estate. Cherry Morris threw modesty to the winds. She pulled up her skirts, exposing perfect silken legs, fastened her shapely hands on the iron bars of the gate, and began to climb.

In a moment she was over.

THE SOFT whir of the motor sounded hushed in the night. The heavy sedan was easing to a stop near the open French door of the *hacienda*. The big man at the wheel ducked out, letting the motor run. Quickly, from beneath the floor mat of the rear seat, he removed a coil of fine, steel wire.

Working quickly, he twisted one end of the wire about the rear bumper of the car. Moving quickly toward the house, he trailed the wire after him. Beside the French door was a window; it was unlatched. He threw it up a few inches, then slipped the looped end of the wire through the crack between the sashes. Then he entered through the French door, made sure the slip-loop was loose, and peered at the still form of Oke Oakley on the floor.

He pulled his hat still lower, and stepped past Oakley, then eased into the hall, toward the lighted door of the bedroom. When he appeared in the frame of the door, Valerie Vance was rising from the bed. She saw him; a stifled cry broke from her lips; she fell back in terror. With a savage bound, the big man was upon her.

He clapped a hand over her mouth. She struggled desperately to tear away from him, but his strength was too great for her. He pinned her to the bed with his weight, lifted his gun. On the point of crashing it against Valerie Vance's head he paused. The actress' body trembled, and went lax. Her eyes closed; she had fainted.

The big man chuckled gutturally. He pocketed his gun, looked about quickly. Jerking open a dresser drawer, he removed half a dozen handkerchiefs. Swiftly he knotted them together, and bound the actress' ankles and hands. Then he forced a gag into her mouth, lifted her, with a heave, and strode out.

He carried her across the library, where Oke Oakley still lay, trudged out the French door, and put the limp body of the actress in the rear seat. Then, turning back, he reentered the library. He picked up the loop of steel wire from the floor, turned toward Oakley, holding the loop to slip it over Oakley's head.

Oakley moved. He opened his eyes to see the immense figure over him, reaching one hairy hand toward his shoulder, to lift him. He saw the steel loop poised above his head. He jerked back, kicked out desperately. His heels thrust against the stomach of the towering man above him. The big man staggered back, gasping. Oakley tottered to his knees, to his feet.

His gun had fallen from his hand; it lay out of reach. The big man was crouching, still holding the loop of steel wire ready—reaching to drop it about Oakley's neck. Oakley saw the shining strand passing through the crack of the window beside the French door. He heard the car running outside. He realized that that glinting circle meant death—the death Stephen Devine had suffered.

Suddenly the big man leaped.

Oakley met the rush desperately. The blow on the head had weakened him, but dizzy, tottering, he grappled. The tremendous weight of the other man bore against him, thrusting him back. Oakley lowered his chin to his chest and struck out blindly.

He beat the hulking body with his fists. He threw his arms up, desperately striving to clinch. The big man shrank under the power of Oakley's blows; twisted to free himself. Oakley flailed him again, madly. Then one of the big man's fists crashed past his arms and clicked to the point of Oakley's chin. Oakley swayed back.

Outside he heard, dimly, a call: "Oke! Oke!" It was the voice of Archibald Brixey.

The huge man jerked about. He snatched at the automatic sagging in his pocket. With a last desperate effort Oakley grabbed for that gun arm.

The big automatic jerked; a blast of fire came from it and a bullet drilled into the floor. A hoarse cry of rage came from the huge, menacing figure. He whirled in desperation, and darted outside as

Cherry Morris' voice called: "Oke! Oke!" from the side of the house. She saw him spring to the wheel of his waiting sedan.

The big car lurched off as Oke Oakley staggered to the window. He caught the glitter of the steel wire in the light—a wire streaking outward through the French door. As the car shot away, the wire snapped tight. One instant it sang; the next the vibrant bell-like tone filled the air.

Oakley was peering at the car. He saw the black figure at the wheel, the head bent forward. And he saw that head disappear as if by some weird magic—vanish off the shoulders of the man who was sending the car hurtling away!

The sedan lurched. It swung crazily. Its twisted front wheels slowed it as it nosed toward an oak. The crash came suddenly—a ringing of metal as the front bumper bent, a rending shock as the fenders crumpled. The car bucked to a stop, its collapsed hood buried against the side of the tree.

Cherry Morris cried out.

Brixey's call came again—"Oke!"

"Here," Oakley answered. Then said in a breath: "He got it—as he gave it to Vance and Driscoll and Devine—as he tried to give it to me!"

Archibald Brixey ran into the light and stopped short. "Good Heavens!" he blurted. "The man at the wheel of that car hasn't any head!"

Oakley took a deep breath. "I know," he said. "He had the wire run in through the window, all set to decapitate me. While he was fighting with me, the loop went over his own head. He didn't know it, but it was still around his neck when he ran out the door and started the car. The wire coming in the window and out the door—one end fastened to the car and the other to his neck—that did it."

"Oke—are you all right?" Cherry demanded.

"Almost all right," he said.

"Who is it—out there in the car?"

"Madtz," said Oakley. "Sam Madtz."

IN McCLANE'S office at police headquarters, Oakley explained it all again. Vladimir Kostov was there, and Valerie Vance; and, of course, Cherry Morris and Archibald Brixey. McClane listened glumly.

"It was pretty well known, wasn't it," Oakley asked the police detective, "that Mrs. Madtz had a habit of playing around with handsome young juvenile actors—that she was two-timing Madtz right and left?"

"Yeah. That's why we suspected him of bumping off his wife at the Malibu Beach cottage nine months ago," McClane answered. "But Madtz had an iron-clad alibi, and we had to let it go as a burglar job, even though it looked fishy to me."

"An iron-clad alibi—and a fake," Oakley said. "A faked alibi supplied by Maurice Vance. Vance said Madtz was with him the entire evening, when Mrs. Madtz was killed—but it wasn't true. Vance's diary proves that. He was at Santa Monica Beach, alone—the entry he made under that date proves it.

"There's the picture. Madtz, in a fit of jealousy, killed his wife. He made Vance supply him with an alibi. Vance was fading out of pictures—he helped Madtz, and Madtz helped him by giving him new contracts. It wasn't blackmail on Vance's part—Madtz was buying him. Vance's fake alibi saved Madtz—but Madtz brooded—he was worried."

"He was never the same after the death of his wife," Kostov agreed.

"Worried," Oakley went on, "because he feared that Vance might make a slip—in one of his bursts of temper. Vance was a continual menace to Madtz. One word from Vance, one slip, and Madtz would go to the chair. He brooded over it until he was half mad, and determined to save himself in the only way possible—by silencing Vance.

"So he killed Vance. He was forced to kill Driscoll and Devine because they both had seen him on Sound Stage Seven the night he rigged up the decapitating machine. Even that didn't clear him. He had been forced from one murder to three—and yet he wasn't safe. Vance's diary was also a menace. He went to the Vance place last night to get it—and that was the end of him."

Kostov sighed. "Perhaps," he said, "I did not behave like a good citizen, Oakley, in calling you off the case so suddenly. But as soon as you discovered how the murders were committed, I knew Madtz had done it. Why? Because Madtz had a small cut on his hand. I'd noticed it once, in the studio room, when the bandage slipped off. It wasn't a knife cut—it looked like a burn made by a cord. When you discovered the machine of death, I knew a wire had made that cut on Madtz's hand and—I only wanted to save myself, my job, like everyone else working in the studios. Madtz was the most powerful executive in Super-Classics and—"

"You wanted to protect him, the same as Devine did," Oakley nodded. "You weren't absolutely sure, but sure enough to know that if Madtz chose to get rid of you, he'd do it instantly. In a way, I don't blame you for wanting to avoid trouble with him. He was a madman— desperate to save himself. If Driscoll and Devine hadn't happened to see him on the set that night, he probably would have gotten away with it.

"And I probably would never have doped out how it was done if I hadn't happened to order a sliced-egg sandwich in a restaurant and seen a little contraption with wires cut an egg into slices at one stroke!"

McClane sighed deeply. "Shamus," he said. "I hand it to you. You cracked the case. But then I always take my eggs scrambled."

SKELETON WITHOUT ARMS

NO ONE WAS NEAR THEM
WHEN THEY WENT—NO
WEAPON VISIBLE AFTER
IT WAS OVER. AND
YET THEY LITERALLY
EXPLODED IN A RAIN
OF BLOOD. WHAT WAS
THIS GHASTLY HORROR
THAT HAD COME TO
STATION KSPS? WHO
WAS THE FIEND WHO
TURNED MEN INTO
LIVING FIRECRACKERS—
LEFT THEM FLESHLESS
SKELETONS IN A SPLIT
SECOND?

CHAPTER ONE

MURDER AT THE MIKE

IN THE SHADOW of the twin black towers of Radio Station KSPS, which reared above the building that fronted the Stupendous Productions Studios on Santa Monica Boulevard, a roadster braked to a stop. Evening traffic whizzed past as two men and a woman left the car and strode toward the ornate gate.

To the studio cop who peered through the bars, the taller of the two men announced: "I'm Clay Oakley. These are my assistants, Miss Charmaine Morris and Mr. Archibald Brixey. We're expected."

The studio cop unlatched the gate. "You're a private detective, ain't you, Mr. Oakley? I bet you've come here to try to find out where Rex Bartell disappeared to."

"That," said Oakley, passing through, "is not a bad guess. Mr. Sartman, I take it, is inside?"

"Yes, sir. Go right on in."

Clay Oakley followed the gravel path toward the neon-decorated doorway of the studio broadcasting station, his arm linked with that of Cherry Morris. With the pert, slender red-head on one side of him, and the aristocratic Mr. Brixey on the other, Oakley was truly flanked by elegance.

"Cherry darling," he remarked, "I should never take you with me on trips like this one, especially when you look as beautiful as you do tonight. Some day a movie executive is going to get your signature on a five-year contract, and then what will become of Oke?"

"Oke, my dear," answered Cherry, "I wonder. But it will take more than a five-year contract to lure me away from you."

"I say!" exclaimed the immaculate Archibald Brixey. "Are we investigating a mysterious disappearance or attending a meeting of a mutual admiration society?"

"Both," said Oakley, and he stopped, peering down at the broad mat which lay outside the bronze door.

An envelope was lying there. He picked it up and turned it over. It was plain and cheap and sealed; and across its face was scrawled a name—Max Sartman. Below was printed—Private. Oakley inspected it as he opened the door.

ACROSS the luxurious reception room of the radio studios hurried a squat, paunchy man. He gripped Oakley's hand and wheezed, "I'm glad to see you!" He gave a tug at Brixey's fingers, devoted a moment

Smoke and flame gushed
from his mouth and nose.

to admiring Cherry Morris' bright beauty, and said breathlessly: "We must go somewhere to talk privately, Mr. Oakley."

"For you, Mr. Sartman," Oakley said, proffering the envelope. "I found it on the door mat."

He looked about as Sartman ripped the envelope. The lobby of the broadcasting studio was, like the rest of Hollywood, pretentious, garish and modernistic. Most of the talkie-producing companies had annexed radio stations, and the Stupendous Productions organization was no exception. Its antenna shot music and advertising into the ether eighteen hours a day, and the programs were garnished with bits done by the studio stars. Within these walls there was the same feverish tension which characterized the big sound stages while scenes were being shot.

A voice issued from a loud-speaker in the lobby while Sartman peered at the letter. Oakley noted the cultivated enunciation and the superabundance of first-person-singulars which issued from the cabinet.

Sartman turned to him with a start and said with a gasp: "Read that! Read it!"

Oakley read it.

> If you want Rex Bartell back alive get ready to pay a big ransom. Keep the police out of it. Get $100,000 in small bills and have them ready. The next letter will tell you what to do with it. If you don't obey orders your handsome young actor will be sent back to you piece by piece.

The letter was unsigned.

Peering over Oakley's shoulder, Archibald Brixey observed: "A hundred thousand? I jolly well think no actor is worth that much!"

"This is the first—" Oakley began to ask.

"The first we've heard, yes! My God, Mr. Oakley! Do you think they'll do it?" Max Sartman put the questions gaspingly. "Do you think they'll kill him? A hundred thousand dollars! My God! That's ten times more than we pay Bartell in a year!"

"Anything is possible," observed Oakley, "in Hollywood. Let's get to work, Mr. Sartman. The studio is retaining me. You want to get your young actor back safely. But you've already notified the police and—"

"The police—pah!" spat Sartman. "That big ox, McClane—what can he do? He couldn't find the Pacific Ocean. You must find Rex Bartell, Mr. Oakley, and get him back. We have parts ready for him— small parts, but—" Sartman made a frantic gesture.

"Just what," asked Oakley, "happened to Rex Bartell?"

"Come with me, Mr. Oakley."

Sartman led the way up richly carpeted steps. Cherry Morris stayed at Oakley's side, her svelt evening gown trailing. On the second floor of the building glass doors looked into the broadcasting studios. In one an orchestra was tuning up, preparing to go on the air. In another a young man, painfully handsome, was seated at an antique Spanish table, reading from a script into a microphone.

"Richard Marsh," Sartman said, passing the door. "He's broadcasting now."

Marsh was one of Stupendous Productions' juveniles, of minor prominence. Because it was his business to keep up on all news of the film studios, Oakley remembered that Richard Marsh was under contract personally to Max Sartman, chief supervisor of Stupendous. He had attracted notice first as a radio singer, and the appeal of his voice had brought him a chance in the talkies.

SARTMAN pushed open the door of a studio on the opposite side of the hallway. Oakley and his assistants entered. The room was garishly decorated. It contained a grand piano and folding chairs, and a standard microphone. Otherwise it was empty.

"Here, in this room, Mr. Oakley," Sartman stated, "Rex Bartell was seen for the last time."

Oakley extracted a notebook from his coat. "I've noted down a few facts on the case. Bartell was due to broadcast at nine o'clock night before last. He was to use this studio, you say. He came in here a few minutes before nine, and—"

"He was early," Sartman interrupted. "The control man wasn't in the monitor room yet." He indicated a cubicle in the corner of the studio windowed with a double pane of glass, in which were black-paneled instruments. "The announcer wasn't even ready. So he went to that table and sat down and began to read over his script—and disappeared."

"Really!" said Archibald Brixey.

Oakley walked about the studio, glancing out the windows. "Two stories up," he observed. "A good thirty-foot drop. There's another story above, isn't there?"

"Yes. The master control room is upstairs. It's crazy to think that Bartell jumped out of one of those windows, just before he was ready to go on the air. Anyway, he was kidnaped. But there wasn't any way he could get out—none!"

"Couldn't he have simply walked out the door?"

"No. There's only one door. While Bartell was still in this studio, I came upstairs. I was talking a minute with Arthur Claxton, the studio director, right outside the door. I looked in, and saw Bartell here, reading over the script. Then, when I came in a minute later, he was gone."

"He couldn't have got past you without your seeing him?"

"No. He couldn't have got out at all—but he was gone. Even if the kidnapers got him out of the room somehow—how did they get him off the lot? There were a dozen cops on duty night before last, because two of the sound stages were in use. All the gates were locked. The fence is too high to climb over. It just couldn't happen, Mr. Oakley—but it did!"

"One other note I have here," Oakley pointed out, "concerns Bartell's car."

"Yes. Bartell drove into the studio and parked behind the building. One of the cops saw his car here just before nine o'clock. The cop noticed that the rumble seat had three or four suitcases in it. After Bartell disappeared, we found the car still there, but the suitcases were gone. I tell you, Mr. Oakley, this is driving me crazy. The police are getting nowhere. I've asked questions myself until I'm losing my mind. Not even Bartell's friends can guess what happened."

"As for instance?"

"Richard Marsh."

"The juvenile who's broadcasting now? They were friends? I thought they were rivals—both the same type and wanting the same parts and—"

"Professionally rivals, yes—but not personally. Marsh and Bartell and Sidney Wheaton share the same dressing room. Bartell didn't seem worried that day, they told me. Of course, he didn't know what was going to happen. The kidnapers must've taken him by surprise—but how they got into the studio, and how they got Bartell out of here, I don't know!"

"Suppose," said Oakley, "I talk with Marsh."

Sartman peered at the electric clock in the monitor room. "He'll be finished in five minutes. We can go in then."

THEY crossed the hall to find a young man in evening dress looking through the glass door of the studio opposite. Sartman absently introduced him as Arthur Claxton, the studio director. In the room beyond, the young actor was reading from a script in a voice that reeked with artificial cultivation.

Claxton smiled and observed to Sartman: "Sounds just like Sidney Wheaton, doesn't he?"

In the hallway a loud-speaker was reproducing Marsh's stagey accent. "And now, dear friends, as I approach the end of my allotted time—"

Suddenly the voice died out of the loud-speaker. Marsh's lips continued to move, but his voice was lost behind the sound-proof walls. Arthur Claxton glanced with quick anxiety at the dead reproducer, then back into the room. Marsh was looking up, troubled, passing a hand across his forehead.

And suddenly—

The thing that happened was paralyzing in its frightfulness. Richard Marsh was jarred from his chair by some explosive force that struck him. His mouth flew open and flame gushed out of it. Smoke spewed out of his nostrils. As reflexing muscles threw him upward, and flung him across the table, wisps of smoke rose from his body.

"Good God!" gasped Claxton. "What's happened?"

Sartman, muttering, thrust at the door. Oakley shouldered in behind him, glancing swiftly about. In the monitor room in the corner of the studio, a technician in shirt-sleeves was half risen from his chair, peering in terror through the double pane of glass, his hands rising automatically to the phones clamped on his ears. Halfway across the studio, Oakley stopped.

The room was stiflingly hot. The air was filled with the stench of burned things—of, Oakley thought, scorched flesh. As he paused Cherry Morris' hand slipped behind his arm. Sartman lumbered across the room with Arthur Claxton and they peered in dismay at the motionless form of the young man stretched across the table.

Smoke still curled up from him into the air. His hands hung limply. From his nostrils and mouth blood was trickling. Sartman backed away from him and gasped a whisper: "Good God, he's dead! Oakley, he's dead!"

"I should think he was dead," Oakley said quietly. "That young man exploded—literally exploded."

CHAPTER TWO

THE BURSTING DEATH

OAKLEY crossed the hot, fume-filled room and bent over the smoking body. At his gesture, Sartman fumbled with window catches and thrust sashes upward. Oakley turned to see Arthur Claxton hurrying from the room, his face beaded with perspiration.

"Wait a minute!" Oakley snapped. "Where're you going?"

"The station's off the air," Claxton answered breathlessly. "It's my job to—" He broke off and, dabbing a handkerchief at his face, pushed out the door.

Oakley bent low to peer at the body again. What he saw made him grimace. He straightened toward Cherry Morris. Her face was white, and her eyes widened into Oakley's.

"Better get out into the air, Cherry," he told her. "This is not pretty. This young man's body is split open."

"I," Cherry said in a whisper, "am quite all right, Oke."

"I say!" Archibald Brixey blurted. "You mean he actually burst?"

"Burst is the word. See here, Sartman." Oakley turned. "Call the police. We'll need the medical examiner. And I want Claxton back here at once."

"What in God's name happened to him?" Sartman demanded with an intake of breath.

"I don't know! Get busy!"

Sartman burst out of the studio. Oakley saw faces pressing against the glass of the door; already word had circulated through the building that something had happened. He latched the door, put Brixey in charge of it, and returned to the table where the body of Richard Marsh lay.

"The first rule in a case of this kind, Cherry, my dear," he remarked as he bent over, "is 'Never touch the body.' Which rule I will now proceed to break."

Cherry Morris stood her ground as Oakley went to work. He turned the body face up, and his fingers went red. He did strange things. He pulled up Richard Marsh's trouser legs; he removed one shoe; he loosened the young man's vest and shirt; he inspected the fingers. Seeing that one of Marsh's vest pockets was ripped and charred, he fingered into it.

What he removed was the fragment of a small cardboard box. Blackened as it was, Oakley could make out the name printed on the label—*Madame Midnight*.

A knock at the door brought Oakley up. Sartman and Claxton were outside. At Oakley's signal, Brixey opened the door. The supervisor and the studio director came in nervously.

"The police are coming, Oakley. God, this is horrible! Did you see—the flame gush out of his mouth and nose? He seemed to—to go off like a fire-cracker!"

"Very much," said Oakley, "like a fire-cracker." He was peering about the table. "Is the station functioning again, Claxton? If so, come here and look and tell me what this means."

Claxton gazed at the microphone and the length of rubber-covered cord which led from it to a plug in the wall. Half the length of the cord was charred, and the insulation had melted onto the floor. The microphone was still hot to the touch.

"Short circuit?" Oakley asked.

"It isn't possible!" Claxton answered. "The microphone leads carry only a low potential—about the same as an ordinary telephone. Even if a high potential got into these wires, somehow—which isn't possible, either—a short circuit couldn't burn the leads only part way. The whole length would heat up. And anyway—Marsh wasn't touching the microphone at all."

"No go, then," Oakley observed. "But there's a strange thing. Claxton. Marsh's body is covered with burns. There are burns on his insteps, and heels, and calves, and over his chest and abdomen. When the medical examiner looks further, he'll find more, I'm sure. What could have done that?"

"I've no idea!"

"There's no possibility at all that he was killed by a high charge getting into that microphone?"

"None at all—none. I've told you, Oakley, he wasn't even touching the microphone."

"No accident could account for it?"

"I can't conceive—"

"Then," said Oakley, "we may put it down as a fact that Richard Marsh was murdered."

Max Sartman stepped quickly to Oakley. "Murdered? For God's sake—how?"

"How," said Oakley wryly, "and why and what and who are a few details I haven't cleared up yet!" He glanced at the door. "Who's that trying to break in? He looks like Marsh."

Sartman turned. "Marsh's father. He's a radio engineer here. God, it's awful."

"Go out and calm him down," Oakley suggested. "He's got to be kept out of this studio. The rest is up to the police and the medical examiner."

SARTMAN edged out of the room, thrusting back the man who attempted to enter. "My son, my son!" Oakley heard in an anguished voice. With a sigh he stepped to Cherry Morris, fingering the bit of pasteboard that had been part of a box.

"Somewhere in the files in the office, Cherry, you'll find a folder about Madame Midnight," he said. "Look it up and have the dope ready for me when I want it. You know anything about her?"

Cherry's composure had returned. She powdered her patrician nose as she answered. "Only that she's another of the fakirs that infest our fair city, Oke. She specializes in herbs, I believe. The movie people go for her. She sells love potions and what not—stuff that is supposed to make old actors young and young actors irresistible. Am I off now?"

"You're off."

Oakley led her out. Sartman was in the corridor, attempting to calm the father of the dead young actor. The elder Marsh was lean, with bushy hair, and his eyes were now widened wildly. Pale as death, he peered through the glass door and seemed to hear nothing Sartman said. As Cherry Morris hurried down the stairs, Archibald Brixey and Arthur Claxton left the studio. Claxton locked the door behind him.

"Stay on the job until the police get here, Claxton," Oakley directed. "Archie, you're coming with me."

As they turned toward the stairs, a young man ran up to them. That he was another juvenile in the movies was apparent from his appearance. His blonde hair was meticulously waved; his color was high; his features perfect. Oakley recognized him as Sidney Wheaton. Wheaton hurried to the door of the studio, where Claxton stopped him short.

"Great Heavens, what's happened to Dick?" he demanded.

"Nobody knows, Sid," Claxton answered. "Maybe it's damned lucky for you you were late tonight."

Oakley pondered over that remark as he went down the stairs with Brixey. Sartman hurried after them, having left William Marsh with Claxton.

"What is happening here?" he demanded, almost hysterically. "First Rex Bartell disappears—then Richard Marsh gets killed. Two of my three juveniles—it's horrible. Mr. Oakley, what can we do?"

"One thing you can do," Oakley suggested, "is take me to Marsh's dressing room."

"Yes, yes!"

Sartman led the way out the rear door of the radio station. The building which housed it was the highest on the Stupendous lot. Within the walls of the studio streets led past the huge sound stages and executive offices. Company cops were on the prowl as Sartman led the way deeper into the lot.

"I say, Oke," Archibald Brixey spoke up, "are we to believe what you said—that Richard Marsh literally exploded like a fire-cracker?"

"You are. Flame gushed out of his mouth and nose because something inside his body exploded. Naturally, it killed him instantly. What's more, he's covered with strange burns."

"And it's murder?"

"Undoubtedly it's murder. It certainly isn't either suicide, or natural death, and Claxton claims it couldn't be an accident. Therefore, murder. Marsh's father is taking it pretty hard, Sartman."

"Yes, poor chap," Sartman said breathily. "Marsh was his only child. The boy was not very popular in pictures, but he might have become a name in time. He got his start in radio, you know. He was a technician, in New York. Once when a singer didn't show up to broadcast on time, Marsh was rushed in at a moment's notice to take his place. He'd had an audition, but a place hadn't been found for him; and that one chance broadcast started him. He built up a following."

"And from radio he went into pictures."

"Yes. His father has been in charge of the radio research laboratory. Working on direct transmission via short waves for network broadcasts of television."

"Television research going on here?" Oakley asked. "Why?"

SARTMAN laughed wryly. "Ever since Warner Brothers beat out everybody else on the talkies, Hollywood has been grabbing at every new development. We put William Marsh to work here because it was a chance of controlling something big. Television is coming, and his system, if it worked, would put the studio first in the movie field, and save us tremendous expenditure for films."

"How?"

"By broadcasting movies direct to theatres. The players would act here in the studio, and thousands of people, in hundreds of different theatres, could see the same thing at the same time—and the cost of millions of feet of film would be saved. But Marsh has been working on it for years, without getting anywhere. The expense has been too high. The research laboratory will be closed up when Marsh's contract ends in a week."

"Tough on Marsh—losing the lab and his son at the same time," Oakley observed.

"He will be a broken man. Here, Oakley, is the dressing room."

Sartman's passkey opened the door. Lights snapped on to disclose a long room, its walls covered with photographs. Closets standing open disclosed extensive masculine wardrobes. Three dressing tables, framed with glowing bulbs, were lined along one wall.

"Marsh and Bartell and Wheaton used the same room, you see. The farthest one is Marsh's dressing table, and the middle one is Wheaton's."

Oakley looked them over. Sticks of grease paint and bottles of liquid face powder cluttered them up. Unceremoniously Oakley opened drawers. In Marsh's he found nothing out of the ordinary. But as he was fingering through Wheaton's he made a noise denoting sudden interest, and picked up a small pasteboard box.

Archibald Brixey leaned close and read aloud the name printed on the label—*"Madame Midnight."*

"Again," said Oakley.

He opened the box. Inside lay a number of large capsules, filled with what seemed to be crushed herbs, brown and dry. Oakley separated one into halves and picked the dusty leaves out. Abruptly he bent close, peering.

"So!" he said.

He removed a small, metallic cylinder from the capsule. It was cup-shaped and just large enough to be inserted into the container and covered with the herbs so that it could not be seen. Oakley's eyes raised to Sartman's.

"Know anything about these things?" he asked.

"Why—" Sartman fumbled with words. "I was in this dressing room only this afternoon. Wheaton and Marsh were here. Marsh was downcast because he'd lost a part to Wheaton in the new picture, *Odds Evened.* Wheaton was trying to cheer him up. And he suggested that Marsh try taking some of those capsules."

"Wheaton urged Marsh to take them?"

"Yes. Marsh laughed at the idea. Wheaton declared he believed in Madame Midnight's herbs. He said the preparations she gave him accounted for his vigor and youthfulness—even his success. He wanted Marsh to try them to see if they'd help. Marsh agreed to do it, not believing in it at all, and Wheaton gave him a full box of the things."

"Sounds exactly like the Hollywood mentality!" Oakley observed sourly. "These movie stars go in for the damnedest beliefs and superstitions you ever heard of. And in Marsh's case, it was just too bad. Very much too bad."

"Why?"

"Because these capsules, Mr. Sartman, contain fulminate caps."

"Ful—"

"Explosive caps. Damned powerful. Taken into the stomach inside the capsules, they would probably stay there. It was one or more of these things, exploding inside Marsh's stomach, that killed him."

"Good Lord, Oakley! But how—how could the things be made to explode?"

"Damn it, I don't know! The fact is that Marsh had swallowed one or more of these miniature infernal machines, and somehow they were set off. As for Wheaton—it looks bad for that young man."

"Wheaton wouldn't do a thing like that! Murder Marsh in that horrible way? No, Oakley! It's—"

"Sartman, beat it back to the broadcasting studios and get Wheaton aside somewhere. I'm coming in and grill him."

"Yes—yes, if you wish."

Sartman breathlessly sidled from the dressing room. Oakley, while Brixey watched, pried open several more of the capsules. In each he found a fulminate cap. Grimly he inspected the label on the box.

"But, I say, Oke," Archie Brixey observed. "If Wheaton were intent on murdering Marsh that way, he wouldn't have given the poor lad the capsules while Sartman was watching, would he?"

"Not unless he thought he was completely covered—and it's a method of murder that's never been used before, Archie, don't forget. But in case Wheaton was sincere, and didn't know the caps were in the herbs, this woman, Madame Midnight, becomes a very interesting person."

OAKLEY opened the door and clicked it behind Brixey. They walked down the dark studio street toward the broadcasting building.

The towers reared high into the sky above them as they entered the open space flanking the rear of the radio station.

Oakley's hand was on the knob when a sudden sound surprised him. Turning, he saw a movement in the darkness behind the building. A vague form was crouching at the rear wall, huddled down; Oakley saw, dimly, a face shaded with the bill of a cap.

"Strange, Oke," said Brixey quickly. "We went right past there a moment ago and there was nobody there."

Oakley stepped aside. "Who's that?" he asked.

And instantly the figure sprang off.

Oakley swung long legs after it. Archibald Brixey saw the figure whisk out of sight at the corner of the building, and darted toward the rear door. He plunged along the hallway, toward the front entrance, as Oakley sprinted past the corner. The dark figure was making a queer, whimpering sound as it ran.

Brixey dashed out the front door as the figure emerged from the gloom beside the building with Oakley in swift pursuit. Brixey leaped to block the way. He reached out to grab, and an amazing thing happened. His face was resoundingly slapped. The nature of the blow startled Brixey so completely that he brought up, arms dropping.

Oakley crashed against him as the figure swerved. His hand shot out, and his fingers closed upon the patterned cap on the fugitive's head. It slipped off in his fingers; and in the light, long, golden hair spilled over the shoulders of the one running.

"A girl!" gasped Brixey.

She was running wildly toward the gate. The studio cop who officiated there heard her quick footfalls and turned to block her way. She shoved at him in desperation; and another slap rang. The next moment she was running through the gate, and across the sidewalk, toward a car waiting at the curb.

Oakley sprinted out. The car, with the girl at the wheel, spurted into the traffic. Oakley wrenched open the door of his roadster and the starter ground. The roadster swung sharply past parked cars and accelerated after the coupé in which the disguised girl was fleeing. Through the window he glimpsed her head, the golden hair streaming down. He jumped a red light to keep her close, then eased down to make it not too apparent that he was following.

"In any other town a cop might stop her," he observed, "but not in this mad hamlet."

"Look here!" Brixey exclaimed. "Are you grilling murder suspects tonight or chasing women dressed like men?"

"Wheaton can wait," Oakley answered. "I want to know why that girl came to the studio dressed in man's clothes. I want to know why she popped out of nowhere behind the broadcasting station. You see, Archie, blondes have an attraction second only to red-heads."

CHAPTER THREE

HAG'S MASK

OAKLEY spent half an hour following the coupé through winding roads in Beverly Hills. The girl was driving more slowly now, apparently in the belief that she was not being followed. Along Wilshire Boulevard they rolled, Oakley keeping a safe distance behind. A turn took the girl toward Hollywood, and when she reached the front of a small apartment house she slowed.

Oakley parked a block behind. He saw no movement about the girl's car for long moments. When, finally, the door swung open, and the girl alighted, she was no longer wearing male attire. Garbed in a smart sports suit, a jaunty hat on her head, she strode to the apartment entrance carrying a small suitcase.

Oakley and Brixey walked along the opposite side of the street after she entered. Presently they saw lights appear in a corner room three stories above the street. Oakley promptly crossed, and entered the apartment house. In an automatic elevator he rode with Brixey to the third floor.

Above the bell button of the corner door was a card. *Alice Westmore,* it read.

"The name," said Oakley, "is slightly familiar."

The knob would not turn. Oakley pressed the button. In a moment he heard quick, soft footfalls on the floor, and the latch clicked.

"Come in, Art!" a girl's voice called. "I'm bathing!"

Oakley looked interested. He opened the door to find the living room empty. The girl's footfalls were crossing the floor of the bedroom beyond. Another latch clicked, and there was the faint sound of streaming water in a tub. The voice called again: "I'll be out in a jiffy!"

"This," said Brixey, "is very embarrassing."

Oakley smiled as he walked into the bedroom beyond. Across the spread lay the suit the girl had been wearing, and silken underthings. A pair of shapely slippers had been kicked into a corner. Beside the bed sat the overnight case. Oakley clicked it open, and saw a man's coat and a pair of trousers rolled up in it.

Inside the bathroom the water kept splashing.

Oakley looked about the dressing table. He lifted a bottle of perfume and breathed of it happily. Its label read—*Seductiv.* Oakley silently agreed and replaced it.

Suddenly the bathroom door clicked. Steam issued out as the girl called: "Art! Aren't you early tonight?"

Oakley sighed again. "I regret very much," he said, "that neither of us is named Art."

There was a gasp from the bathroom. The shower stopped streaming. The girl peered out through the crack of the door. Only one side of her face was visible, and a section of towel which she had draped around herself, and beneath it a shapely, nude leg.

"Why, I— Who are you? What do you want?" she asked quickly. "How dare you—"

"Miss Westmore," sighed Oakley, "we are sorry that business brings us here at such an inopportune time. You see, I am a private detective. I am very interested in your recent appearance on the Stupendous lot dressed as a man. You're not working there, are you?"

The girl gasped again. "I don't know what you're talking about!"

"Now, really," said Brixey. "You do, quite."

"Is," asked Oakley, "an explanation forthcoming?"

"Why should an explanation be forthcoming to you, may I ask?" the girl retorted. "You might explain why you've invaded my bedroom. No, don't explain. Just get out!"

"But I will explain," Oakley persisted. "The matter involves a kidnaping and a murder."

"A—"

"Murder. A particularly nasty murder. Richard Marsh exploded in the broadcasting studio tonight, and since you made such a strange appearance and disappearance there immediately afterward—"

"Dick Marsh! Mur—"

"Oke," sighed Brixey as the girl stammered into silence, "it is obvious that the young lady is not implicated. I am becoming more painfully embarrassed every moment. I suggest we leave."

"On the other hand, I suggest," said Oakley to the girl behind the door, "that you come out and talk the matter over."

"I won't come out!"

"We will stay," Oakley countered, "until you do come out."

"I'll stay here until you go!"

Oakley sighed. "That obviously brings us to an impasse. I won't go until you come out, and you won't come out until we go, and I'm afraid that if we persist, nothing will ever come of it. One of us must unbend. Suppose, then, I behave more like a gentleman and come back later, at a time when you are not in the tub."

The girl began to sob softly. "Please don't come back," she pled. "Please don't!"

"I'm sorry," said Oakley. "I must. Good night."

He left the bedroom with Brixey at his heels. Closing the door, he breathed one last time the fragrance of *Seductiv*. They rode in silence to the ground floor and walked in silence to the car. Oakley's eyes were troubled when he started off.

"I remember her name. Several years ago she was in pictures, but she dropped out all of a sudden. There was something about an accident she suffered which kept her from going on."

Brixey glanced up at the shining windows as they passed.

"She is," he said softly, "a very luscious young lady—what I saw of her."

OAKLEY parked at the curb in front of KSPS. Uniformed policemen eyed him as he passed the gate. In the lobby he found more policemen and plainclothesmen. Ignoring them, he wriggled into a phone booth and called the number listed under Secrets, Inc.—his office.

"Cherry, darling," he said when the connection went through, "Oke wants to know what you've learned about Madame Midnight."

"Not much more than I've already told you," Cherry Morris answered. "She opened up shop about a year ago. Stars began coming to her and made her famous. Some of the biggest names in Hollywood drink tea made from herbs she sells them. Have no dope on the woman whatever—where she came from, or what her right name is. Want the address of her place?"

Oakley jotted it down.

"Since you need no beauty naps, Cherry, here's a job for you. A young lady named Alice Westmore has caught my fancy—professionally only, of course. I want your gorgeous blue eyes kept on her until I can question her outside of a bathtub. Better skip over there right away." And Oakley told her where to go.

"A red-head?" asked Cherry.

"A blonde," said Oakley.

"Then I've still got a chance."

Oakley grinned as he left the booth. With Brixey he climbed the stairs. There was a crowd in the studio where the mysterious death of Richard Marsh had occurred, but the body had been removed. Oakley edged in to find Sartman there, with Claxton, and Sidney Wheaton, and a mass of brawn known as Detective Lieutenant McClane. The plainclothesman grinned sourly at Oakley.

"Try to figure this one out, shamus!" he greeted. "Or maybe you have already."

"Not quite. See here, McClane. I've helped you out in the past, and I'd like a little reciprocity. What's been learned?"

"Little or nothing. If I'm to believe eye-witnesses and the medical examiner, this bird Marsh simply exploded. Inside of him is a mess. Died instantly. And as for burns on his body—listen.

"On the insteps, little round burns in two rows, running parallel with the foot. On the heels, little dots of burns. On both calves, triangular burns. On the abdomen, a square burn. On the thighs, round burns. On his chest, a hole was blown into him. On his neck, a round burn in the front and another in back. None of 'em very deep, and they couldn't've killed him, but all those funny burns are queer."

Oakley nodded. "Anything else?"

"No. What do you know?"

"I saw it happen. The radio power failed at the exact moment Marsh died. When we went into the room, it was hot as blazes, but you see the heat's not turned on. That's all I can contribute at the moment."

OAKLEY detached himself from McClane. His gaze centered on a young man sitting miserably at the side of the room—Sidney Wheaton. Wheaton looked worn; his pleading eyes kept to Max Sartman. Sartman merely shrugged and sighed as Oakley came near.

"See here." Oakley bent close over Wheaton so that his voice would not carry. "Have you any idea what killed Marsh?"

"No—of course not."

"He died at about twenty-six minutes past the hour. About ten minutes before you came into the studio. Where were you then?"

"I—I was in Santa Monica. I was driving to the studio from the beach, and I ran over a broken milk bottle, and both right tires of my car were punctured. I must have been there at the time—held up."

"How about proving it?"

"You can check up on the garage I phoned. The Speedee, on Wilshire. They came to get my car, and I went ahead in a taxi. Why— why are you asking that? For God's sake, you don't think I had anything to do—"

Oakley opened a hand near Wheaton's face. On it lay the little cardboard box labeled *Madame Midnight*.

"These yours?"

Wheaton looked dazed. "Yes. I suppose so. Where—"

"Suppose you take one. Archie! A glass of water, please, for Mr. Wheaton."

The young actor shifted uneasily in his chair as Brixey shouldered from the studio. Oakley watched his reaction keenly. From the box he removed a capsule—one which, he was sure, contained a fulminate cap. When Brixey returned with a brimming glass, he passed the capsule to Wheaton with the water.

Wheaton placed the thing on his tongue. He was about to sluice it down when Oakley gripped his wrist.

"That's far enough," he said. "Spit it out!"

Wheaton looked amazed. He brought the capsule from his mouth. Oakley took it, frowning, and turned to Brixey. Leaving the juvenile peering after him puzzledly, he strode to the door with Brixey at his side.

"Come along, Archie," he said crisply. "The night's just begun."

He said nothing more until his roadster was purring along Santa Monica Boulevard. It was late, but the thoroughfare was still streaming with cars. Hollywood's lights glared in the sky as Oakley wheeled past corners, turning toward Culver City.

"You seem to have lost interest in young Wheaton, Oke," Brixey observed.

"The young man either doesn't know there are fulminate caps in the herbs, Archie," Oakley answered, "or he's a far better actor than he's given credit for."

"I watched him when he began to swallow the capsule," Brixey put in. "Maybe if he knew the explosive was inside, he had nothing to worry about. Those things have to be set off somehow, you know, and if he simply didn't set off the one he was about to swallow—"

"There," Oakley interrupted, "is the well-known rub. Those things have to be set off. How could it have been done? Usually a fuse is used, but obviously there was no fuse in this case. Anyway, at the time of Marsh's death, Wheaton wasn't anywhere near the studio. And, lastly, we have no idea of why he would want to kill Marsh."

"Which leaves us nowhere," said Brixey. "Where, may I ask, are we going?"

"We're going," explained Oakley, "to pay a visit to Madame Midnight."

OAKLEY stopped at the curb on a street which was not yet built up. Only a few houses spotted the block. Near his car sat a squat, square building, perhaps once intended to be a store. Its front window was curtained with black cloth, behind which there was a dim gleam of light.

Oakley noticed, as he trod to the door, that there was another car parked ahead of him at the curb. He stopped to read a card behind the pane—*Madame Midnight. Hours, Twelve Midnight to Three A.M.*

"Hocus-pocus," said Oakley. "Archie, grace the landscape with your presence until I come out."

"Pshaw!" Archie deplored. "Am I not to meet the lady?"

"You're to keep an eye on possible visitors."

Oakley knocked. There was no answer so he turned the knob and pushed the door open. He stepped into air thick with the fumes of incense—yet it was a pungent scent unlike any he had smelled before. The room was draped with black cloth which was covered with glittering, silver symbols of the zodiac. And in the ceiling above, light issued from a replica of the full moon.

Except for a table and two chairs, the room was unfurnished. The black curtains hung all around. Through them came the sound of something boiling, and Oakley sensed that he was smelling the vapor of some herbaceous brew. He waited, and presently the black curtains at the rear of the room parted, and a face looked out.

It was the face of a hag. A black shawl bound the head, and from it strayed wisps of coarse unkempt hair. The dark, mottled skin looked age-old; the eyes sagged, the mouth drooped. Oakley said nothing while the woman regarded him coldly.

"What do you want?"

"Madame Midnight?"

"What do you want?"

"I am in trouble. I need help."

The woman seemed to stiffen. "No," she droned. "Not tonight. I cannot help you."

She turned, and the black curtains flipped into place, blotting away her mask of a face.

Oakley muttered maledictions. "But I want you to help me. Can't you give me something to help me?"

Through the curtains came, "Go away! Go away!"

Oakley reached out and lifted the curtain. There was an old stove in the rear room, and the woman was bending over it. A huge iron pot was bubbling, and vapors were rising from it. The woman, fullish in loose skirts, was stirring the mixture. On the walls around her were shelves loaded with bottles and small boxes like the one Oakley had found in the Stupendous juveniles' dressing room.

The woman sensed the movement of the curtains and turned on him.

"Stay out! Go away!" she screeched. "I'll call the police if you don't go away!"

Oakley backed. "I'm sorry. I only came for help. I feel so low in spirit, I—I'm afraid. Everything has gone wrong. Fortune has turned against me. I've even thought of taking my life because it looks so hopeless. If you won't help me—" he ended with a shrug.

The woman was peering at him, the dripping spoon in her hands. Oakley felt uncomfortable under her stare. She said, in a husky tone: "Then all right. Sit down. I will see if I can help you."

OAKLEY waited in a chair. The cauldron in the rear room kept bubbling and steaming. The hag-woman came through the drapes, and seated herself on the opposite side of the table. She gestured for Oakley's palm, and he spread his hand before her.

She studied the lines silently, her head bent low. "Yes—yes, you are facing grave misfortune. It is because you are not equal to the tasks put upon you. Your mind and body need stimulation."

"Yes—you are right," Oakley said, spurring her on.

"I cannot help you if you do not believe."

"I believe that you can help me."

"I will give you herbs. You are to make tea with them. Three times a day drink the tea and—"

Oakley was smiling. Peering at the darkly mottled face, he chuckled. The woman's head jerked up and the shaded eyes peered into his, startled.

"Not bad, Miss Westmore," Oakley said. "Not bad at all."

A choking sound came from the woman's throat as she tensed to spring from the table. Oakley reached out quickly. His hand snatched at the shawl which covered the woman's head as she whirled away. And again, as she rushed to the rear door, Oakley saw flowing, golden hair spill into sight.

Oakley leaped for the curtains. He brushed through them as a door in the rear of the kitchen slammed. He sprang at it, and pushed—and found it fastened. Behind the door were quick voices. Oakley pounded a fist.

"Open up!"

Another door slammed. Someone had hurried out a rear entrance. Oakley whirled, dashed back—and stopped short at the street door through which he had entered. It resisted his effort to open it.

"Archie!" Oakley shouted. "Stop that woman!"

Somewhere outside he heard a moan. It was followed quickly by the snarl of a motor. A car spurted away from the curb, not far off, went racing down the street as Oakley struggled with the door.

"Archie!"

There was no answer. Oakley turned angrily, trod back to the kitchen, and found the rear way still locked. Jerking aside more black drapes he found windows, all of them nailed down. He snatched up a chair which sat beside the stove and thrust its legs against the panes. Glass cracked. Oakley broke his way clear, and stepped over the sill.

"Archie!"

This time there was another moan. Oakley rounded the little building quickly. The car which had rushed off was the one that had been parked in front of his. It was out of sight now. Oakley's attention shifted quickly to a figure squatting on the sidewalk.

It was Archibald Brixey, sitting and holding his head. Oakley grabbed his collar and jerked him up.

"What the devil happened to you? Why didn't you stop that woman?"

"He hit me, Oke!"

"Who hit you? I wanted that woman! It was Alice Westmore—the luscious young thing we surprised having her bath. Made up as a hag and selling herbs."

Brixey sighed. "I shall have to quit my job, Oke, really I shall. My skull can't stand it."

"Damnation!" Oakley boomed. "Archie, gather your wits! Did you catch the number of that car? Answer me!"

"I really am trying, Oke," Brixey sighed. "It was that girl—that delightful blonde? Dear me, what is she up to? How did you know it was she?"

"Simply because the old hag had the fragrance of *Seductiv* perfume about her. I caught it even through the smell of that damned mess she was cooking on the stove. I took a chance, that's all, and it worked. This thing is connecting up!"

"It's jolly well connecting up!" Brixey sighed. "I saw the face of the man who hit me, Oke. He came out of the rear of that place and when I made a pass at him he knocked me down, and my head hit a stone. It was that chap we met at the studio tonight—the studio director. What's his name—Arthur Claxton."

"Claxton?"

"Claxton," said Brixey.

Oakley snorted. "Something's damned funny. Archie, get into that car and drive to the apartment house where the girl lives. Find Cherry and demand to know how that girl managed to slip past her. Then camp there yourself. When that girl shows up again you grab her. I'll look for Claxton myself."

"Very well, Oke. I wish," moaned Archie as he moved toward the car, "I had an aspirin."

OAKLEY went back into the black sanctum of Madame Midnight as Brixey rolled off in the roadster. Legging across the sill of the broken window, he regarded the shelves filled with bottles and small boxes. He opened several of the containers, found them filled with black pills, and searched further.

The girl, Alice Westmore, had recognized him immediately, of course—he realized that. Hence her refusal to see him. On his insistence, she had yielded in the hope that it would mean less trouble—that was obvious. Claxton, of course, had been waiting in the rear room; the car at the curb had been his. Oakley mulled it over as he snatched open boxes.

He found one containing huge capsules, like those identified with Sidney Wheaton. He parted the capsules and picked the herbs out of them. They contained nothing but dry, brown leaves. Oakley settled down to a thorough investigation. He pried into every capsule, into every box he could find. But in none of them was there more than dried herbs.

He was crawling out the window again, disgusted, when he saw his roadster roll to a stop at the curb. Cherry Morris was at the wheel. As he climbed in, she fluffed her hair in place with a gesture of annoyance.

"I understand," she said, "you have made unkind remarks about me."

"You let that girl slip past you."

"She was gone, really, Oke, before I got there. Her windows were dark. I've been on the job ever since, but she didn't show up. Men," she added, "can be so unkind."

Oakley settled down in the seat as the car started, and gazed at Cherry's colorful hair fluttering brilliantly in the reflected glow of the dash. His hand closed warmly on hers.

"Not," he said, "for long."

CHAPTER FOUR

HEAT FROM HELL

BRIGHT California sunshine streamed through the windows of the sanctum sanctorum of Secrets, Inc., as Clay Oakley sat at his desk next morning, poring over sheets of notes taken from his files. In an easy chair Archibald Brixey, a lump on the side of his head, was relaxed in sleep. He jerked when the telephone rang.

Oakley took the call.

"This is your undying passion calling, darling," came the voice of Cherry Morris. "I am still camped near the Westmore girl's apartment house. I've eaten forty chocolate sodas so far, and six men have tried to pick me up. There's nothing doing anywhere, except a faint uneasiness behind the belt."

"Swell!" said Oakley sourly. "I've just had KSPS on the phone, and they're going crazy over there trying to locate Claxton. He hasn't shown up. Well, honey, parade your lovely feet up and down that sidewalk some more, and keep watching."

"Though my lovely feet are full of unlovely aches, Oke, I'll do anything you ask."

Brixey yawned resoundingly as Oakley pushed the phone back. "Now that I've had a sleep on this," he announced, "it's in a worse muddle than it was before."

"Then drink lots of coffee," Oakley retorted. "Archie, this murder is getting in my hair. I didn't go to that studio to find out why a young actor gets blown mysteriously to pieces. I went there to locate the missing Rex Bartell. We seem to have overlooked that."

"But surely," said Brixey, "the two are linked together. First one young actor vanishes, and then another bursts with a loud noise. There seem to be dark designs on the Stupendous juveniles."

Oakley fingered the fulminate cap he had found inside one of the herb capsules. "Very nasty, Archie," he said, "one of these things going off inside of one. And the fact that we know several of these things, exploding in Marsh's stomach, killed him, is only part of the answer. The most important thing is—who made it go off, and how?"

"They don't explode spontaneously?"

"No, certainly not. A blow will explode them, or heat applied, or open flame, which amounts to almost the same thing. Obviously, a blow couldn't have set off the one or more of them that were in Marsh's stomach. There's no way that I know of that it could have been exploded. Yet that murder, Archie, was committed according to plan."

"Plan?"

"Certainly. First, these things were introduced into Marsh's body without his being aware of it. Secondly, somehow, they were exploded. Just why that outlandish means of murder was chosen is beyond me at the moment, except that it could be done without the murderer's being present. Marsh was alone in that room—absolutely alone."

"And all at once—*pop!*" said Archie.

"*Pop,*" said Oakley, "and he was dead in an instant."

The phone rang again as he spoke. An excited voice came over the wire. "Oakley? This is Sartman talking—Max Sartman. I've received another letter—a threatening letter—"

"From Rex Bartell's kidnapers?"

"Yes. It instructs me to put the hundred thousand dollars in a bundle, and charter the advertising blimp that's always sailing over this city. It says for the blimp to fly from Santa Monica Beach south to Oceanside, above the beach road, tonight, and that I'm to toss the money overboard when I see a light flash seven times."

"That's a hell of a way," Oakley exclaimed. "Any bird who tries to pick up that money will get caught. A car can follow that blimp easily."

"But the letter says if there's any interference, Bartell will be killed. Oakley, what can we do? God knows few actors are worth that much money, let alone Bartell, with as many juveniles running around without jobs as they are—but I can't have that boy's blood on my head."

"Regardless, plan to go through with it. Have that car trailed by headquarters men. Make 'em grab anybody who tries to get the money, and it might as well be fake money at that. If anybody's picked up, those cops'll make him talk. In the meantime I'm coming over to the radio station to look the place over. I'd like to meet you there in fifteen minutes."

"Yes, yes! I'll be here."

OAKLEY, signaling Archie, stepped out of the office and locked the door behind him. Crossing Hollywood Boulevard into the parking space beside Grauman's Chinese Theatre, where banners were fluttering in the sea air, he climbed into the roadster. Neither Oakley nor Brixey spoke as they crossed to Santa Monica Boulevard and drove toward the Stupendous Productions lot.

The studio cop at the gate admitted them. They entered the ornate lobby to find Max Sartman pacing the carpet. He came to them wringing pudgy hands.

"I will do as you say, Oakley," he declared. "If we get that boy back safe—what a relief! And what publicity! It's all over the country in the papers—Bartell's being kidnaped. We've got a bushel of telegrams from women begging us to get him back safe. What publicity!"

"I thought you'd realize that sooner or later," Oakley observed. "See here, Sartman. If this is one of your press-agents' stunts to work up a little notoriety for an actor—"

"No!" Sartman exclaimed. "It is nothing like that! I swear it! The boy has been kidnaped."

"All right," Oakley retorted. "Where's Claxton? Has he shown up yet?"

"No—no, he has disappeared, too. We can't find him anywhere. Oakley, for God's sake, what is happening here?"

"Don't worry about Claxton. He'll show up sooner or later. I want to go to the studio where Marsh died."

"Yes. Right—"

"Mr. Sartman!"

Sidney Wheaton came running down the stairs, calling the supervisor's name. His face was flushed with anger, his movements quick. He strode to face Sartman with fists clenched.

"You gave me the part, and now you're kicking me out of it? Is that fair? Haven't I earned it? Have you anybody better for the part? I won't stand for that kind of treatment, Mr. Sartman! My public knows I was given that part—"

"My boy." Sartman placed what was intended to be a soothing hand on Wheaton's shoulder. "We are switching you to a better part, aren't we? You're losing nothing. What difference—"

"I refuse to be changed over!" Wheaton snapped. "It is my part! Who could you put into it that—"

"We are postponing the picture a little, Wheaton. We must use you in the meantime. Perhaps, when the picture begins, we will put Rex Bartell in the part—"

"So that's it!" the juvenile almost screeched. "You're postponing the picture until after Bartell is back. You're going to capitalize on the publicity he's getting—all that rotten notoriety! You want to get your hundred thousand dollars' worth of free advertising! You have no regard for acting ability—you put Bartell in my part. That's despicable, Mr. Sartman! That's—"

"Now, now!" Sartman's face was flushed. "You go up into Claxton's office, and I'll talk with you about it. Not now. I must take Mr. Oakley—"

"Nothing is more important to me than this now, Mr. Sartman! I'll tear up my contract! I won't stand for such treatment!" Wheaton's voice was still screeching. "We'll settle this right now—right now!"

Sartman sighed. "Very well, Wheaton. Excuse me, Oakley. I—I must—"

He broke off in confusion. Wheaton paced back and forth, in a turmoil of anger

"In Claxton's office, Wheaton," Sartman pled again.

The juvenile ran up the stairs. Sartman shrugged at Oakley. "What can I do with these temperamental kids? All of them think they're the best actors in the world. Wheaton—he's the worst I ever saw. You heard him say 'my public.' When an actor begins to talk about 'his' public, he's half crazy."

"A very interesting and tempestuous young man," Oakley observed. "And ambitious. Perhaps, after all, I'd better talk with him again."

"Yes—if you like. Go ahead. I'll wait until he's calmed down."

OAKLEY climbed the steps, and turned forward. With Brixey beside him, and Sartman following, he walked toward a door labeled *Studio Director.* He pushed in to find the reception room empty. An adjoining door was open, and through it Oakley could see Wheaton angrily pacing back and forth in front of a desk.

Oakley half crossed the office—and stopped. He jerked stiff in his tracks. For the thing happened with paralyzing suddenness.

Wheaton turned quickly, peering around. Breath went into his lungs sharply as a puzzled expression crossed his face. And the next instant—

A muffled explosion sounded in the inner office. A tongue of flame licked out of Wheaton's mouth, gushed from his nose. For an instant he seemed to be a rigid image filled with fire. He made pawing, clutching motions in the air, and toppled forward. And when he struck the carpet he lay flat, motionless—smoke whirling up from his body!

"Good God!" Sartman burst out. *"God!"*

A scream sounded in the inner office as Oakley leaped through. Immediately he felt again an intense heat in the room, suffocating and close; and it was filled with the nauseating odor of scorched flesh. The scream sounded again as he stopped at the prostrate body. It came from a girl—blonde, wide-eyed, frightened—who had risen from a typewriter desk near where Wheaton had been pacing.

She blurted: "My typewriter got hot! All of a sudden! It burned me!"

Oakley glanced at the desk on which the machine was sitting. Fumes were rising from it. Oakley gestured Brixey to take care of the girl, and bent over Wheaton.

He turned the young man face up. Wheaton's condition was a thing of horror. The mouth was torn, the nostrils scorched black. Smoke was weaving up from the broken cavity of the chest. The power of the explosion had literally burst Wheaton open. Bones lay stripped of their flesh, and both Wheaton's arms had been blown almost off—they dangled to the body on torn ligaments. And from the entire body fumes oozed.

Oakley straightened, grim and cold. "Dead," he said. "He got it worse than Marsh."

The telephone rang shrilly. Oakley ignored it, and turned away. Brixey was forcing the secretary into an adjoining office and closing the door; the girl was staring at the horror on the floor and babbling hysterically.

Oakley snapped at Sartman: "Get the police in here again! Take another phone. I'll answer this one."

As Sartman, stunned and moving automatically, strode through the outer door, Oakley took up the desk instrument.

"Mr. Oakley, please."

"Cherry? Oke talking!"

"Oke!" The girl's voice rang with excitement. "They've come back—both of them. Claxton and Alice Westmore just went into the apartment house. They ducked out of their car as though they wanted to avoid being seen. Better snap it up if you want 'em."

"Lord; what a time for them to show up!" Oakley moaned. "Cherry, if they start to leave before I get there, and there's no other way of stopping 'em, call a cop and have 'em arrested. I'll clear out of here as soon as I can—"

He hung up while talking, and peered again at the form on the floor. Sobbing noises were coming from the adjoining room. Oakley pushed through the door. Claxton's secretary was blurting unintelligible sounds into a handkerchief.

"It's quite true," said Archie. "She was burned. Not only the hand that touched the typewriter; but her—on the thighs, just above the knees. In, you might say, the position of her garters. She—ah—showed me."

"Some guys get all the breaks," Oakley said sourly as he went back and bent over the typewriter.

The machine still felt hot to the touch. Every inch of the black enamel on it was blistered. The celluloid disks on the keys were charred. Oakley went back to the adjoining room, took the secretary's right hand, inspected the burns, and let it go at that. "As long as you'll vouch for the others, Archie," he explained.

He reentered the office where Sidney Wheaton lay dead. A door swung open as Sartman entered from the hall. The fattish supervisor was mopping at his sweat-beaded face and breathing hard.

"I got McClane. He's coming. God, I could hardly talk. It's the same thing all over again, Oakley—the same thing!"

"Not quite," Oakley answered. "I'd just about decided Wheaton was behind the murder of Richard Marsh, when this happened. Wrong hunch. No doubt of his innocence now, because he got it the same way Marsh did—which is God knows how. Poor chap."

"Oakley—the third juvenile is gone!" Sartman was staring. "One kidnaped—two killed. What can it mean?"

"More than I can tell you at the moment. I've chased hunches on this case and got nowhere. There's just one lead left, Sartman—just one, and I've got to follow that fast. I can't stay here. You've got to tell McClane about this until I get back. Archie!"

Brixey's head came out the door.

"If you want a chance to return the clip you got on the head last night, come with me!"

They bounded down the stairs three steps at a time, headed for the roadster at the curb.

CHAPTER FIVE

BLIND-ALLEY CLUES

OAKLEY braked to a stop directly in front of the apartment house in Hollywood where Alice Westmore lived. He noted grimly that the car sitting ahead of his at the curb was the same which had been parked in front of Madame Midnight's establishment the night before. He slipped from the wheel as light footfalls tapped on the pavement.

Cherry Morris pattered across the street. "They're upstairs now, Oke," she informed her boss. "Better get up there in a hurry. The bedroom light just went out, and that looks like they are getting ready to leave."

"Stick around, darling," Oakley answered briskly, "and we may celebrate the capture of a murderer and a murderess by having a hamburger sandwich together."

"You're too good to me," she observed as Oakley strode into the apartment lobby.

Cherry Morris remained in the door as Brixey entered the automatic elevator beside Oakley. Oakley gave a tap at the automatic nestling under his left arm. He was reaching for the button which would start the cage toward the third floor, when gears whirred somewhere, and the car began to move.

Oakley was satisfied to ride with it. His satisfaction became keener when the cage stopped at the third-floor level. The door slid open quickly; and Oakley's hand slipped to his automatic.

Arthur Claxton stood in the light, a suitcase in each hand. Behind him was the girl, Alice Westmore, blonde and lovely. Something like a gasp came from her when she saw Oakley.

Oakley kept the gun inside his coat and said: "Sorry to interrupt your leave-taking. I suggest you go back."

Claxton blurted angrily: "See here, Oakley—"

"Go," said Oakley with a snap, "back!"

A sob came from the girl's lips. Claxton straightened, his face suffused with wrath. The pair exchanged a glance of hopelessness, and turned without a word. Oakley nudged them to the corner door. The girl unlocked it. Oakley followed them in and Brixey clicked the latch behind him.

"Now," he said, "let's talk."

"Oakley, don't be a damned fool!" Claxton exclaimed. "Alice and I have nothing whatever to do—"

Oakley was studying the girl's face, and feeling pity for her. She had been a very beautiful girl, but on one cheek was a livid scar. The disfigurement was a surprise to Oakley. Through the bathroom door, the night before, he had seen only the opposite side of her face; and the grease-paint of the Madame Midnight masquerade had blotted it over. The girl's sensitive features reddened as Oakley looked at it.

"Sorry," he apologized. "Must ask questions. Where are you two heading?"

"We— I was only taking Alice away until this thing blows over," Claxton answered stiffly.

"Why?"

"Because she has nothing whatever to do with it. God, Oakley, you're making a mess of this thing! Are you crazy enough to think that Alice had a hand in Marsh's death?"

"I'm crazy enough to follow hot leads when I have 'em," Oakley answered. "Now, let's sit down and act civilized. You've got a hell of a lot of explaining to do. Shall we?"

Alice Westmore was gazing at Oakley resolutely. "We'd better, Art," she said. "We've got to make a clean breast of it, even if—"

"Good girl," said Oakley. "Who starts?"

The girl said firmly: "I will." She sat down and lighted a cigarette. Claxton paced. "I'll explain why—why that little episode transpired last night."

"I'm listening."

"You see—" The girl hesitated. "Two years ago I was just getting my start in pictures. I think I had a future—I was told so. I had looks, and I could act a little, but the looks were far the more important of the two. Then—a year or so ago—I was in an automobile accident—"

THE GIRL shuddered as she remembered it. "The car I was driving ran into another on the road to Malibu. My windshield was non-shatterable, but the other car's wasn't. It flew to pieces as the two cars sideswiped, and some of the flying glass struck my face. You see—the result of the cut."

"Regrettable—very," said Archie Brixey sympathetically.

"The scar that was left," Alice Westmore continued, "ruined my chances in pictures. Of course, I couldn't get another job. Well, I had no money. I haven't any folks, either. It was up to me to make a go of it myself, somehow, and I preferred to stay in Hollywood. So, in desperation—in order to earn enough money to get along on—I became Madame Midnight."

"I see. There was no other way?"

"No other way that would let me—hide my face," the girl explained. "You see, I was born and raised in the Southwest. My nurse was an Indian woman. She doctored the men on the ranch with herbs, and as I grew up she told me all her secrets. I remembered all that, and decided to use my knowledge. I got friends of mine to send me the herbs, and I began to sell them.

"Sometimes they helped the people who came to me. At least, there was a helpful psychological effect. My business grew, and I began to make money. I was satisfied to keep it up—anyway, I could do nothing else. I've kept to myself by day, and at night I've been Madame Midnight, selling herbs to movie people who had fame that was denied me because of this—scar."

"Very well," said Oakley gently. "I understand that much. But—you knew Richard Marsh and Sidney Wheaton? Wheaton, you know, was killed tonight, only a short time ago, in the same horrible way. If you—"

"Good Lord, Wheaton too?" Claxton exclaimed. "See here, Oakley. I was at the studio last night, and Sartman told me about the box of capsules you'd found in Wheaton's dressing table. I knew you'd be following up that Madame Midnight lead. My only intention was to keep Alice out of it—I had to do that."

"Romance," sighed Archie.

"Alice is dependent on her Madame Midnight shop for a living. I felt that if you began to investigate her, and learned who she really is, the whole thing would be blown up. She'd have no more clients. That was my only reason for going to the shop and warning her, Oakley— believe me!"

"Does no one else know she is Madame Midnight?"

"I've kept it a secret from everyone except my two closest friends," the girl answered. "Arthur and Rex Bartell."

"Ah?" said Oakley. "So, Claxton, when you heard about the box of capsules I found, you beat it to warn Madame Midnight, Miss West-more. And when I came and found out who she really was, due to the exquisite perfume she uses, you were so desperate that—"

"Don't you see, Oakley?" Claxton demanded. "I was willing to do anything to keep you from linking her with the murders. That would be far worse than simply ruining her business. I was desperate, yes. I took Alice away from there, with the intention of keeping her in hiding until the case blew over—until you found the real murderer, and she could come back without facing disaster."

"Not quite wise," Oakley commented. "And not quite understand-able. Miss Westmore is a charming and attractive young woman, in spite of her slight disfigurement. She would have no need to keep up the hocus-pocus of the Madame Midnight shop if, say, she married a successful young man."

Alice Westmore's face flushed. Claxton looked sheepish.

"I have begged Alice to marry me and leave all that behind," he explained, "but she won't have me. She doesn't love me. It's—"

"Rex Bartell? Then, Miss Westmore," Oakley asked, "why not marry Rex Bartell?"

"Oakley, leave her alone!" Claxton snapped. "You're going too far!"

"I'll explain," the girl answered. "Rex, you see, is only just getting a start in pictures. Whether or not his option will be taken up is always a question. He has been told that his next one will not be. That means Rex will be out of a job—and since he is no better off than most young actors, it means that we'd starve if we married, probably. And Rex will simply not marry me until he is able to provide a decent living."

"Very commendable, too," remarked Brixey.

"Which explains why I have continued to be Madame Midnight, and all the rest."

"Not quite all the rest. It doesn't explain why you popped out of nowhere on the Stupendous lot last night, dressed in man's clothes, and made a desperate attempt to escape us," Oakley pointed out.

ALICE WESTMORE came quickly to her feet. "Mr. Oakley, I swear to you that I know nothing about Richard Marsh's death—or Sidney Wheaton's. Whatever I've done has no connection. Please, please, believe me—and let me alone!"

"The fact remains," said Oakley calmly, coming also to his feet, "that both young men died because fulminate caps exploded inside them, and the caps were contained inside capsules of herbs which came from your shop."

"Good Lord—Alice didn't put them in!" Claxton exclaimed. "Why should she? She scarcely knew Marsh and Wheaton! Why should she want to kill them?"

"I can't answer that question, and you haven't answered mine," Oakley remarked. "Why were you on the Stupendous lot last night, dressed in man's clothes. Where did you come from when I saw you first, and why were you so desperate to get away?"

"I—I can't tell you that!" the girl cried. "But please believe me, it—I—" And she sobbed, pressing a handkerchief to her face.

Arthur Claxton pushed a threatening finger at Oakley. "Oakley, get out of here! Leave Alice alone! If you implicate her in this dirty case, I'll beat you to a pulp!"

Archibald Brixey stepped forward. "See here, my good man," he said. "Mr. Oakley rarely handles such matters as you have just brought up. He refers them to his Fisticuff Department. I," he explained, "am the Fisticuff Department, and ready to function."

Smiling, Oakley rose and gestured the irate Brixey back. "It's all right, Archie," he said. "Suppose we take the hint and depart. Provided," he added, turning to the girl, "I have your promise not to run away. I'll keep quiet about this if you'll stay here."

The girl dried her eyes resolutely. "I won't run away again," she said. "I promise that."

"Then, Archie," said Oakley, "let's take our leave."

The amazed Brixey watched Oakley step out the door. He gave one last glance at the girl, and followed. Riding down in the automatic elevator he regarded Oakley in surprise.

"Have you parted company with your senses?" he inquired. "Can you actually believe that neither the girl nor Claxton is mixed up in the murders?"

"Silly as it sounds, Archie, I believe it," Oakley answered as the car stopped and he stepped out. "Which leaves us with no more leads to follow. The case of the bursting deaths is as much of a puzzle now as it ever was."

Cherry Morris took Oakley's arm as they crossed the sidewalk to the car. "How about the hamburger?" she asked.

"No murderers, no hamburger," Oakley answered. "Cherry, grab a taxi, go home, and rest those shapely feet of yours. Archie and I are wallowing in uncertainty and we must work the night through. Please brighten the office with your resplendent hair at the usual time in the morning."

He drove off with Cherry gazing after him hungrily. Without talking he wound his way to the entrance of Radio Station KSPS and the Stupendous lot. Brixey followed him through the gate and the neon-decorated door of the building.

Again Oakley found the place overrun with patrolmen and plainclothesmen. They allowed him to pass up the stairs. In Claxton's office he found Sartman pacing the carpet.

"Hello—where's McClane?" Oakley asked. "I expected to find him grilling hell out of somebody."

"He's doing it—upstairs," Sartman answered wearily. "I tried to keep him from it, but I couldn't. The way he's been handling that poor old man—"

"Who?"

"William Marsh—Richard Marsh's father. As though the man killed his own son in that horrible way!"

OAKLEY sighed and went out the door. He climbed carpeted stairs into a long corridor which ran along the rear wall of the third floor of the broadcasting building. Three doors opened into it, and one of them was standing ajar.

McClane's voice was booming out: "Somebody's got to know why the station went off the air when those kid actors were killed! Come on—come clean!"

"I don't know—I don't know," was the moaning answer.

Oakley entered a bizarre room. Its walls were covered with black composition panels. On them small bulbs were glowing at dull red heat; meters were flickering; switches and fuses glittered in the light. This was the master control room of the studio, and two men were keeping their attention on the panels as best they could with McClane's bawling voice battling with the music which issued softly from a loud-speaker on a cabinet.

In a chair in the center of the room, William Marsh was sitting, slumped down, his face wan and drawn, his lean hands folded in his lap. That he was a man grief-stricken over the death of his son could not be doubted. That McClane's hammering had worn him still worse was plain to see. Marsh's eyes rose pleadingly to Oakley as McClane straightened.

"Having another brain storm, I see, McClane," Oakley said wrily.

"Listen!" McClane bellowed it. "Twice this station has gone off the air a few minutes, and each time a guy died. The switches that control the power are up here, in the farther room that Marsh uses as a research laboratory. He was the only one near the switches at the time. Does that spell anything to you or not?"

"You're sure that the station's going off the air has something to do with the deaths, McClane?"

"Something's got something to do with the murders, and what other lead is there to follow up? I tell you, there's only one switch that controls the power going to the antenna from the amplifier. It's in the next room, and Marsh was alone in there both times when it happened."

"But the fact remains that you're a bit batty, McClane, if you believe that Marsh deliberately killed his only son."

Marsh moaned: "No—no. I—I loved Richard. He was more to me than anything else in the world. I loved Richard."

McClane growled. As Oakley started for the connecting doors, McClane opened the way. The next room was a clutter of apparatus. Panels glittered in the light, benches were a maze of coils and amplifiers, and numerous radio tubes of all sizes and shapes were in evidence. None of the apparatus seemed to be in use. McClane escorted Oakley through to the adjoining room.

At one end of it two gigantic amplifying tubes were glowing, with water flowing steadily through their cooling jackets. Others were functioning also, building up the powerful potential that the station antenna sprayed into the air pulsing with music and voices. Even larger switchboards were installed here.

A broad bench along one wall was also covered with strange apparatus. In the center of the room, on a tripod pedestal, glistening in the light, was a tremendous cone-shaped coil of heavy, bare copper wire spiralling in the tracks of an insulated shell, shaped like a floodlight reflector. Another tapering coil backed it. This, Oakley presumed, was a piece of apparatus which Marsh had built in his research.

"You see," McClane pointed out, gesturing toward a huge black handle on a panel, "this switch controls the amplified power going to the antenna. Marsh was alone in here both times when the station went dead. Now, I ask you, if there isn't some connection—"

"McClane, be yourself," Oakley chided. "That man's grief is real. He's stricken with sorrow over the death of his son. You're going too far when you suspect him of deliberately killing that boy. When you stop and think it over, doesn't it really seem so?"

McClane grunted. "I can't overlook any chances. But if you think I'm being too hard on the old guy, all right."

Oakley smiled, and returned to the master control room. Placing a sympathetic hand on William Marsh's shoulder, he said: "Don't mind McClane. You'd better go home and get some rest."

Marsh came unsteadily to his feet. "No—no, I can't rest. I must work, to keep my mind off—what happened. I must work because I have only a few days left—only a few days."

THE WORN old man ambled slowly through the center room, and into the laboratory beyond. He closed the door, and a latch slid in place as McClane chewed worriedly on his cigar. Oakley turned and regarded the other technicians in the room.

"I suppose you've grilled them, too?"

"Sure—why not?" The two men glanced warily at McClane as he growled. "I'm going to find out who shut the station off the air if I have to third-degree every one of these radio nuts. I tell you there's some connection."

Oakley sighed, signaled Brixey away, and trod down the stairs. He found Sartman still pacing back and forth across the studio director's office. Sartman stopped and wrung his hands.

"Again I must remind myself that I'm here to find out what became of Rex Bartell," Oakley said. "What're you doing about the ransom letter?"

"I've made all arrangements, Oakley," Sartman answered. "Because I couldn't go myself, I sent a detective with the money. It's fake money, of course. They're probably going up in the blimp right now, ready to follow the beach road and drop the bundle when they see the light flash. I pray to God we get Bartell back safely!"

"Men ready to grab whoever picks up that money?"

"Yes, yes! But if they carry out their threat and—"

"Don't worry about Bartell. In spite of the fact that we can't figure out how the kidnapers grabbed him, they're not so bright if they can't think up any better way of having the ransom money passed to them. If things get too hot, they'll let Bartell go. How, by the way, did that second ransom note come? By mail?"

"No—no! It was found out on the door mat, just as you found the first."

"How'd it get there? Nobody could get in through the gate to leave it, or throw it in, without the cop's seeing something. Did he?"

"No. I'm afraid, Oakley, that somebody who comes and goes unquestioned has left those letters there. Somebody here, in this studio—"

"Just tell McClane that," Oakley commented, "and he'll grill the gizzard out of everybody in the place."

McClane lumbered in as Oakley spoke. He was fumbling with a notebook. Oakley asked him for details, and McClane grudgingly gave them.

The body of Sidney Wheaton had been found covered with strange burns, exactly as Marsh's had been. McClane had a list of them—small burns, circles, two rows of them, on both insteps; pin-point burns on the heels; irregular-shaped burns in front of the calves; a square burn on the pit of the stomach; round burns on the thighs, and another at one side of the abdomen; gash-like burns on each wrist, on the underside, and two circular burns on the neck, one in front and one in back.

"They mean plenty, of course," Oakley said. "The hell of this case is that things have been happening so fast that we've had no time to try to figure them out. I'm going to the office for a session of brain-racking. Besides, I have an appointment this evening, and it's almost due."

The inner door opened, and a girl came out. She was the secretary whose burns Archibald Brixey had so sympathetically investigated. She was still pale and shaky, but artificial color on her face, and her smart suit, made her an attractive figure.

She stopped and said: "Perhaps—maybe I could give you an idea."

Oakley regarded her with interest. "Yes. An idea about what?"

"About what happened to Mr. Wheaton."

"For God's sake, let's have it!" McClane blurted.

"Why—why, I saw Mr. Wheaton come into the office. He was mad—awful mad. I never saw anybody so mad in my life. I said to myself, 'He looks—'"

"Well?" McClane demanded.

"I suggest, McClane," said Oakley quietly, "that you're expecting too much."

"Well?" McClane demanded again.

"Well, I said to myself, 'He looks mad enough to burst'—and then he did!"

Oakley moaned. "Good night, McClane," he whispered.

CHAPTER SIX

INVISIBLE POWER

WITH Archibald Brixey behind him, Clay Oakley unlocked the door labeled *Secrets, Inc.* Surprised to find lights burning in the reception room, he pushed into the *sanctum sanctorum.* There he discovered Miss Cherry Morris, relaxed in the easy chair, wriggling the toes of her stocking feet.

"I sent you home," Oakley chided her.

"I'm waiting," said Cherry, "for that hamburger sandwich."

Oakley sighed as he settled into a chair. "Look here, young woman. The brain inside that head of yours is as bright as the hair which decorates it. Got any ideas?"

"Cherry is stumped, Oke," said the girl.

"You went into that studio, when Marsh was killed, as soon as I did. It was stifling hot, though the heat was turned off. Any guesses why?"

"Marsh, I've been told, was very hot stuff," said Cherry.

"No cracks! The station went off the air at the time of the murders, but of course your mind is still dwelling on hamburger sandwiches. Cherry, I'd like nothing better than to go over to the Twin Barrels with you, but I've got an appointment."

"Important?" asked Cherry.

"More important than hamburgers, sweetheart."

Oakley trod into the adjoining room, which housed his voluminous files, and came back bearing several thick folders. Settling at his desk, he removed papers and newspaper clippings from them, and studied them. Archibald Brixey settled in another chair and yawned. Cherry kept wriggling her alluring toes. Oakley concentrated until, at last, he sat back with a sigh.

"Nothing anywhere," he said.

A knock sounded on the door. Cherry slipped into her slippers, entered the reception room, and opened the way. A tall man, carrying a briefcase, was outside. He asked to see Mr. Oakley, and Cherry brought him into the inner sanctum.

"Mr. Cartwright?" Oakley asked. He introduced the gentleman to his assistants. "Mr. Cartwright is a consulting radio engineer." As he gestured the man to a chair he inquired: "What have you found?"

"Very interesting data."

Cartwright brought papers out of his briefcase, and among them a magazine. He passed them to Oakley, and Oakley studied them. Presently the private investigator turned bright eyes on his assistants.

"Have you," he asked, "ever heard of a bevy of gentlemen named McLennan, Bunton, Gosset, Cutwhilst, Lakhowsky and Schere-schewsky? I thought not. I have here, thanks to Mr. Cartwright," Oakley explained, "a copy of *The Canadian Journal of Research*, Volume Three. Turning to page two hundred and twenty-four I find an article called *The Heating of Electrolytes in High Frequency Fields.* It is written by J.C. McLennan, F.R.S., and A.C. Bunton, M.A."

Archibald Brixey was leaning forward. "It sounds very imposing."

"And interesting. I'll read you the first paragraph of this paper.

" 'Considerable interest has been aroused by the discovery that curious and unexpected physiological and biological effects are produced by short electromatic waves of wave-lengths fifty meters and under. Gosset, Cutwhilst, Lakhowsky and Magram, in 1924, reported an effect on plant tumors, while Schereschewsky in 1926 noted their lethal effects on mice and inferred that certain wave-lengths have a specific effect on living cells. The production of fever in men has been observed. Later experiments show that the phenomenon observed so far can be explained as due to simple heating effects.'"

"Which means what?" Cherry Morris asked, perking up.

"Mr. Cartwright will be able to explain it better than I. Let's have it, Cartwright."

The radio engineer sat forward in his chair. "Experiments concerning the effects of short-waves on living tissues have been going on for some time," he began. "In the General Electric plant at Schenectady there are a number of such contrivances. They have been put to therapeutic use. That is, human bodies, subjected to very short radio wave-lengths, generate artificial fevers, and this is one way of combating disease."

"We're more interested in how people are killed than how they are cured," Oakley remarked.

"Quite. I want you to know first that the use of short-wave-lengths in this manner has been going on for some time. There are electrical furnaces, too, which make use of the eddy-currents generated in the fields of high-frequency coils. These eddy-currents, passing through conductors, generate heat. They are used for the final elimination of residual gasses in the manufacture of radio vacuum tubes, but I won't go into that."

"Don't," said Archie Brixey. "Get to the point."

"Yes. We know, then, that powerful short-waves generate heat when they are absorbed by conductors. The better the conductor, the more absorption of the radiating short radio waves, and the more heat developed. So copper, iron, all metals, when in this high-frequency field, become hot."

"A copper fulminate cap—"

"Would become heated."

"Even inside a human body?"

CARTWRIGHT was emphatic in his reply. "Of course," he said. "The short radio waves penetrate all substances, exactly as ordinary radio waves of the broadcast band do. At this moment, your body is being shot through and through with radio waves, and this has always been true, especially since commercial broadcasting began. It's harmless, of course—except that very powerful short-waves generate heat."

"Then, if these waves were powerful enough, and were made to pass through the body of a person in which was contained a copper fulminate cap—"

"The cap would explode."

"But—"

"The very short wave-lengths," Cartwright continued, "are directional in the same sense as light. They can be shot along a certain path, like the beam of a searchlight, although, of course, they are invisible. It's possible, Mr. Oakley, that this was done in the case of the two murders. A beam of powerful short radio waves was half the instrument of murder. The fulminate caps in the stomachs of the victims was the other half."

"I say!" blurted Brixey.

"The source of these short waves could have been anywhere close at hand—possibly in another building?"

"Yes—but the likelihood is that the source was in the same building. The most probable place is the control rooms upstairs in KSPS. I know the layout well; I've even seen some of the apparatus William Marsh built. If a beam of short radio waves was shot downward from a parabolic repulsor, the beam, like invisible light, would penetrate the ceiling, and the full power would strike upon the young men below and—"

"I've heard enough!" Oakley exclaimed. "Thanks, Cartwright!" He jerked up, gesturing. "Cherry, write the gentleman a check." As Cartwright withdrew, he paced the floor. Pausing in the corner, he clicked the switch of a radio and turned the dial to the position of KSPS. As music floated into the room, and the outer door closed, Oakley turned to face Brixey.

"That's it, Archie! Somebody upstairs in KSPS did exactly that— paved the way for murder by getting Marsh and Wheaton to swallow fulminate caps without knowing it—then bumped them off by drilling them with a focused beam of short-waves, intensely powerful. God, what a way to kill a man!"

"Devilish!" Brixey exclaimed. "The murderer was nowhere in the room, but upstairs, out of sight. I say, Oke. Who could have done it? You can't suspect Marsh, who probably rigged up the apparatus, of deliberately killing his only son. It's obvious he's all broken up by it. Then who—"

"Somebody else in the place—somebody who understood the apparatus that Marsh built. The damnedest, most devilish—"

Oakley broke off as a voice issued from the loud-speaker of the radio. "This is Station KSPS, Stupendous Productions broadcasting, ladies and gentlemen. We have just completed the last broadcast of the evening—"

"The station's shutting down!" Oakley exclaimed. "Archie—come along!"

He started for the door and stopped short, facing Cherry Morris. She was powdering her nose and adjusting wisps of bright red hair.

"Cherry's coming too, Oke."

"You're going home to bed!" Oakley snapped. "This damn thing is too dangerous, Cherry. We're probably dealing with a madman. I certainly don't want you burned to a crisp, darling, if it should come to that."

"Cherry," said Cherry, more firmly, "is going along!"

"Nix! Come on, Archie!"

Oakley sped out the door, with Archie leaping at his heels. He ignored the call from Cherry Morris that echoed after him. Quickly dodging through late traffic, into the parking space beside Grauman's Chinese, he ducked into his roadster. The next moment the car was whizzing along a cross street toward Santa Monica Boulevard and the Stupendous studios.

"But Oke!" Brixey gasped as he clung to his hat, "what has this to do with Bartell's disappearance?"

"Not a damned thing that I know of, Archie," Oakley answered, as the tires whined around a corner. "But it explains a hell of a lot else. How the fulminate caps were exploded. Why the burns on the corpses. See that? The burns on the feet were caused by the eyelets and nails in the shoes getting red hot, instantly. The burns on the legs, from the metal in the garters. The burns on the thighs from coins in the pockets. The burns on the abdomen from the belt-buckle, and possibly a watch. The burns on the front and back of the neck due to collar buttons. Tremendously powerful short-waves were shooting into those rooms for a moment.

"That's why the rooms were so hot! That's why the secretary's typewriter sizzled—some of the waves reached it, and she wasn't burned otherwise because she was wearing nothing metal, except the clasps of her garters. And the studio going off the air—

"Somebody switched the entire power of the station into the short-wave apparatus—thousands of watts!" Oakley exclaimed. "That's the answer, Archie—that's how those boys were killed. But who did it? *Who?*"

The wind tore past them as they sped.

OAKLEY and Brixey pushed through the gate and door of the broadcasting building. The reception room was deserted. Oakley ran up the stairs to the second floor, with Brixey at his heels. A quick look through the glass doors of the studios disclosed them all empty.

Up the next flight went Oakley. He stepped into the master control room to find it deserted. The bulbs on the panels were no longer glowing. He pushed into the center room, then into the far room which served as the research laboratory. It, like the others, was empty.

Oakley regarded the towering piece of apparatus which sat on a castered tripod, its helixical wires glittering in the light. It looked strange and ominous. He stepped past, glanced at the huge switchboard, and saw that the power was off. With a sigh he turned back.

"Is that the thing that was used, Oke?" Archie inquired.

"Probably, though God knows who used it. What's directly below here? The studio in which Marsh died! And just ahead, on the front corner, Claxton's office! Both could be reached easily by direct beams. We'll check up on that, Archie!"

Oakley passed through the control rooms, and down the stairs. When he reached the base of the flight, the door of Claxton's office opened, and Max Sartman stepped out. He gestured nervously as he strode toward Oakley.

"I've been trying to get you on the phone. The men who took the money along the shore road in the blimp have just reported. Nothing happened—no lights!"

"What?" Oakley exclaimed. "Nobody signaled for the money to be dropped?"

"Nobody! They're onto us, Oakley! They know a trap was set for them. We'll never see Rex Bartell alive again—never!"

"I'll be damned." Oakley's eyes glittered. "We've got to forget Bartell for a minute, and hope that he's safe. Sartman, upstairs is a machine that was used for killing your two juveniles. They were murdered by—"

Oakley pushed into the studio in which Marsh had died as he spoke. Sartman followed, listening intently. Oakley strode to the table, studying its position.

"The research laboratory is diagonally above. Nothing between this table and that machine but a floor and a wall, and the short waves penetrate those as though they did not exist. Claxton's office—just a swing of that parabolic repulsor, a throw of the switch—and it was done!"

Sartman was mystified and silent. Quickly Oakley covered the theory behind the weapon of murder. He pointed out that it explained every strange aspect of the victim's body, and even the length of microphone cord which was only partially burned because only part of it lay within the beam of invisible power. Sartman listened aghast, as Oakley paced back and forth and talked.

"The man we want was in the research laboratory, upstairs, alone, at the instant death hit those juveniles. He used the machine Marsh built, throwing the entire power of the station into it. It was all over in a few seconds."

"But the capsules—"

"Somebody hid the caps in the capsules as the first step in the murder. The next was to get the victims within the bounds of the short-wave beam so that the power would be sufficient to explode the caps in their stomachs. Insane as it sounds, it was a damned clever weapon of murder to choose—because the murderer needn't be present, and the effects were so puzzling—"

Sartman, pacing while he listened, paused beside the window of the monitor booth in the corner. His jaw sagged as he gazed at a panel inside.

"Who could have done it, Sartman? Who could have been within reach of that piece of apparatus upstairs, other than William Marsh? I say 'other than William Marsh' because it's impossible to believe

that man deliberately murdered his own son. One of the technicians—somebody who—"

"Look!" Sartman blurted.

Oakley stepped close beside him. He saw, inside the monitor booth,
only a dim red glow on the panel. A tiny signal bulb was burning.

"The mike in this studio is alive!" Sartman exclaimed. "Somebody's
turned on the juice. Somebody's listening in—they've heard everything
you said!"

"What? Where? Upstairs? I was just up there—the place is empty."

"No, no!" Sartman exclaimed. "Someone is up there now. The power
is on. I tell you, somebody's listening in—somebody's heard every
word you said!"

Oakley's eyes narrowed as his hand slipped beneath his coat toward
his armpit holster. "Glad to hear it," he remarked tartly. "We're going
up!"

OAKLEY swung out of the studio and bounded up the stairs. At
the head of the flight he paused, peering up and down the narrow
hallway which ran the entire length of the building. Archie Brixey
paused beside him, and Sartman followed, wheezing.

There was no sound. Oakley stepped into the master control room.
Now he saw that a single vacuum valve on a panel was glowing; one,
obviously, which connected with the microphone in the death studio.
But there was no one in the room; and the door leading into the next
was wide open.

Oakley's gun slipped out as he stepped to the sill. A swift shift of
his head, and he saw that no one was hiding behind the wall or the
open door. The grotesque radio apparatus glistened in the light. Quietly
he crossed to the farther door, which connected with the research lab.

He twisted the knob and pushed. The door was firm. Stepping
back, he eyed it.

"Who's in there?" he called.

There was no answer. Oakley turned, and signaled Archie Brixey.
"Ease around to the hallway door which connects with that room,
Archie. If it's open, go in, and go ready to shoot."

Brixey's aristocratic features hardened as he slipped his own automatic out, and strode quietly back into the master control room.
Oakley watched him pass through the door into the hallway, and

heard his footfalls on the carpet. A moment of quiet passed before the footfalls came again. Brixey walked quickly into the middle room.

"Locked," he said.

Oakley's eyes sought Sartman's. "It may please you to know," he said quietly, "that the murderer is in that room. He slipped in there while we were talking downstairs. He knows he's trapped and—anything may happen."

Sartman asked in a breathy whisper: "Who?"

Oakley smiled tartly. "It's got to be someone who knows the studio thoroughly, somebody who can use Marsh's apparatus. One possibility occurs to me—the only possibility."

Again Sartman whispered: "Who?"

"Arthur Claxton."

Sartman merely stared. Oakley took a moment to slip from the room, into the hallway, and try the other door which connected with the research lab. It was still locked; and there was still an ominous silence behind the panels. He retraced his steps to find Sartman coming into the hall.

"Stay out here," Oakley told the supervisor quickly, "and guard that door. If anybody tries to get out—"

"You think Claxton did it? You think he's the one who's in that room?"

"I think—"

Oakley broke off, peering down the stairwell. Red suffused his face. A man was running up the flight from the second floor. He was looking up, and his face was clearly visible in the bright light.

The man was Arthur Claxton.

"—not!" finished Oakley with a snap.

CHAPTER SEVEN

SKELETON WITHOUT ARMS

CLAXTON paused at the top step. Oakley regarded him angrily, Sartman in amazement. Claxton demanded: "What the hell's the matter? Can't I come into my own studio without being stared at like a ghost? Or are you going to get nasty again, Oakley?"

"I feel," said Oakley, "very nasty. I'd just decided you were a murderer, Claxton, and your appearance shows me I'm wrong. Unless you just dropped out of the window of that research lab, leaving it locked, and came in here to try to fool—"

"I've been dropping out of no windows, Oakley," Claxton answered frigidly. "I came here to catch up on lost time in my work, since you've insisted that Miss Westmore stay in town and we can't leave. She's downstairs in my office now. The cop at the gate will tell you—"

"Never mind," Oakley sighed. He gestured to Sartman again. "Stay out here in the hall and keep an eye on that door. Whoever's in there, I'm going to get him out if I have to tear down a wall." And he turned, tramping angrily back into the master control room.

Claxton followed him. Brixey was at the locked door of the middle room. Oakley was about to speak when a sound came through the panel—a faint creaking. Brixey jerked and Oakley's eyes widened.

"Still in there!" he exclaimed.

He turned quickly at a new sound behind him—quick, light footfalls. They came across the hallway, and into the master control room, and Miss Cherry Morris came with them. She paused, smiling, puckering her patrician nose.

"I will not," she declared, "be left behind!"

Oakley moaned. "Cherry, get out of here!" he ordered her. "The man we want is in that room. He's trapped. If he starts shooting, I don't want any bullets burying themselves in your beautiful young body. Beat it!"

"Now that I'm here," Cherry said firmly, "I'm going to stay. Just let your murderer start shooting, and I'll flash a knee at him and disrupt his aim."

Oakley gave it up. Grimly he whirled back to the door. He twisted the knob again, and pounded knuckles on the panel. "Open up!" he commanded. "Come out of there, or we'll break in and get you!"

The only answer that came from the sealed room was another soft creak, Oakley drew back. Gesturing, he directed Brixey. "Let's have that chair. That door's going down."

Brixey shifted it toward him. Oakley gripped its back, swung it up. It was poised above his head when his muscles suddenly tightened. For one instant he kept the position, while strange expressions crossed the faces of the others in the room.

Swiftly Oakley dropped the chair. He snatched at his vest pocket. From it he jerked the small box labeled *Madame Midnight*. With the same movement, as a gasp escaped him, he twirled it across the room, into a corner.

Instantly an explosion rang. The pasteboard box flew into fluttering fragments. Fumes puffed into the air. The report rang sharply from the walls. In the corner, where the box had fallen, there were now only a few flakes of paper and a floating fog.

"He's turned on the machine!"

Oakley blurted it as he peered at the others in the room. He was feeling suddenly hot, as though a fever had seized his body and was mounting by the second. He half shouted: "Get any metal off of you! Free yourself of metal or you'll be burned!"

Crazily he began fumbling through his pockets. Oakley's warning gained significance immediately in the minds of the others. The girl gasped and tore at a tiny necklace dangling about her neck. She flung it away, and a red mark was left on her skin.

It was a weird, half-comical moment that passed within the room. Money scattered as Oakley, Brixey and Claxton turned pockets inside out. Two watches thumped to the floor. Cherry Morris slipped a ring from her finger and then, with celerity, snatched up her skirts and tugged herself free of a pair of garters while displaying enchanting legs.

As Claxton's cigarette case fell to the floor, a wisp of smoke curled from inside it. Oakley's belt and Brixey's suspenders followed it. Quickly they kicked off their shoes, ripped off collars, tore out buttons. In a moment they were freed of all things metal.

During that ludicrous moment, they had worked their way from the middle room into the master control room; but the growing heat followed them. The air was stifling. Oakley felt his body burning with terrific fever. The wall they placed between themselves and the door of the research lab did not diminish the power of the invisible beam in the slightest.

"Cherry, get out!" Oakley shouted. "Claxton, go with her. Archie and I are tackling that door!"

Cherry Morris pattered in slipperless feet into the hallway, her stockings slipping down. Claxton backed out, his face beaded with sweat. Oakley glanced around swiftly.

Everything metallic in the room seemed to be radiating heat, sizzling. A coil of wire that lay on a desk was giving off fumes as its insulation melted. Oakley had slammed the door shut during the retreat; as he moved to twist the knob, to jerk the door open again, the intense radiation from it stopped his hand.

Brixey was gasping for air. Oakley tore off his coat, covered his hand with it, and grabbed the knob. As the door swung open, smoke puffed up from the fabric, and he dropped it. He hurried into the inner room, sweat pouring down his face, as Brixey gasped in after him.

The center room was filled with scorched fumes. The apparatus on the table was crackling with the increasing heat. Oakley could feel it penetrating his body, a heat that crowded around his heart and upset the working of his lungs. The organs within him seemed to be blistering, his blood coming to a boil.

With growing intensity, the invisible power was beating through the door of the research lab.

"Oke! Oke!" It was the frantic call from Cherry Morris. "Come away! Please come away!"

Oakley gasped an unintelligible answer as he snatched up the chair. He swung it swiftly against the panels of the connecting door. A leg snapped off, but the panel held. Oakley swung again, feeling that the terrific, penetrating heat was sapping all strength from his body.

Brixey, panting, dragged another chair from the master control room. He straddled beside Oakley, and whacked it against the door. Alternately they crashed the chairs against the panels. The wood of the door cracked; a slat of it fell out. A bright light shafted through as Oakley dropped his chair and stumbled forward.

In the research lab he could see the gigantic, tripoded piece of apparatus, turned toward him. The heat was beating out of it. He hung to the door, gasping, as he reached through the crack toward the latch. And as he fumbled, his watering eyes stared—stared at the man inside.

That man was standing calmly, looking through the broken door. He was making no attempt to attack Oakley and Brixey. He was holding something in one hand, and the other was moving toward his mouth. The regular, even gesture was absurdly like that of a person eating nuts. And, seeing him, Oakley's eyes widened in amazement.

Oakley found the blistering hot catch and drew it back. He kicked the connecting door open with one savage thrust. He was lurching across the sill, when the man in the lab moved. That man's hand raised a last time to his mouth as he stepped forward, to a position directly in front of the powerful, radiating apparatus.

"Back!" Oakley gasped. "Back, Archie!"

He stumbled out the door, pulling Brixey with him. Keeping his feet, he stared in mute horror. For a second now the man in the lab had been standing directly in the beam of invisible power. And suddenly—

A muffled, horrible explosion sounded. The man in the next room disappeared in a cloud of smoke. Liquid spattered through the air as the thump of the falling body sounded. Looking down, Oakley saw spots on his hands—spots of red—blood. Through the doorway fumes gushed, awful and nauseating.

Through the mist of fog, Oakley stared. Brixey was hanging to him, gasping. On the floor now was a widening pool of red.

Oakley gasped: "He killed himself!"

Thrusting forward, he stumbled through the connecting door, beyond the horror on the floor. As he passed outside the beam of invisible power, the terrific heat abruptly disappeared. With his body bathed in perspiration, his skin still smarting, but breathing more freely, Oakley moved toward the switches on the board which were thrown on.

He snatched the handles down. A crackling sound came from the tripoded apparatus. Assured that the power was off, Oakley turned back.

Brixey was grimacing as he peered at the thing on the floor.

It had been the body of a man. Now it was ripped asunder, a thing of horror. Bathed in blood, with fumes oozing up from it, it lay weltering. The head, disfigured beyond recognition, had been blown off. The upper part of the body had been denuded of flesh by the terrific power of the internal explosion, and the broken ribs lay white and bare. The arms had fallen aside, with the upper parts also stripped clean. In an instant a man had been turned into a skeleton—without arms.

"God!" Brixey gasped. "I didn't even see his face before it happened."

"I saw his face," Oakley answered tightly. "It was William Marsh."

"Marsh! Marsh, after all?"

"Marsh, after all," said Oakley.

A new sound startled him. It was a crash of breaking glass, and it came from the middle room. Oakley stepped over the sill, and saw the glittering fragments on the floor. They had flown from one of the windows—and outside that window now, a window three stories above the ground, there was movement.

A man was dangling in space. A rope was whipped about him, and he was clinging to it. He was swinging, twisting; one of his feet, out-thrown, had struck the window and broken the pane.

Oakley sprang to the latch, and slid up the sash. As he reached out and closed arms around the dangling body, he heard a startled gasp. Urgently, Oakley dragged the dangling man in through the window. He forced the hands to let go of the rope. There was a scramble—and a young man sprawled on the floor.

He dragged himself up, panting.

"My word!" exclaimed Archibald Brixey.

"I'll be damned!" blurted Oakley.

It was the young man whose mysterious disappearance had first brought Clay Oakley to the Stupendous broadcasting station—Rex Bartell!

OKE OAKLEY grabbed Rex Bartell's arm. "Cherry!" he called. The young man breathed hard and looked frightened as the red-headed girl hurried, still slipperless, into the room. "Take him to Claxton's office and keep him there till I come down!"

"Listen!" Bartell begged. His was a brunette handsomeness well adapted to the screen, though now his clothes were wrinkled and dirtied. "I can explain—"

"You bet your life you can, and you'll do it in a minute," Oakley told him grimly. "Cherry, lure him away."

Oakley stepped to the door of the research lab and closed it, giving one last, grimacing look at the thing, half man, half armless skeleton, which lay inside. He picked up shoes, money, anything he could find and, padding in his stocking feet into the master control room, sank into a chair, and breathed in cool air.

Brixey was looking blank. "Oke," he said, "I'm all in a muddle."

"Stay in it a while!" Oakley snapped, drawing on a shoe. "We'll have the answer in a minute."

He refused to say more, though Max Sartman lumbered in, ges-ticulating, half crying, half sobbing. The supervisor trotted behind Oakley down the stairs. Oakley stepped into Claxton's office on the second floor to find Rex Bartell and Alice Westmore wrapped in each other's arms.

"This," Cherry Morris remarked, "is some clinch. It's been going on for minutes."

Oakley snorted. He tapped Bartell's shoulder, and the young man drew away from the girl. Immediately he began to blurt: "I know it was a crazy idea, but—I did it because—well, I was fading out and I thought if I got lots of publicity the studio would—"

"You did *what* because?" Oakley demanded.

"Kidnaped myself."

"Kidnaped *yourself*?"

"Why, sure." Bartell's was the naiveté of youth. "You didn't think somebody really grabbed me, did you?"

"To tell the truth," Oakley said grimly, "we did think that. And now you pop up here and tell me you kidnaped yourself!"

Alice Westmore exclaimed: "It was a wild, impulsive thing to do, Mr. Oakley—but I can understand why Rex did it. I was just as desperate to get ahead in pictures when I began. Once he started it, of course, he had to go on with it and—"

"Suppose," said Oakley with a sigh, "you begin from the beginning, young man."

"Sure." Bartell grinned impulsively. "You see, I wasn't doing so well. I'd had a few small parts, but nothing new was coming along. In fact, Mr. Sartman told me only a week ago that he wasn't going to take up my option. Well, I got desperate—because I had to keep my job—I had to make big money so I could marry Alice—and I just planned it out."

"To kidnap yourself," Oakley said sourly.

"Sure. My idea was to get a lot of swell publicity. The newspapers would play it up big. My name would be all over the front pages. Then, afterward, I'd have such a big publicity value that I'd stay in pictures. People would be sure to come and see Rex Bartell in any picture, after all that. So I—"

"You got the publicity, all right—millions of dollars worth of it," Oakley said. "If you don't get thrown into the jug on top of it."

Bartell paled; but he went on. "I was to broadcast that night, you see—studio talk, you know—and I had it all planned out. I left my car in back of the studio, with grips in it. There were blankets in the grips, and cans of food, and water, and enough to keep me comfortable for days while I was on the roof—"

"On the roof!" Oakley moaned. "You mean to tell me that all the while we were looking for you, you were on the roof of this very building?"

"Sure. It's the highest on the lot, there wasn't any danger of anybody's seeing me. So I parked the car. With the grips in it. I had a rope tied to the handles of the grips, and I threw the rope up on the roof. After three tries, it stayed up there. So then I went into the studio, and when I saw my chance I climbed out the window, and up on the awning—"

"And onto the roof—yes," Oakley added.

"It wasn't hard. I'd done harder stunts than that before the camera. Once I was on the roof, I pulled the suitcases up. Then I just planned to stay there until I reappeared—until it would look like the kidnapers released me. Those ransom letters—why, I just dropped them off the roof so they fell near the front door. I just stayed up there and ate and slept and—"

"Drove people crazy. Nice idea!" Oakley commented.

Alice Westmore spoke earnestly to Oakley. "He didn't tell me about it first, Mr. Oakley, or I wouldn't have let him do it. The first I knew was when I got a letter from Rex, telling me what he was about to do, and by then he'd already done it. He told me where he was. Because I wanted to go to him, to tell him he couldn't go on with it, I came to the studio dressed as a man."

"Because you were known as Bartell's fiancée?"

"Yes. I told Arthur about it, and he'd gotten me the pass, in a false name. I called to Rex, and he let down the rope. He hoisted me up there with him. I was scared to death, but I was so worried about what Rex was doing I—I tried to induce him to give it up, but it was too late then. When you saw me, I'd just been let down again by the rope and—"

"And," Oakley supplied, "you led me a merry chase! All right. One publicity-crazy young actor accounts for one hell of a mess. But it doesn't explain why Marsh deliberately killed his son—"

"Deliberately?" Arthur Claxton said. "Certainly not, Oakley! Marsh couldn't have known that his own son was broadcasting from that room."

"What!"

"Not at all. It was Sidney Wheaton who was scheduled to speak on that program in the first place. He didn't show up in time. We had his script here and when I saw Richard Marsh in the place, I induced Marsh to take Wheaton's place on the program."

"Oh, God!" Oakley moaned. "Marsh was in the spot that Wheaton should have been in?"

"Certainly. Marsh was an expert mimic, and I'd often heard him take off Wheaton's theatrical accent. I introduced Marsh as Wheaton, and Marsh read Wheaton's speech as Wheaton would have done it. Anyone listening in wouldn't have known the difference."

Oakley was staring. "Good Lord! William Marsh was listening in, upstairs. He heard Wheaton announced and thought Wheaton was speaking. He turned that machine on, and Marsh died instead of Wheaton. No wonder Marsh was broken up—realizing he'd killed his own son by mistake!"

"You see, Oakley," Sartman spoke up, "Wheaton was entirely innocent in the matter of the explosive in those capsules. He didn't know the stuff was in there, certainly. He'd already taken some of them. The caps must've been lodged in his stomach, so that when the short-wave power hit him later—he died the same way Marsh died."

"Then William Marsh put the caps in Wheaton's capsules. They were intended for Wheaton only!"

"Say, I saw"—it was Rex Bartell again—"I saw Marsh's father in the dressing room several days ago. He was alone in there when I went in. I thought I saw him closing the drawer of Wheaton's dressing table. He pretended he was doing nothing out of the way—but he was upset and nervous. I didn't think much of it at the time—"

"William Marsh," broke in Alice Westmore quietly, "came to my studio almost a week ago, and asked for some of the same herb capsules that I had given Sidney Wheaton. Obviously he loaded them with caps and switched the loaded ones for the ones in Wheaton's dressing table. But why? Why was William Marsh going to kill Wheaton?"

"For the same reason," Rex Bartell said, "that I was crazy enough to fake my own kidnaping. Because Sidney Wheaton was the pet of this studio. He was getting all the best juvenile parts, and Dick and I were being given the air. Dick Marsh's option wasn't going to be taken up, either. Dick's father—

"The man was mad about Dick—his only son. I've been to their place several times, and the mere mention of Wheaton's name was enough to make William Marsh rave. Wheaton was getting all the breaks, and Dick was suffering for it. Wheaton was being built into a star, and Dick was getting thrown out of work. William Marsh hated Wheaton. Because he was so crazy about Dick, and wanted Dick to reach the top—that's why.

"Another thing—William Marsh was through here—at the studio, in his research work. He was broke because the studio appropriation wasn't enough to pay all the costs of his work, and he used all his salary for the expenses. And when he saw that Sidney Wheaton was costing Dick his job, too—that both of them would be left without work and without money—he killed Wheaton. To eliminate the competition, of course, so Dick would stay with the studio, and get the big parts. It was more important than life or death to William Marsh—I know."

Oakley sighed and rose. "Damned sad," he said. "Ironic that circumstances brought it about so that Marsh killed his own son instead of the man he planned to kill. It must have broken his mind. His killing Wheaton afterward must have been a crazy gesture of revenge."

Oakley paused, and eyed Cherry Morris. She had replaced her slippers and garters and was rouging her lips.

"I suggest, Sartman," said Oakley wearily, "that you think up a good string of lies to make McClane believe that Bartell was actually kidnaped, and that the kidnapers released him. You don't want that kid in trouble. You want him in pictures, don't you?"

"Yes—yes! All the publicity he got! A fool trick, but—what publicity!"

"And what would Hollywood be without publicity?" Oakley asked. "Come, Cherry. Come, Archie."

Wearily Oakley walked out the studio door, and through the gate, with Brixey on one side, and Cherry's arm on his.

"Now," asked Cherry, "what?"

"We shall go," smiled Oakley, "and get us a hamburger sandwich."

THE SILVER DOOM

BENEATH THE SUN-WARMED WATERS OF THE CARMORE POOL IT LURKED—A SILENT, SCAVENGING HORROR THAT TURNED MEN TO SKELETONS IN SPLIT SECONDS—THEN VANISHED INTO THE UNKNOWN. WHAT WAS THIS DEATH-DEALING SILVER CLOUD THAT BROUGHT DOOM TO THOSE IT SHADOWED? WHY DID IT STRIKE AT ONLY A SELECTED FEW OF THOSE WHO DOVE INTO ITS LAIR?

CHAPTER ONE

DEATH ON THE NEEDLE

CLAY OAKLEY of Secrets, Incorporated, private investigator of affairs Hollywoodian, entered the imposing gate of the great Associated Studios accompanied by his first assistant, the elegant Mr. Archibald Brixey. With passes in their hands they waved studio cops out of their way, strode along the narrow streets of the walled lot, climbed the stairs of the executive offices, and entered a door labeled *Josef Hirsch.*

To a blonde and chilly secretary Oakley said, "To see Mr. Hirsch, please," and handed her his card.

"He just phoned me on a matter of life and death," he added.

A moment later they entered the chromium-and-black modernistic inner office.

JOSEF HIRSCH was reputed to be one of the sternest, most overbearing, and temperamental directors in pictures; yet Oakley found him now to be pale and visibly trembling with fear. His eyes beseeched pity.

"Someone has tried to kill me!" Hirsch blurted. "It was two nights ago. I was just turning my car into the driveway of my home at Bel-Air. I heard a shot. It came from behind the garage. The bullet—it missed me by an inch, Mr. Oakley. It went into the seat cushion. God, I—"

"You haven't told the police?"

"The police? No. I don't trust the police. When I recovered from the shock, I made a search—but there was no one. I tell you, that man tried to kill—"

"Why," interrupted Oakley quietly, "did you wait two days before doing anything about it, Mr. Hirsch?"

There on the brink
they struggled.

"I put three servants to watching the house and grounds night and day. I thought that would be enough—but it wasn't. Just an hour ago—here—"

"A second attempt?"

"Yes! I was sitting here at this desk. Suddenly I heard another shot. Glass broke out of that window. The bullet went past my head. Look there!" He jerked aside the window curtain and disclosed a gaping, ragged break in one pane. He crossed the room with quick strides

and pointed to a black, round hole in a panel opposite. The bullet, certainly, had passed directly over the desk.

"The shot must have been fired from the top of that sound stage. But I saw no one on it, I had the studio cops look around—they found nobody. I've got to have protection, Mr. Oakley—"

"Surely you have some idea who—"

"None—none!" Hirsch blurted. "I don't know who is trying to kill me or why. That is what I want you—"

Hirsch started as the telephone buzzed. His hand trembled as he lifted it. The voice rattling in the receiver was plain.

"Mr. Stengel is on Sound Stage Five, Mr. Hirsch. He wants you to complete the temple scenes this morning."

"Yes—I know. I'll come."

Hirsch nervously left the office, with Oakley and Brixey following him closely. They strode along a studio street to the entrance of the huge, flat-topped, oblong building labeled *Sound Stage 5.* They entered through a heavy, padded door.

In the huge room were a score of technicians, actors and actresses in make-up, a jungle of spotlights, a maze of electric cables snaking over the floor. At one end of the stage a set had been erected—the interior of a Chinese temple. It glittered with gold paint and fantastic designs; but overshadowing all else was a gigantic idol which sat against the rear wall.

Its face alone was the height of a man, and it was one which no Occidental eye could view without shock and revulsion. One eye was partly and leeringly closed; the other was staring wide with a terror-striking wrath. Its mouth was twisted cruelly, its lips loose and open, disclosing darkness beyond. The whole face was a Chinese nightmare.

Archibald Brixey stopped short and gasped. "My word—what's that?"

Hirsch answered as he walked toward the set. "The Taoistic God of Anger. It is a reproduction of an actual—"

A man who strode toward Hirsch impatiently interrupted. His face was Teutonic and florid. Oakley's business was to know Hollywood personalities, and he recognized this man as Ernst Stengel, chief supervisor of the Associated Studios. Stengel drew Hirsch aside, and they talked quickly, in lowered voices, as Oakley and Brixey glanced about.

Scraps of the conversation carried.

"She is not the girl I want. I said so from the start. I must have Fenton." This was Hirsch.

"No—she is perfect, Josef—perfect!" Stengel's insistence was firm.

"I can't work with her."

"But the retakes, Josef! If we made a change, now— You must go ahead with her!"

Hirsch shrugged. "Very well. But she will be in no more pictures of mine!"

Oakley noticed, at the edge of the set, a girl who was watching Hirsch and Stengel anxiously. It was as though she knew they were speaking of her. She was Carlotta Vine, a newcomer; hers was not the typical mask-like beauty of Hollywood, but had a quality that reached deeper. As Hirsch and Stengel ceased talking, she turned quickly away.

"Ready!" Hirsch shouted. "We will rehearse again!"

Technicians moved about, actors and actresses made ready. Hirsch rapidly discarded his coat and rolled up his shirt sleeves. Stengel stepped back, out of the hustle. Further commands from Hirsch cleared the set of all save Carlotta Vine and an actor made up as a Chinese.

His skin was covered with saffron powder; his eyes had been slanted upward by a clever manipulation of invisible fish-skin and spirit-gum; a thin black mustache gave him a sinister look.

"Now!" Hirsch exclaimed. "Dwyer, you get behind the idol. You're out of sight. Miss Vine, the scene begins with you standing in the center of the temple. You gaze, fascinated with horror, at the ghastly face of the God of Anger. You walk toward it slowly, as if hypnotized."

Hirsch turned a fearful glance back at Oakley, and sighed with relief when he saw that he was being watched. The twist of his body disclosed to Oakley that the director was carrying a revolver; its butt protruded from his hip pocket.

"As soon as Miss Vine comes close, Dwyer, your head appears in the open mouth of the image. You place the blow-gun to your lips. You are about to shoot the poisoned dart at Miss Vine when we cut, but you don't really shoot it. Understand? We'll do it with the lights."

Switches clicked, and a weird gloom filled the set. The gold paint glittered; the hideous face of the Taoistic God of Anger seemed to grimace as if alive. As the lights were adjusted, Dwyer, the actor made up as the Chinese, disappeared through an opening behind the shoulder of the idol. Carlotta Vine took her position facing it.

"Go through with the action," Hirsch directed.

THERE was silence on the stage as Miss Vine gazed at the horrible features of the idol. Her hands came up to her throat; step by step, as if drawn by a force greater than her will, she moved toward the image. As she drew closer, attention centered upon the twisted mouth of the God of Anger. A moment of uncertainty passed; Hirsch's voice called: "Dwyer! Aren't you watching her? Now!"

There was no response; no Chinese villain's head appeared behind the image. Hirsch muttered and strode upon the set angrily. He was at the girl's side when, suddenly, the saffron face loomed in the darkness of the idol's mouth.

The black tube of a blowpipe glistened as it was raised to the mouth of the yellow face. There was a sharp intake of breath.

Hirsch jerked as the black nozzle of the blow-gun turned toward him. Terror stamped his face; he grabbed at the revolver in his hip pocket. He swung it up, pointed it toward the saffron head in the mouth of the image.

Swiftly, darkly, a tiny dart sprang from the barrel of the blow-gun and hissed through the air. At the same instant Hirsch fired. Carlotta Vine cried out frightenedly and shrank away as Hirsch's bullet tore a fragment from the mouth of the idol.

As quickly as it had appeared, the Chinese face vanished in the darkness. Hirsch stood motionless, gun still lifted; frozen with terror. A tense moment passed—a moment of silence broken by a low moan of pain that came from behind Hirsch.

Oakley and Brixey had started forward.

"Oke! Something's the matter with that man by the light!"

Beside the light-standard a "gaffer"—an electrician—was standing, head bowed forward, raised on the tips of his toes, both hands clutching at his chest. Suddenly he toppled, and fell to the floor.

Oakley reached him as Hirsch spun about and peered down at the prone gaffer. Oakley turned the man face up; noted the lax face, the closed eyes. And he noted another startling thing.

To the man's chest a tiny fluff of feathers was clinging. Oakley's eyes caught the glint of metal as he bent low. It was the dart from the blow-gun. It had punctured the gaffer's chest and its needle was buried deep; a tiny drop of blood glistened beneath it.

Hirsch blurted: "Oakley! What the devil! I—I shouldn't have used that gun. I'm so damned jumpy— But I told Dwyer not to blow the dart! He's hurt this man!"

Oakley raised grim eyes. "This man," he said, "is more than hurt. He's dead." There was a hush. Oakley straightened, took quick strides toward the idol as Hirsch repeated unbelievingly: "Dead?"

OUT OF SIGHT behind the shoulder of the image, Oakley found an opening. The only light in the space beyond was the dim glow of the spots shining through the open mouth of the idol. The rear view dispelled the horror of the thing. It was built of *papier-mâché,* supported by wooden braces. But it was not this which drew Oakley's eyes; it was the figure of a man lying on the floor, a blow-gun still held in one limp hand.

Oakley bent down as Hirsch hurried up beside him.

"Good God, Oakley! Is that man really dead?"

"Very dead," Oakley said. "This one is only unconscious." It was Dwyer. His black wig was pulled partly off. Oakley stripped it away to find that an ugly blow had been delivered to the actor's head from the rear. A blow powerful enough, Oakley judged, to have crushed Dwyer's skull had the wig not given protection. He came to his feet with Dwyer in his arms. "Lights!" he snapped.

Hirsch choked a command that brought a brilliant glare over the sound stage as Oakley strode into the open with Dwyer. He laid the man on the floor. An excited script girl passed a bottle of smelling salts to him, and he used it. As Dwyer's eyelids began to flutter, Oakley left him and again studied the still form of the gaffer. Brixey was at his side.

"Against all the rules, Archie, but I've got to see this."

Oakley pulled the dart from the dead man's body. The gleaming needle was more than an inch long. Oakley shrugged as he studied it. "It must have been really poisoned, Archie. The needle alone couldn't have killed this poor chap. Poisoned with something as powerful as *curare.*" Oakley turned. He tapped Hirsch's shoulder. "Call the police, Hirsch."

"The—police?"

"A murder has been committed here."

"Murder?"

"Certainly!" Oakley's voice took on an edge. He bent over Dwyer again. The actor's artificially slanted eyes were clouded and uncertain. Oakley waved the smelling salts under his nose and he gasped.

"Why the hell did you do that, Dwyer?"

The actor mumbled: "Do what?"

"Shoot that dart."

"The dart? I—I didn't. Somebody—hit me."

"Who?"

"I don't know. Somebody—slipped up behind me when I was waiting to— Oh, God!"

OAKLEY left Dwyer to his aching head. He shot questions at the stunned Hirsch and elicited scant information. The name of the dead man was Louis Peters, a long-time employe. Dwyer had been borrowed from Super-Classics to play the part of the Oriental and was almost a stranger at Associated.

"Why should Dwyer kill a gaffer?" Hirsch demanded dazedly.

"Dwyer didn't intend to kill the gaffer, Hirsch," Oakley said quietly. "That dart was aimed at you—and missed."

"Dwyer—tried to kill me?" Hirsch gasped. "But he has no reason! I never met him before we started this picture. We've got along pleasantly—"

Oakley interrupted impatiently.

"Look here, Hirsch. It's certain that dart was meant for you. It's not certain who shot it. Dwyer claims he was hit on the head by somebody, from behind, before he could go into his part. That explains his failure to follow your directions. If he's telling the truth, Dwyer didn't do it."

"But—I saw his face!" Hirsch blurted.

"I saw what you saw," Oakley nodded.

"It couldn't have been anybody else. Miss Vine!" Hirsch turned to the actress, who was standing at one side, pale and frightened. "You saw him blow that dart! It was Dwyer, wasn't it?"

The girl whispered: "Yes."

"It was Dwyer," another voice agreed.

Oakley observed: "Chinese faces look a great deal alike to us, you know. Chinese make-up would have the same effect. It might have been somebody else made up the same as Dwyer and—"

"But there was only one actor on the set in Chinese make-up, Oakley!"

"Make sure of that, will you?"

Hirsch hurried off as Oakley surveyed the scene. Dwyer was mumbling, seemingly unable to grasp the situation. Oakley sighed, as Brixey said: "I say, Oke. I had an unobstructed view. It was Dwyer."

Hirsch hastened back. "Dwyer was the only one in Chinese make-up," he declared. "The men at the doors swear nobody else in Chinese make-up was on this stage. There can't be any doubt—"

"In that case," Oakley commented, "we're forced to the conclusion that Dwyer did it and then slugged himself in order to fake an alibi.

It's logical to suppose, then, that Dwyer made the first two attempts on your life, Hirsch, with a gun, and this third one with the poisoned dart. Which means that you need my services no longer, and all that's left is for the police to force a confession from Dwyer."

CHAPTER TWO

THE SKELETON TERROR

CLAY OAKLEY sat at his desk in the office of Secrets, Incorporated, and spoke over the telephone. The voice at the other end was the heavy boom of Detective-Lieutenant McClane, speaking from headquarters.

"I've already told you absolutely everything I know, McClane," Oakley declared. "The strongest proof that Dwyer killed Peters, while trying to kill Hirsch, is eye-witness testimony. Everybody claims it was Dwyer. I'd say so myself. What's the matter—won't he talk?"

"All he'll say is that he didn't do it. He sticks to the story he told you, about getting cracked on the bean."

"Where'd he get that poison?"

"Damned if I know. It's *thara*, used in South America by native tribes—like *curare*. Paralyzes the heart. Well, the case is closed, Oakley, confession or not. You think so, don't you?"

"I wouldn't dare," said Oakley, "disagree with you, McClane," and he hung up, grinning, as a snort answered.

He looked across the desk at the man who had entered his office a moment before the telephone call had come through. He was Ernst Stengel, Chief Supervisor at the Associated Studios; he looked deeply troubled as he placed on Oakley's desk an oblong package.

"I scarcely know what to think," he said vaguely. "The thing that happened in the studio this morning, now this."

Oakley took the package and peeled the wrapping from it. It was a light cardboard box—a container such as florists use, though this one was devoid of any printed trademark—and studied it. He was lifting the cover when Stengel said quickly: "I am placing absolute trust in you, Mr. Oakley."

"If you did not trust me absolutely, Mr. Stengel, I'd suggest that you take your case to some other private investigator."

Oakley's hand was still resting on the cover of the box. "This came to Mrs. Stengel, you say, by messenger?" he asked.

"Yes. Early this morning. It upset her terribly. I did not go to the police with it because I wish to avoid publicity if possible." Stengel shrugged. "It may be only a cruel joke—a ghastly joke."

"We'll see," Oakley said decisively.

He raised the cover of the box—and started. The container was lined with green tissue paper. But it did not contain flowers. It contained the arm and hand of a human skeleton.

"Not," said Oakley with a grimace, "very pretty."

He studied the grisly object. From the shoulder joint to the fingertips it was intact. The bones were dry, yellow and brittle. An offensive odor rose from it. Yet as Oakley studied it he smiled.

"After all," he said, "this is not as horrible as it might be. This arm was taken from a prepared skeleton, it might have been bought from a medical supply house. You see, the bones are old, and absolutely clean of flesh, and are held together by little brass wires."

"Yes, I see. But it is ghastly!"

"Why in the world should anyone send a skeleton's arm to Mrs. Stengel?" Oakley asked.

"I don't know! Of course, I have no idea. But I am worried for her. Not alone because of the skeleton's arm."

"For what other reason?"

"You know, Mr. Oakley, of the disaster that has followed those who made the picture *Hell on Earth?*"

"I know that your studio made the picture and that it was the biggest box-office hit of the past year."

"Yes, it was that; but it was also a tragedy to all who took part in it," Stengel continued. "While the company was on location in the Gran Chaco in South America—you know just where that is, Mr. Oakley?"

"Not exactly."

"It is in the very heart of the continent, lying partially in Brazil on the East; and it overlaps into Argentina and Bolivia. It is a tremendous spread of jungle forest. Until an English expedition went into it, about a year before we made our picture there, no white man had penetrated it for over three hundred years. We were warned that it reeked with death, that we were mad to attempt to make a picture there. But we took the chance.

"We made the picture—*Hell on Earth*—and it was everything we hoped it would be. But the company has paid for it dearly. Amstrom, our director, died of fever on location. Breck, his assistant, came back half blind and in a few months he was dead. Clarissa Brooks, the female lead, found her health ruined, and now she is out of pictures. The male lead, Arthur Bradshaw, suffered sunstroke, and his mind became affected. It is not generally known that now he is insane. The sound engineer also died of a mysterious fever, on the return trip. Some evil influence seemed to exert itself on everyone concerned in the making of *Hell on Earth*. These attempts to kill Hirsch—they must be connected somehow, with—"

"Hirsch helped make the film?"

"Yes. He was on location with the Company in the Gran Chaco."

"But Dwyer wasn't?"

"No. Dwyer had nothing to do with it. That is the strange part."

OAKLEY'S lips pursed. "The poison on that dart, Mr. Stengel, is *thara*, which is used by some native tribes in South America."

Stengel's eyes widened. "You see! It is impossible to escape! Now the curse is—is upon those who are dear to me. Josef Hirsch is my brother-in-law. Now—only two members of the company which went on location have so far been untouched—my wife and her son."

"Karl Stengel played the juvenile in the picture, didn't he?" Oakley asked.

"Yes. And Mrs. Stengel accompanied the party. He is very dear to her, and she wanted to be with him. It was against my wishes, but that does not matter now—she went. She has not seemed entirely herself lately—perhaps it is the after-effects of a light attack of jungle fever which she contracted. I cannot disguise the fact that I have been fearful for her, and for Karl. I cannot help feeling that the curse of *Hell on Earth* may strike them down even yet."

"But what," Oakley asked, "could this skeleton arm have to do with the misfortunes of the *Hell on Earth* company?"

"That I do not know. But you can understand why I have come to you for help since Mrs. Stengel received it. I want you, Mr. Oakley— I want you to keep watch on Mrs. Stengel and Karl. If some danger is threatening them, I want you to guard them from it."

"I'll do that," Oakley interrupted briskly. "I will devote myself to it personally—"

"Yes, you must!" and Stengel drew a checkbook from his pocket and scribbled on it, passed the check to Oakley. "Mrs. Stengel and Karl are both at the home of Richard Carmore this afternoon—there is a party."

Oakley gazed at the words, "One thousand dollars," written on the check. "Might I attend the party, Mr. Stengel—with my assistant, Miss Morris?"

"I will arrange that at once. Richard Carmore is my closest friend, and he will be more than willing. Every precaution must be taken—"

Oakley shrugged. "I'll do what I can. If it's a matter of fever, some ailment contracted in the jungle, I can't help. But if there is something else behind this skeleton arm, if someone is threatening Mrs. Stengel, I'll do my damnedest."

"Good!" Stengel exclaimed. "Good! I will expect you at Carmore's place in Beverly Hills as soon as you can come. Goodbye."

Charmaine Morris, Oakley's red-headed secretary, stepped into the inner sanctum of Secrets, Incorporated. At the same time another door opened and Mr. Archibald Brixey entered. He placed on Oakley's desk half a dozen dictagraph records.

"There's your conversation with Stengel, complete, Oke," he said.

"So," exclaimed Miss Morris gladly, "we're going to a party!"

Oke Oakley regarded her wryly. "The sea-shell ears behind those red ringlets of yours don't miss a thing, do they, Cherry?" he asked. "Well, powder your patrician nose, because we're off for Beverly right away. Archie, you stay here."

Oakley gestured toward the box containing the skeleton arm. "You're to try to locate the messenger who delivered this *objet d'art* to Mrs. Stengel, Archie. Use the phone and check up also on the sources of supply of such things."

Oakley left the office and trod down the stairs with Cherry Morris, leaving Archie with the telephone. They climbed into a sleek roadster parked at the curb, turned into Hollywood Boulevard.

IN A MOMENT they were rolling along broad Wilshire Boulevard. Oakley wound his way up a curving road until he reached the broad gate of a typical movie estate.

A gateman admitted him to the driveway, which curved toward a tremendous white *hacienda* on the crest of a hill. Expensive cars were clustered about it. Oakley left his among them and walked along the side of the house with Cherry.

Through the French doors they saw couples dancing to the soft music of a giant electric phonograph. A Japanese butler appeared and, following him, two men. One was Stengel. The other, young, earnest-looking and handsome, was Richard Carmore, one of the better-known directors. They greeted Oakley and his companion.

"It's my business to remain unknown," Oakley said. "Better introduce me as a scenario writer. It's better not to create talk. Mrs. Stengel—"

"I believe she is out at the pool, Oakley," Stengel told him. "She is still upset. If you could distract her—"

Oakley declared he would try. Carmore offered them swim-suits, which they accepted, and he took them to the bath-house. It was located behind the *hacienda*, near the eternal swimming pool. The pool itself was a beauty, a hundred feet long and fifty wide, of gleaming white and blue tile. Its inviting blue water was still now. The pool was deserted, except for a woman and a young man, both in suits, who were sitting on a metal bench beside it. Mrs. Stengel, Oakley recognized, and her son Karl.

Oke and Cherry stepped into the bath-house and changed into the suits, hurried out. Cherry, in a white, scantily cut suit, was a stunning creature. Her lithe body was a sleek sun-brown. She tucked her red hair under her cap, poised on the diving-hoard, and gracefully plunged into the depths of the pool. Oakley followed her; they raced the length and back and called it a tie. And all the while they were observing Mrs. Stengel.

She was a fattish, dowdy woman, with coarse lines in her face and hard eyes. Spoiled beyond words—that was evident. Too many cocktails had made her even less attractive than she might have been. She kept giggling at the things Karl was saying to her. Not, Oakley thought, an admirable woman.

Two couples hurried from the house toward the pool. They charged at Mrs. Stengel and took her hands, tried to pull her from the seat.

"Do come in, Hilda!"

"You must get dressed, you know—dinner's coming."

Mrs. Stengel's laughter reached a new high pitch. "I don't want to come in. I won't come in. I'm going to take a swim."

SUDDENLY she broke away from them and ran alongside the pool, a heavy, ungainly figure. The two couples chased her while she screamed with mirth. One of the men caught her, and she struggled with him, squealing. Then she tore free again, heaved herself, and splashed into the water.

A strange thing happened.

Mrs. Stengel disappeared beneath the surface. Her fattish body coursed smoothly toward the bottom, its shape distorted by the dancing waves. She almost disappeared from view, for the surface was like broken glass in the brilliant sunlight. But something—something began to happen in the depths of the pool.

A silver cloud seemed to take shape beneath the surface—a cloud that gathered from nowhere and moved across the body of water. The surface became more agitated. The water in the pool seemed to heave, as with some invisible force. And quickly its color began to change—to grow darker.

The two couples were laughing, shouting. "Come on up, Hilda!"

Mrs. Stengel was not coming up. At the spot where her body had plunged down the water seemed to boil. Bubbles of air broke on the surface, and the deeper color grew still deeper. Oakley, alarmed, rose, strode to the edge of the pool, and peered down. He saw then that the water was pink—a pink growing quickly into a pale red.

Now the couple stopped laughing. Karl Stengel rose, peered at the water. He called "Mama! Don't stay down so long, Mama!"

The silver cloud in the water was still moving. Suddenly it seemed to coalesce, to disappear. The tumult beneath the surface died away.

"Something's wrong!" Oakley exclaimed, half-aloud.

"Mama!" Karl Stengel screeched.

Suddenly he leaped into the water, a smooth dive. He shot across the bottom. Oakley could see him swimming underwater, kicking along the center of the pool. A full minute passed while Karl swam the entire length; then he popped to the surface, gasping.

"She's gone!" he exclaimed. "She's not down there!"

He raised his hand and peered at it. "The water's red! It's—" he screeched the words, horribly—"it's *blood!*"

He scrambled out of the pool, crazily, and lay gasping on the cork runway. Oakley peered at him, puzzled. His cry was bringing others from the house.

Oakley said quickly: "There's something down there. I see it!"

He dived. Bluish-green enclosed him as he shot close to the patterned bottom of the pool. Bluish-green tinted with a weird red color. He kicked along, toward the object he had seen, and as it loomed closer, Oakley saw it confusedly.

It looked—it looked like a skeleton!

Crazily, he grabbed at something close to his face. He kicked up, splashed to the rim of the pool, dragged himself from it. He stared at the thing he had in his hand.

The arm of a skeleton! But this one was not old, dried, fastened together with wires. It was fresh-white. Bits of flesh and cartilage were clinging to it. The small bones indicated it was the arm of a woman!

Oakley put it down grimly. He shouted to anyone who could hear above the excited chatter of the crowd that was gathering: "Drain the pool!"

OAKLEY'S shout silenced the group at the other side of the pool, but only for a moment. They began chattering excitedly again, and crowding around Karl Stengel, who still lay gasping on the cork walk. Others came hurrying from the house, and among them were Ernst Stengel and Richard Carmore.

Oakley shouted again: "Drain the pool, I say! Open the valve!"

He waited until Carmore ran to the far end of the pool, threw open the door of a small wooden house, and twisted at a metal ring. He was bending over, studying the skeleton arm, as Stengel hurried toward him.

"Oakley—great heavens, what's happened?"

"Plenty!" Oakley snapped. He turned as Carmore came to Stengel's side. "Get this crowd away from here, into the house. Is that valve open?"

"Yes—the pool will be empty soon," Carmore answered breathlessly. "What the devil is wrong? Where did that ghastly thing come from?"

"From the pool—and there's more on the bottom," Oakley said grimly. "A whole skeleton. Stengel, take hold of yourself. There's every reason to believe that something's happened to Mrs. Stengel—what, I don't know."

Stengel's eyes opened wide. Horror came into them. Carmore hastened to the other side of the pool and began herding the guests into the house. Young Stengel went with them, sobbing. The level of the water had already fallen perceptibly.

"But—but what makes you think—" Stengel began the question falteringly.

"Mrs. Stengel dived into the pool," Oakley told him quickly. "She didn't come up, and your son dove in after her. He couldn't find her. I went—and saw the skeleton on the bottom—nothing else."

"Good God!" the big man breathed. "How is it possible? How could—"

Oakley signaled to Cherry Morris. "Better get back into your clothes. I'm going to do the same thing. It'll take a little while for the pool to drain."

Stengel turned to him dazedly. "Is—is my wife dead?"

"I can't explain what happened." Carmore was returning. "Carmore, take Stengel in hand, will you? Keep him away—"

"No!" Stengel burst out. "No! I will stay here. Whatever has happened—I must know."

Oakley gestured resignedly. Cherry had already gone into the bath-house, and he began to follow. Carmore came with him to the door, agitated and pale.

"Good Lord, Oakley, do you mean that the arm—that arm—"

"It's a woman's; that's all I know, Carmore," Oakley answered. "Except one thing more. If Mrs. Stengel is dead, it's murder."

"Murder!"

"Exactly. That means the police. I suggest that you call them right away."

"Yes—yes, I will."

Carmore hurried away, and Oakley stepped into the bath-house. He was in a compartment, toweling himself, when Cherry Morris spoke to him from the next booth.

"I feel a bit ill, Oke. What could possibly have happened?"

He uttered a bitter laugh. "It's a gruesome business, Cherry, but all that's left of Mrs. Stengel is lying on the bottom of that pool. Nothing but a skeleton."

OAKLEY dressed quickly, and stepped back into the bright sunshine. Cherry came to the door with him, and they gazed at the pool. Its level had already dropped halfway, and the shallow end was almost exposed. Carmore and Stengel were still beside the pool, sitting on one of the benches.

Oakley went to them as Cherry Morris hurried into the house.

"Police coming?" he asked.

"Yes."

Oakley turned away, toward the skeleton arm which still lay on the cork walk. He stooped, examining it closely. He noted that several of the small bones of the fingers were crushed, and wagged his head in bafflement. He brought a towel from the bath-house, wrapped the arm in it, and laid it aside.

Stengel said in a hushed tone: "I was afraid! I was afraid! *Hell on Earth.* The curse—"

"Nonsense, Ernst!" Carmore protested. "Whatever's happened—it can't have any connection."

Oakley looked up as a girl appeared in the doorway, and came toward the two seated men—a strikingly pretty brunette, clad in smart sports clothes—Carlotta Vine. She seized Stengel's hand and said quickly: "I'm terribly sorry! If only I could do something. Richard, can't we take him away?"

"He won't go," Carmore said. "I don't think you'd better stay here, dear."

She turned deep brown eyes on Oakley, and Carmore made a gesture of introduction. "My fiancée—Mr. Oakley." Oakley took her hand, but she turned away at once.

"Perhaps a drink, Ernst?"

"No, *liebchen*. Nothing."

His eyes were fixed on the falling surface of the pool. The sloping bottom was half bared now. Oakley went to the ladder at the dry end, let himself down, and walked to the creeping water line. Beneath the water now he could see the skeleton. Soon it would lay exposed.

Little by little it came out of the water. It was a ghastly thing, twisted, with some of the bones fallen out of place and lying loose on the bottom. A moment later something else came into sight—a sodden mass of fabric. Oakley picked it up. It was a bathing suit, ripped in many places.

"*Grosse Gott!*" Stengel exclaimed, peering down. "It is—it is—"

It was, Oakley knew, the suit which Mrs. Stengel was wearing when she had plunged into the pool!

He looked up to see, at last, Carmore leading Stengel away. The big man was sobbing silently. Carlotta Vine's arm was across Stengel's shoulders.

Oakley grimaced, and turned back. The water had fallen away from the skeleton now. He bent over it, examining it closely. He noted, first of all, that many of the smaller bones, like the fingers of the hand he had already seen, were crushed.

CHAPTER THREE

THE SILVER DOOM

OKE OAKLEY climbed from the drained pool as a police car whizzed up the drive. Four men hurried around the house. Carmore met them, talked to them rapidly, then led them toward the pool. One of them smiled crookedly at Oakley—McClane, from headquarters.

"I might have known you'd be here," he said sourly. "What's happened?"

"Murder," Oakley said.

"Yeah? Where's the body?"

"There. That skeleton is all that's left of Mrs. Ernst Stengel. An hour ago she was a whole woman. If you want the facts, McClane, I'll tell you everything I know."

McClane wanted them. He listened to Oakley's account with growing impatience. At last he burst out: "I don't believe it! How can it be? What became of the flesh that was on her bones?"

"Gone—somewhere."

"You said that you and your girl friend'd just been in the pool. Nothing happened to you and her. Then Mrs. Stengel jumps in and turns into a skeleton. Next Karl Stengel goes in, and you go in again, and nothing happens again. There's no sense to it."

"But there's murder in it, McClane," Oakley said quietly. "And there's one other item you may be interested in. The left hand and the right foot of the skeleton are missing."

"What!"

"I've checked over and examined the whole pool—but they're gone."

McClane peered at the skeleton, then climbed down the brass

ladder and hunched over it. Oakley, at his side, pointed out that his observation was true.

"Where'd that silver cloud you saw come from?" McClane asked.

"It appeared suddenly all around Mrs. Stengel, and in a short while it disappeared—that's all."

"What could it have been?"

"I don't know."

"Well, something happened to the woman in this pool, all right, and there's one guy who ought to know what it was—and that's the bird who owns it."

"Carmore? Perhaps," Oakley admitted.

McClane looked up, and saw Carmore looking at them from the top of the ladder. The big detective climbed up, and Oakley followed. Carmore was pale. Carlotta Vine was standing beside him, her dark eyes clouded with worry. McClane faced them stolidly.

"Now," he demanded, "what happened to Mrs. Stengel, Carmore?"

"I can't tell you."

"No?" McClane drawled. "It happened in your pool, didn't it? Who's in a better position to know? When it comes right down to it, Carmore—why did you kill Mrs. Stengel?"

"I?" Carmore gasped. "You're mad!"

Carlotta Vine exclaimed swiftly: "How can you say such a thing?"

"Easily," McClane answered. "If you're going to make it hard, Carmore, all right. You and I are going to talk this over. Go on into the house, where we can be alone."

THE PAIR disappeared into the house with Carlotta Vine following. Oakley sighed, perched on a bench, and stayed there until Cherry Morris came out and sat beside him.

"Let's check over possibilities," Oakley suggested. "What could reduce a human body to a skeleton in a very short while? Acid? That's out. You and I were in the pool immediately before it happened, and it seemed all right—not even chlorine in the water. Fresh as a spring. Nothing in it afterward, either, except the skeleton—and the blood." Oakley shuddered. "Maybe we shouldn't have drained that pool. A chemical analysis of the water—"

"You can wring enough from Mrs. Stengel's suit," Cherry Morris reminded him; and then they lapsed into silence.

It was perhaps half an hour later that Ernst Stengel hurried from the French doors toward Oakley. "They are arresting Richard!" he exclaimed.

"Yes? And what does Carmore say about this thing?" Oakley asked.

"He knows nothing! Nothing! No matter how it was done, Richard Carmore could not be capable of such a thing. Oakley, I beg you—I beseech you—keep them from arresting him if you can!"

"I'll do my best."

Oakley stepped into the house. The guests were in the great living room, gathered in groups, talking nervously. In an adjoining room, a study, Oakley found the four plainclothesmen, together with Carmore and Carlotta Vine.

He eyed McClane keenly. "Sure of what you're doing?" he asked.

"I'm sure there's nothing else to do, if it's any of your business, Oakley!"

"Carmore hasn't confessed, has he?"

"What of it? He'll come through."

"You have no evidence against him, have you? Any motive? The opportunity, the means, the motive, McClane—have you checked them all over?"

McClane's eye flared. "Carmore owns this house and has owned it for a year. Mrs. Stengel was killed in his swimming pool. I don't know how or why, but the rest holds. Carmore's coming to headquarters with us, and he's going to talk!"

Carmore turned, took Carlotta Vine's head in his hands, and kissed her gently. "It's all right, darling. They can't hold me. I'll phone my lawyer before we go—and there'll be nothing to worry about."

"Won't there, though!" McClane sneered.

AT MIDNIGHT Oke was sitting in the inner sanctum of Secrets, Incorporated, reading the headlines of the *Examiner. Carmore Released Under Bond!* the black type screamed. Another—*Dwyer's Denial of Guilt Unshaken.* Oakley tossed the paper away, pushed aside several reports still unread, and gazed at Archibald Brixey.

"Suppose," Oakley suggested, "that Dwyer is telling the truth. Suppose that twelve eye-witnesses are all wrong. Suppose he was actually hit on the back of the head, knocked out, and his place taken by someone else—"

"But Oke!" Archie protested. "Everything points to his having done it. Perhaps he didn't slug himself to fake an alibi, but tripped over a brace and hit his head and—"

"All right, but suppose he didn't. What other possibilities are there? McClane tells me there are no fingerprints on the blow-gun other than Dwyer's and the property man's—and the property man wasn't on the stage. No clue there. Is Carmore implicated? No; he's proved he wasn't on Stage Five at the time, either, and witnesses substantiate him. The only other possibility is that we didn't see the man we thought we saw."

"I'd swear it was Dwyer, especially since nobody else in Chinese make-up came onto the stage, Oke—"

"Picture that scene," Oakley said. "Dim light. A long wait while the girl was walking toward the idol. Now a question, Archie. Could someone on that stage, someone already there, quickly make up his face, in the dark, to look like Dwyer's, then take Dwyer's place, and after it was all over, remove the make-up without leaving a trace?"

Brixey's head wagged. "No, Oke. It couldn't be done."

"I'm afraid you're right, Archie. It couldn't be done. And yet I'm becoming positive that Dwyer didn't do it."

A sudden knocking interrupted them. At the same time a hushed, strained voice carried in from the outer door. "Oakley! Are you there! For God's sake, let me in!"

Oakley rose quickly. Immediately the latch of the office entrance was drawn back, a man shouldered in—Josef Hirsch. He was white as death, trembling, gasping so that he could hardly mouth: "Oakley— he's tried it again."

OAKLEY grasped Hirsch's right wrist. In the fingers of the director a tuft of feathers was gripped, a bright needle protruding from them. A dart! Oakley noted its filmed point, judged that it was covered with *thara*, and gingerly took it from Hirsch.

"Just as I was leaving the studio—a few minutes ago!" Hirsch sputtered. "I was getting into the car—and this thing went past me. It hit the shoulder of my topcoat—went into the padding. Oh, God, Oakley—you promised to protect me!"

Oakley frowned in distaste. "Hirsch," he said quietly, "we all like to go on living. None of us would welcome being made a pincushion for poisoned darts. Pull yourself together, man!"

"I saw no one—no one!" Hirsch sped on. "It came out of empty air. Oakley, I—I can't stand it. If you don't stay with me—"

Oakley made a disgusted noise and strode into the inner office. "We'll have this needle analyzed, of course. I warned you to stay indoors as much as possible, Hirsch. And I must say that this case is developing in such a way that I can't very well give all my time to following you around like a watch-dog."

Hirsch's eyes popped. "You mean you're going to leave me to the mercy of—" Anger flared in his eyes. "You're failing me! You—you're double-crossing me. You're afraid you'll be hit yourself by one of these things!"

Oakley's lips thinned. "Mr. Hirsch," he said quietly, "I don't believe I like you very much. In fact, I'm sure of it."

The telephone jangled. Oakley dropped the dart into an envelope, passed it to Brixey, and took up the instrument. A strained, hushed voice came over the wire.

"I've got to talk to Mr. Oakley at once!"

"Speaking. Who's calling?"

"Karl Stengel. Mr. Oakley, I—my father told me before he left for the studio this evening that I should phone you in case anything unusual happens."

"Yes?"

"I have just received a box containing the arm and hand of a human skeleton!"

"When did it come—and how?"

"Just a few minutes ago, by messenger. It's the same as—as my mother—"

"Steady," Oakley encouraged. "Stay where you are. I'm coming right out."

He turned from the instrument to reach for his hat and coat. "Come along, Archie. We've got another skeleton arm in the case—this time the woman's son."

Hirsch looked horrified. "Where are you going? You can't leave me now! Oakley—I beseech you—"

"Sorry, Hirsch," Oakley retorted. "I suggest another investigator, one who won't double-cross you and is not afraid to go with you." His voice was sharp-edged. "I'm in this business for money, of course—more or less—but, you haven't got enough to hire me. Good night, Hirsch."

Hirsch flared: "Damn you, Oakley—I'll make you sorry for this!"

"I wonder," Oakley rejoined quietly.

He drew on his gloves while Hirsch slammed out of the office. Archibald Brixey grimaced his disgust. Oakley snapped off the lights and strode out with Brixey at his side. He did not speak again until his roadster was shooting along the almost deserted Hollywood Boulevard toward Beverly Hills.

"Archie, what's in those reports of yours? I want the dope before we get to Stengel's place."

Brixey answered as the car swung toward Wilshire. "First, the messenger who delivered that grisly thing to Mrs. Stengel—I found him. He was given the box in downtown Los Angeles. He can give no decent description of the man.

"Next, about that damn skeleton. I haven't found where it came from. All places that supply such things haven't sold one in months."

"Possibly it came from the property room of one of the studios. Checked on that, Archie?" Oakley asked.

"Hadn't time," Brixey answered. "To go on—no fingerprints on the box except possibly those of Mrs. Stengel. As for the chemical analysis of the water from Mrs. Stengel's suit, I had that rushed through. Nothing there except slight traces of human blood."

OAKLEY drove the car along a winding way. Some of the gaudiest estates lay in this district, and Stengel's was one of them.

Oakley found the big gate of the estate closed but unlocked. He swung toward the impressive entrance to the house, stopped the car, walked to the door, and rang.

"Place looks asleep," Oakley observed. "Why doesn't someone come?"

His second ring brought no response. Oakley grasped the doorknob, turned it, and found the heavy portal unlocked. He stepped into a spacious, tapestried hall.

"Hello!" he called.

His voice echoed; and as the echoes died away, Oakley stiffened. He heard, not far off, a strangled moan.

"I say!" exclaimed Archie Brixey.

Oakley trotted toward the tremendous dining room at the rear of the hallway. Inside the door he stopped short.

A girl lay on the floor, bound hand and foot. A strip of cloth covered her mouth; her eyes were popping in terror. She was wearing a maid's costume.

Oakley stooped, quickly unknotted the gag. The girl gasped for breath as he shot questions at her and loosened the strips that bound her limbs.

"What happened to you? Where's Karl? Is the whole damn place empty?"

"Somebody grabbed me from behind!" the girl gasped. "I was coming from the kitchen. Somebody was hiding behind the door. He—"

"See him?" Oakley interrupted.

"Just a glimpse. He was wearing a dark topcoat, and he was masked with a handkerchief. I don't know how he got in. Karl—Mr. Karl was upstairs, and this man went up. I heard him coming down in a little while, like he was carrying something heavy. I—I couldn't do anything. All the other servants are out of the house and—"

Oakley demanded: "Where's Karl's room? I'm a private detective retained by Mr. Stengel. Hurry it up!"

THE MAID fluttered into a central hallway into which a broad staircase descended. As she ran up it, Oakley and Brixey kept at her heels. The upper floor was dark except for a single light shafting from one open door into the hallway. The maid hurried into it, calling: "Mr. Karl! Mr. Karl!"

She stopped short. "He isn't here!"

Oakley had expected that. He made a circuit of the room quickly. By a dresser he paused, peering at a light cardboard box which lay among stiff brown wrapping paper. Its cover was off and, resting on a ruffle of tissue, he saw the skeleton arm.

It was like that which Mrs. Stengel had received—old, brittle, its component parts fastened together with little brass wires. The woman had received the right arm, and this was a left.

Oakley bent, peering at a dark spot on the rug. He touched his finger to it, and his eyes glinted. It was red and wet. Fresh blood!

"Outside, Archie. Start searching the grounds. Snap into it!"

As Brixey hurried out, Oakley stared at the maid. "Did you hear a car start up after the man who attacked you went out?"

"No."

Oakley waited to hear no more. He hurried down the stairs and out to his car. He saw a light flashing across the grounds—Brixey carrying an electric torch. Oakley pulled another from the pocket of his car, and ran in the opposite direction.

Suddenly his foot met something solid, yet yielding. He stumbled over it, whirled about, flashed his light down.

The bright cone disclosed a young man lying on the grass, under the shadow of a huge bush. His eyes were closed; there was a gash across his forehead where he had been dealt a severe blow. It was Karl Stengel—unconscious.

"Archie! Here!" Oakley called.

He dropped to his knees beside Karl Stengel. The young man was breathing almost imperceptibly; his pulse was erratic. Oakley was rising when Brixey hurried to his side.

"Dear me!" he said. "That young man has been dealt a nasty blow."

"He'll be coming around soon, I suppose, Archie. We'd better get him back into the house and call a doctor. See anybody prowling about?"

"Not a soul, Oke."

"Lend a hand."

Oakley stooped to lift Karl Stengel's shoulders; but abruptly he paused.

From the house came a shrill scream!

Oakley whipped about. His hand flashed toward his arm-pit and reappeared gripping a neat little automatic. He ordered over his shoulder tersely: "Stay with him, Archie!"

HE RAN swiftly across the lawn toward the tremendous house. As he swung through the door and hurried along the hallway, the terrified maid rushed forward from the dining room.

"I-I saw him!"

"What?" Oke snapped. "Saw who?"

"The man! The man who was in here—the one who tied me up! I was in the kitchen, and he came past the window outside. I saw him—wearing a white mask!"

Oakley raced to the rear of the house into the kitchen. Above the sink was the open window through which the maid had evidently seen the masked man. He hurried out the rear door and loped toward the corner of the house.

The darkness was quiet. There was no sign of movement around the house. Oakley's light was not burning now, but his gun was ready. Ducking low to avoid silhouetting himself against the window, he peered at the ground. It was all grass; no footprints would have been left.

Oakley rose, listened, moved again. He trotted to the far side of the grounds, silently. He was proceeding quickly along the edge of a garden when he heard a metallic sound—a dull clank—and paused. It seemed to come from the opposite side of the estate. As Oakley turned, he heard the starter of an automobile grind, a motor purr softly. The sounds were coming from the public road which flanked the estate on the far side. Oakley went running.

He saw a car, without lights, glide swiftly past one of the gates. He raced to the gate, but the distance was not short. By the time he reached it, and sidled through, the car was gone.

Oakley hesitated, then grimly turned back. It struck him as odd that the gate was unlocked. He flashed his light and found the chain dangling loose, the padlock open. It had not been opened with a key. Some strong tool had twisted its hasp loose. Having seen that much, Oakley stepped through again, and hurried toward the spot where he had left Brixey.

There was no light shining in the shadows. Oakley called in a hushed tone: "Archie!" Brixey did not answer. Oakley moved quickly into the shadows, filled with misgivings; but he breathed a sigh when he saw a dark form on the ground, lying motionless. That would be Karl Stengel. Brixey must have dashed off, to give pursuit to the masked man.

Oakley stooped, gathered the limp form into his arms. A queer expression crossed his face. Karl Stengel was a stocky, heavy young man; the body in Oakley's arms was thin and light. With a sharp exclamation, Oakley lowered the form to the ground, whipped out his light, flashed it into the unconscious man's face.

"Hell!" he said.

The glare showed him the placid, aristocratic features of Archibald Brixey!

Brixey mumbled and writhed. Oakley felt of a bruise on his forehead, then roughly shook the man.

"Archie!" Oakley snapped.

It was a moment before Brixey could answer. He wriggled as

consciousness returned. Then his eyes popped open and he stared into Oakley's grim face. He gasped: "Awfully sorry, old man!"

"Never mind the regrets, Archie!" Oakley snapped. "I want to know what happened."

"So," said Archie Brixey with a sigh, "do I!" He rubbed his swollen forehead, struggled to his feet, tottered a bit. "Oke, at first I thought it was the unconscious man that blipped me, but it wasn't. I was watching the house, wondering what the soprano screaming was about, and then I turned to pick up young Mr. Stengel. At that point I suffered shameful abuse. I was struck on the head and rendered *hors de combat,* and that's really every bit I can tell you."

"Whoever did it took Karl Stengel with him!" Oakley snapped. "Archie, we've got to get going."

OAKLEY had whirled about and was running across the lawn. Brixey trotted waveringly after him, toward the roadster at the door. When he reached it, Oakley was coming out of the house. He climbed behind the wheel hurriedly, and Brixey scrambled in beside him.

"What is our destination?"

"Carmore's place. We're in this case to prove Carmore innocent. We've got to check up on him fast."

"But what about Karl Stengel?"

"We haven't got a prayer of tracing that car tonight," Oakley answered as he shot the roadster into the road. "That's McClane's job, and the maid is phoning headquarters now."

Oakley sent the car swerving around curves so rapidly that the tires whined. Carmore's place was not far away: it would take only a few minutes to reach it. In a moment he was swinging the car off the road and nosing the roadster toward an iron gate which was closed.

He hopped out and found the gate locked. "Over the fence, Archie," he suggested. In another minute, side by side, they were moving across the lawn, toward the *hacienda.*

The house was dark, the grounds silent. Oakley led the way across the grass to the rear of the place. Near the swimming pool they paused, peering at the dark reflections in the water. They started away again when Oakley, peering at the house, suddenly gripped Brixey's arm.

"Somebody over there!" he whispered.

He swung around, ran alongside the edge of the pool, and skirted toward the rear of the house. For a moment the shadows seemed empty. But suddenly a movement flashed in the black depths of them; a figure leaped away and began running swiftly alongside the house.

Oakley went after the man swiftly. Brixey speeded his long legs into a run. The chase led quickly along the dark side of the house. Oakley leaped forward. He threw his arms around the man. Archibald Brixey came to a gasping stop in front of him, shutting off all escape.

For a brief moment the man in Oakley's arms struggled. Brixey's flashlight splashed into the fugitive's face, and the silent battle quickly ended.

"I say, it's Carmore!" Brixey exclaimed.

Oakley released the man. In the shine of the light Carmore's face was pale. He was breathless and trembling. Oakley glared at him grimly. "Sorry, old man," he said. "But what are you up to?"

Carmore answered angrily: "A man has a right to move about his own house as he pleases, hasn't he?"

"Stengel's retained me to prove you're not mixed up in this, Carmore," Oakley answered. "That's why I'm here, and that's why I want an explanation."

Carmore breathed heavily a moment. He was garbed in pajamas and robe and slippers. He pushed Brixey's light out of his face and said: "The explanation is very simple. I was going to bed when I thought I heard water running in the pool. I hadn't turned it on, and I wondered who had. Naturally, I didn't know what to expect."

Oakley nodded. "All right—it sounds plausible. There is water in the pool. It's almost full. You didn't turn the water on or order it done?"

"Scarcely. Nobody will care to use that pool for some time. But somebody turned the valve. The pool must have been filling for hours."

"Strange," Oakley observed. "How long does it take the pool to fill?"

"About six hours."

"It's almost one now. Somebody must have turned on the valve at about seven tonight—" Oakley broke off as a shriek came through the night. It was an ear-rending cry of terror. It seemed to come from the rear of the house. And instantly it was followed by a loud splash as something fell into the water of the swimming pool!

"Good God!" Carmore gasped.

Then came another piercing cry. In high-pitched tones two words seemed to be distinguishable. "Peer Anna! Peer Anna!"

OAKLEY broke into a run toward the rear of the house. As he rushed within sight of the pool, he saw that its surface was broken by small waves. Something was flailing through the water in almost the center of the pool.

Then, suddenly, a head popped through the surface. Oakley's light was shining across it as the face appeared.

The face of Karl Stengel!

Almost as quickly it vanished, as though drawn down by some power beneath the water. Oakley's last glimpse of it was a horrible picture. The eyes were closed, the face a mask of agony.

Oakley sprang to the side of the pool, his light turned onto the surface. Brixey crowded beside him, his torch also blazing. Carmore breathlessly paused at the rim, peering down.

The water was in turmoil. Faintly in the light of the torches shone the same silver cloud which Oakley had seen envelope Mrs. Stengel. It was a fury beneath the surface, mysterious and terrible.

Carmore flung off his robe, poised to dive into the pool. Whirling, Oakley caught his arm. "Stay out! For God's sake, stay out!"

Suddenly the silver cloud in the water moved. It drew together and swept into the depths. Abruptly it was gone, and the water became quieter.

Carmore was peering in horror. Oakley looked around swiftly. An exclamation shot through his lips. "Carmore! Did you leave that door open?"

In the rear of the house a black, empty rectangle was visible. Carmore peered at it and gasped: "No!"

Oakley ran toward it. He burst into the house, stopped, leveled his gun. The darkness inside was broken only by the sound of the softly lapping waves of the pool. Carmore came in behind him and snapped a switch. Blinding light flooded the room.

"Nobody here," Brixey announced from his position behind Carmore.

"But somebody was here!" Carmore explained. "I left the door closed. Somebody—" He strode into the adjoining room, the study, and snapped another switch. Soft lights appeared on the walls. Carmore stopped just inside, pointing aghast.

"That chair—someone's moved it!"

The antique piece of furniture had, Oakley remembered, stood against the wall. Now it was almost in the center of the room. He turned away, quickly, and stepped outside. The two men followed him, quietly.

"The gate's locked. We climbed the fence. Any other way of getting in or out?" Oakley demanded.

"No," Carmore answered.

Oakley paused beside the pool, flashed his light, hesitated. Quickly he ordered Brixey to skirt the grounds, and asked Carmore to assist. As they ran off through the darkness, Oakley turned to the opposite side of the estate.

Minutes passed while the hunt went on. Oakley reached the gate and turned back while Brixey continued to search.

Near a corner of the iron fence Brixey stopped dead. His light flashed up and down the iron rods. Two of them were not in place. They had been loosened and lifted through the lower rail. Now they were pulled aside, and the opening made was large enough to pass the body of a man easily.

He turned, and hurried back to the house. Oakley was standing at the edge of the pool, pointing his light deep into the water. Brixey and Carmore stopped beside him, breathless.

"Opening in the fence, Oke!" Brixey exclaimed. "That explains it. Somebody was in the house. And somebody must have thrown Karl Stengel into the pool."

Oakley nodded, still peering into the depths. "Did you hear what he cried out? It sounded like 'Peer Anna.'"

"Yes—that was it."

Oakley rose and sighed. "It will be necessary for you to call the police again, Carmore. And you might begin draining the pool at once, too. There's another skeleton lying on the bottom. And this time it's all that's left of Karl Stengel."

CHAPTER FOUR

SKELETON IN THE CLOSET

OAKLEY gazed across his desk into the haggard face of Ernst Stengel. "Karl must have regained consciousness just before he was thrown into the water. I heard him cry out 'Peer Anna!' Does that mean anything to you, Mr. Stengel?"

"No—nothing. I do not understand—"

"Nor I. After throwing Karl into the pool, the murderer slipped into the house for some reason, then out again. There was no trace of him. It was too late to save Karl. When the pool was drained, after the police arrived, we found him in the same ghastly condition as Mrs. Stengel. There is very little more than that to tell you."

"But—Richard Carmore—"

"Did not throw Karl into the pool—certainly not. Brixey and I were with him at the time. It was someone else. Can you tell me, Mr. Stengel, who would wish to do this to you? Have you any idea—"

"No—none! I could not think anyone capable of it. It is the act of a lunatic—but—" Stengel broke off. "You do not know what killed them both."

"No definite idea," Oakley answered. "If I have any theories, I prefer to keep them to myself. I suggest that you go home and get some rest, Mr. Stengel—you need it. I assure you, I'll follow this case through to the end."

"Yes." Stengel rose. "Thank you." And like a broken man he left the office.

Miss Charmaine Morris was tapping a typewriter in the reception room as Stengel went out. She spun a page from the machine, clipped it to others, and stepped into the inner sanctum. She proffered the typewritten sheets to Oakley. "There's the report on Mrs. Stengel you asked for, darling. Also a preliminary note on Carmore. I'll get more on that later."

"Thank you, precious," Oakley said quietly. "Stick around. Archie and I are going out in a moment, and I want you to hold down the fort."

"Yes, Boss," said Cherry, and fluffed her red hair pertly.

Oakley skimmed through the report on Carmore first.

Hard-working, steady, conscientious, rates one of the best directors in films at present. Engaged to Carlotta Vine, about whom there is some mystery. Carmore bought his house about a year ago and did extensive remodelling. Nothing, so far as I can find out, was done to the pool, though.

Concerning Mrs. Stengel, Oakley read:

Did some acting six years ago. Karl her son by a previous marriage to William Brandz; divorce. Brandz died in auto accident year later. Mrs. Stengel pampered her son, spoiled him thoroughly. Married

Stengel four years ago, after Stengel began making name for himself. Tolerated by film people only because of husband's influence. Stengel's present gorgeous estate is a result of her selfish desire for show—had to have one of the costliest places around here. Stengel, a simple man apparently not very happy with her, but humored her by giving her everything she wanted. All three Stengels friendly with Carmore, especially Ernst. No possibility that Stengel is philandering with other women—not that sort.

"Oke," said Oakley. "Archie, have you all the passes we need for our excursion to the Associated Studios?"

"I jolly well have," said Brixey.

IN THE ROADSTER again, they swung out of Hollywood Boulevard to La Brea. In a short while Oakley brought the car to a stop in front of the Associated lot, and they got out.

At the desk in the reception room they presented passes. Once past an electrically controlled door, a studio cop pounced upon them and they produced the passes again. He directed them along one of the lot streets toward a large building in the corner. At a door labeled *Properties* still another cop stopped them, and examined their passes.

"My word!" said Archie. "I expect the militia to close in on us at any moment."

They pushed inside the building, and showed another pass to a man at a desk, and stepped into the huge warehouse beyond. It was crammed full of every conceivable type of furniture.

Through it they were conducted to a smaller room at the rear, in which was clustered a weird assortment of properties—chemical apparatus, electrical contraptions, cauldrons, boilers, wax figures; and on a shelf sat a row of skulls. The custodian of the inner room, a young man in shirt sleeves, looked at their passes again and asked: "What can I do for you, Mr. Oakley?"

"Got any skeletons on hand?"

"A few."

"Let's see."

The young man opened a closet, an appropriate place for skeletons, and disclosed several hanging from hooks by wire loops fixed through the tops of the skulls. Oakley bent over, examining them. An exclamation of surprise came from him. He lifted one off its hook and drew it out. It rattled as he moved it.

"This one," he observed, "has no arms."

The young man looked surprised. "That's right. It should have arms!"

"What's become of them?"

"I don't know! When I stowed those things in there last, they were in perfect shape. All of them had arms. But—"

"Can somebody have gotten in here and detached the arms?" Oakley demanded.

"It's not likely, but it's possible."

"Who has been in here lately?"

"This stuff hasn't been used in any picture in some time. Let's see. Several days ago Mr. Carmore came in."

"Carmore! What did he want?"

"Nothing, apparently. He came in and looked around. I stepped out of the room while he was here, to help them move a row-boat out, and when I came back he was gone."

Oakley peered grimly at the skeleton. "I want to take this along with me."

"That can't be done, sir."

"It can be done, sir," Oakley answered. "Archie, show him the letter from Mr. Stengel. It gives us the key to the place—anything we want. We want the skeleton."

Brixey produced the letter; the custodian of the properties read it and handed it back. "All right," he said. "If you'll give me a receipt."

Oakley wrote on a pad, "Received, one skeleton minus both arms, C. Oakley," and let it go with that. He folded the skeleton as best he could and carefully placed the bony remains in Brixey's arms.

"I say!" protested Archie as they went back to the car.

"Grab yourself a taxi and take this to a chemist, Archie," Oakley told him. "I want it compared with the arm we have in the safe. Very possibly the arm belongs to this skeleton. Run along, now."

"Where the deuce are you going, Oke?"

"To the customs house," Oakley answered. "See you later."

IT WAS PAST ten that night when Oakley returned to the office of Secrets, Incorporated. Both Brixey and Cherry Morris were waiting for him.

"More work, Archie," Oakley announced. "Come along. Cherry, you had best apply your pearly ear to a pillow for the rest of the night."

"If you think you're sending me off to bed, you might as well know I'm ready for a big evening, Oke," Cherry answered. "Wherever you're going, I'm toddling right along."

"Your company, my dear, is irresistible," said Oakley. "Come on."

They snapped out the lights of the office, locked it, and hurried down to the car. Oakley took the wheel, turned toward Beverly Hills.

"What's up?" asked Cherry.

"A further check-up on Carmore. Things aren't looking so good. How about the bones, Archie?"

"They're the same. The arms came from the skeleton. I was never so embarrassed in my life," said Archie.

"Tonight may not lead to a thing, but we're keeping Carmore in sight," Oakley said as they swung into the winding road which passed Carmore's place. When the estate was behind him, Oakley turned about, and parked on the opposite side of the road, near the gate. With the lights out he settled down to wait.

"May I ask why you paid the customs house a visit, Oke?" Brixey inquired.

"Checking up on the *Hell on Earth* company," Oakley answered. "Stengel still thinks there's a lot in the curse that seemed to hit everybody connected with that picture. I must admit that what happened to Mrs. Stengel and Karl makes the score a hundred per cent."

"But what has the customs to do with it?"

"One of the men—a sound engineer—died on the boat coming back, I found out. I was interested in what happened to him and the stuff he brought back with him. I— Steady!"

A pair of headlights swung around the *hacienda* on the hill. A car rolled down the driveway, and a man left the wheel to open the gates. After rolling the car through them, he locked them again. Oakley could see that it was Carmore.

Carmore sent the car winding down the road, and Oakley noted its number. "Out, Archie," he said. "Stay here and watch the place. Cherry and I are off together."

"Pshaw!" said Archie.

"And here—take good care of this." From his hip pocket Oakley removed a fat bottle some six inches high. "Don't open it, for God's sake. It'll kill you."

"My gracious! What is it?"

Oakley did not answer. He sent the car rolling down the hill after Carmore's. He kept well back of it until it swung into Wilshire and turned toward Los Angeles. Then he speeded closer, in the swiftly moving traffic.

Carmore's car turned quickly into Beverly Boulevard. Oakley kept silent as he followed it. Soon it turned again, into La Cienega, which led into Culver City. But before the car driven by Carmore covered the few miles which separated the two towns, it turned again, into a quiet side street.

It stopped abruptly in front of a modest little house, and Carmore got out. Oakley rolled his roadster past, slowly, waited until Carmore disappeared into the house, then stopped. With a word to Cherry to wait, he walked back to the dwelling Carmore had entered.

He paused, made sure he wasn't watched, then slipped along the driveway at the side, slid close to a window across which the drapes were not tightly drawn.

HE SAW four people in the room—Carmore, and Carlotta Vine; Ernst Stengel and a gray-headed woman seated on a davenport.

Oakley's surprise grew. He drew back, annoyed. He disliked this eavesdropping business, but he sensed strange connections between the people in the room. Deciding to have done with sneaking, he strode around the house to the front door and rang the bell.

Carlotta Vine answered it. When she saw Oakley she gave a little gasp; but she stood back, and he stepped inside. Ernst Stengel rose quickly.

"Oakley! What is it brings you here?"

"The job you gave me to do," Oakley answered. "I've been keeping an eye on Carmore. But if I'm not completely trusted, Mr. Stengel, I'll drop the case."

Stengel looked anguished. "Do not say that, Oakley. I have been keeping nothing of importance from you. I am willing to tell you everything."

"I'm sorry to come busting in like this," Oakley said. "But go ahead—I'm listening."

"This—this little girl," Stengel said, indicating Carlotta Vine, "is my daughter, Oakley."

"Your daughter! I didn't know—"

"No. My daughter by my first marriage. She came with me from Germany with her mother. We did not stay married long after that— we became estranged. Carlotta and her mother went to New York, and two years ago Carlotta came back, this time with my sister. Her mother is in New York now. This is my sister, Oakley—Henriette Stengel."

The gray-haired woman bowed graciously to Oakley.

Stengel continued: "Carlotta is a splendid girl, a brave girl. She did not tell me she returned to Hollywood. She began to make her way alone in the films. It was my sister who told me she was here, only after months. Carlotta will not let me tell anyone that she is my daughter, because she does not want to be favored, she wants to succeed on her own ability, and she will. I am very proud of Carlotta—I should want the whole world to know—but I respect her wishes."

Oakley looked sheepish. "I see. That's why you're so eager to prove Carmore innocent. He's not only your best friend; he's engaged to marry your daughter."

"Yes, Oakley. Yes." Stengel sighed. "I have come here tonight because I cannot bear to be alone. You understand that, don't you, Oakley?"

"I," said Oakley, "understand I've made a fool of myself. I apologize to all of you. And good luck to you, Miss Vine. You deserve it. I'll withdraw as gracefully as possible. Good night."

OAKLEY drove quickly back to the Carmore estate in Beverly Hills. When he got out, Brixey materialized from the shadows.

"Greetings," he said. "Oke, what the devil is in this bottle?"

"High-powered death," answered Oakley. "Let's have it, Archie. We're going here apparently as guests, but we're going to take a good look at that pool."

The Japanese manservant appeared at his ring. Oakley asked to see Carmore, and when he was told, as he knew he would be, that Carmore was out, he declared that Carmore was expecting him and they would wait. The gate swung open, and Oakley drove to the house. There the Jap ushered them into the exquisitely furnished living room, withdrew.

Oakley waited until the servant was upstairs before he moved. Then he opened the French doors which disclosed the pool beyond, and stepped outside. "Stick in the house, Archie," he said quietly. "Warn me if anyone comes."

He regarded the pool curiously. Again it contained water. He listened, and heard the faint rippling which meant that water was still flowing into the pool. Crossing to the little house and opening its door, he found that the valve was turned to the open position.

An area of cement separated the house from the edge of the tiling that framed the pool. Oakley removed a small flash from his pocket and flicked its light along the paving. Cherry watched him curiously.

He followed the cracks which separated the cement into squares; they were tinted various colors, a mosaic pattern. Oakley was halfway between the house and the pool when an exclamation escaped him. Cherry Morris hurried to his side.

"What is it?"

"Notice this square," Oakley said. "No dirt in the cracks around it. Dirt in all the others."

He turned, went into the house, went to the study. From the desk he took a steel letter-opener. Glancing through the window, he saw that the square of cement he had noticed was directly between the window and the pool. He went outside again quickly, and stooped over the section which interested him.

He thrust the thin blade into the crack at one side of the rectangle. When he pried it moved slightly. Eagerly he lifted it—it seemed light. As he raised it, he saw that it was a wooden frame thinly coated with cement—that there was a cavity below. Cherry leaned over breathlessly as he turned the light down.

A foot beneath the surface, the light shone on rusty metal. There were two leaves, hinged, their edges flush. From both of them short levers extended, and to the levers were attached a steel wire. That wire and another disappeared underground, in the direction of the house. Oakley reached down, and pulled one of them.

The hinged iron flaps swung downward, disclosing a greater depth. The rippling surface of water lay under the beam of the flashlight. And beneath the surface, moving slowly, ruffling the water as with some weird power, there seemed to be a silver cloud.

OAKLEY straightened alertly. He stepped away from the cavity beneath the paving, leaving Cherry in darkness beside it, returned to the house. In the doorway he paused, beckoning Brixey.

"Down to the car, Archie," Oakley said briskly. "Beat it to headquarters and get McClane. It's highly important."

Oakley watched him leave the house by the front entrance. Turning, he detached a cord which was affixed to one of the window drapes. It was a silken rope perhaps three feet long. Carrying it, flashing his light, he returned to the spot where Cherry Morris was waiting.

He turned the light again into the hole. The hinged and counter-weighted leaves of iron had swung back into place. Reaching down, Oakley tugged at the wire which swung them open. Again the water below was disclosed, and in the water that strange silver mass.

"What is it, Oke?" Cherry whispered.

"Small underground tank connecting with the swimming pool through a watertight trap, probably," Oakley answered. "The trap must be in the near wall with its edges hidden in the colored pattern. This other wire probably swings it open."

"But the silver cloud in the water, Oke," Cherry insisted. "What is it?"

"Horrible death," Oakley answered. *"Piranha."*

"What's *Piranha?*"

"Fish, one of the most deadly creatures of South America. It's more terrible than a man-eating tiger. It is known as the man-eating fish of the Rio Paraguay.

"It swims in swarms, and preys on every sort of flesh. Anyone not knowing about them, who attempts to take a swim in the Rio Para-guay, never comes up after the first dive. The *Piranha* attack like lightning, like a pack of ravenous wolves. A swarm of them will strip the flesh from an animal or a human in an incredibly short time, and leave nothing but the skeleton."

"They are what killed Mrs. Stengel and Karl? Where did they come from, Oke? How did they get here?"

"Yes, they are what killed Mrs. Stengel and Karl. They came from the Gran Chaco, the Rio Paraguay, in South America. That's where *Hell on Earth* was filmed, you know. Checking up at the custom house, I found that the sound engineer who died on the return trip had trapped some *Piranha* fingerlings, and was bringing them back. He had taken notes about them and was going to present them to some museum, but he never lived to do it. The studio took over his affects—"

"Fingerlings?" Cherry asked.

"Very young fish. At the time, this swarm of them was contained in a small tank. They've grown to maturity since then—a year and a half ago."

"Then this secret tank must have been built especially for them!"

"Without a doubt, it was. Those fish were taken, and placed here, and raised—as a living instrument of murder. The man who used them to kill Mrs. Stengel and Karl has had his plan of murder hatching a long time.

"The whole arrangement must work something like this. A pull on one of these wires opens the water-tight door connecting this hidden tank with the swimming pool. The fish swarm out, instantly, and attack the victim. In only a few seconds, nothing is left by them except a skeleton."

"But how do they get back, Oke?"

"This arrangement takes care of that—the trap right below us. It must be closed, and a huge piece of raw meat left on it in readiness. As soon as the fish have killed the person in the pool, a pull on this second wire drops the meat into the tank below. Scenting fresh food, the fish swarm back into the tank like lightning. Then the water-tight door connecting with the tank and the swimming pool is closed again, and no indication of what has happened is left."

"Horrible!"

"All of that," Oakley said quietly. "That's why some members of the victims were missing—the parts from which the flesh was most difficult to remove. The fish dragged the parts back with them into this hidden tank.

"That's why, too, Karl Stengel cried out when he was thrown into the pool. He'd been to the Gran Chaco with the *Hell on Earth* company and he must have known about the fish. I thought he shouted 'Peer Anna' but it was really *Piranha,* of course."

OAKLEY was gathering together the silken rope he had removed from the curtain inside the house. He dropped one end of it quickly into the water below, and instantly flicked it up again. Like a flash of silver, something sprang through the light of the electric torch. It was a silver fish, gripping the tassel of the rope in its mouth. Oakley pulled it aside, and it lay flapping on the pavement.

They peered at it. It was a blunt-jawed, deep-bellied fish, with a grotesque head, all white, which looked as if it might have been carved from alabaster. Oakley stooped and looped the silken rope into its snapping mouth. Its teeth caught into it. In an instant the heavy rope was bitten in two!

"There are at least a hundred of those deadly things down there in the tank," Oakley declared.

Cherry Morris rose, shuddering. "It looks bad for Carmore, Oke," she said quietly.

"Carmore, or whoever it is, I'm following this through," Oakley declared. "I'm going to try to find the place where those wires end. Keep an eye out, Cherry, while I take a look inside."

Oakley stepped toward the *Piranha,* which was still flapping viciously against the pavement. He gave it a swift thrust with his shoe. Its swift jaws nipped the edge of his sole, and a bit disappeared from the leather, instantly. The fish flapped again, fell through the hole in the pavement, flashed into the water below.

Grimly Oakley touched the fat bottle in his pocket, then turned toward the house. He stepped through the French doors, paused, and moved toward the small room which adjoined—Carmore's study. Snapping on the lights, he paused again, and glanced about the room.

Against the rear wall a chair was sitting. After the visit of the mysterious prowler to the house the previous night, that chair had been found in the center of the room—for some reason it had been moved. Oakley lifted it, set it aside. Then he dropped on his knees and began examining the floor.

He saw no suspicious cracks. But when he turned toward the wainscoting, his eyes sharpened. There was a short section of it beneath the window, apparently pieced in. Oakley pried at its upper edge with his fingernails. Suddenly the board came loose, dropped down on hinges.

Behind it a small space was disclosed. And in that space lay two small iron rings. Attached to them were two stout wires, which entered pipes tilted down at an angle. Oakley examined them.

A pull on one of the rings, he knew, would open the water-tight door connecting the swimming pool with the underground tank. The other would release the trap below the movable section of cement, and drop into the tank anything resting upon it—fresh meat, to draw the *Piranha* back into their lair. Which was which? Oakley could not tell; but he had seen enough. Grimly he began to rise.

A swift, silent movement behind startled him. He sensed rather than saw it—a quick step from the darkness behind the desk. He whirled half around, snatching at the automatic in his arm-pit holster—but it was too late.

A heavy blow caught him on the side of the head. He spilled backward, with a gasp, the world spinning around him. Another heavy blow followed the first. Oakley went lax on the floor, and blackness flooded over him.

OAKLEY heard a stifled moan from Cherry as a glimmer of light reentered his brain. Swift footfalls tapped across the cement. He raised himself, gripped with a sickening dizziness, and tried to shout a warning.

His voice was only a husky whisper. He dragged himself up desperately and peered through the window. What he saw sent a shocking chill through him.

A black figure was moving between the window and the water, a stooped, menacing form. It was coming from a corner of the pool where the brass ladder ran down into the water. And to that ladder Cherry Morris was bound!

A gag was thrust into her mouth, and it was held in place by a length of the silken cord which the *Piranha* had snipped in two. Only Cherry Morris' head was visible above the water: she was struggling to free herself from the bonds which fastened her to the ladder. Her desperate efforts were fruitless, she could scarcely move.

The black figure was leaving her now, moving toward the house. Oakley, staggering, stumbled toward the door. He groped for the automatic nestling in the holster under his arm. The lights spun about him like whirling stars as he thrust himself into the large room beyond.

Instantly a powerful fist struck Oakley in the face. He lurched back, glimpsing as if in a nightmare a white-masked man. Crazily he tried to disengage the catch of the automatic, to fire, but the punishing fist struck him again, ramming him against the wall. He felt the automatic torn from his hand; and as he fell, he sensed that the masked man was rushing into the study.

To open the trap! To swing wide the water-tight door connecting the hidden tank with the pool, to release the swarm of ferocious *Piranha!* Instantly the trap was open, the cloud of fish would dart out—strike at the bound girl—

Madly Oakley dragged himself up. He glanced about for his automatic, it was gone. Tottering toward the door of the study, he saw the masked man kneeling beside the wall under the window, reaching for one of the release rings.

Oakley whirled away. He thrust himself out the French door, toward the pool. As he moved he dragged from his hip pocket the fat bottle he had been carrying. He ripped the cork from it and poised above the opening of the hidden tank. Quickly he spilled half the contents of the bottle through the hole.

Whirling away, he stumbled toward the brass ladder. Cherry's head was turned, she was peering at him frantically. Hanging to the ladder, Oakley poured the remainder of the contents of the bottle into the water around her. He dropped it as he turned away, peering into the depths.

Faint silver was moving through the water—*Piranha* swarming into the pool!

Oakley fumbled with the silken ropes which bound Cherry to the ladder. They were tied tightly; the knots would not come undone. As he heard a heavy step behind, he whirled.

The dark figure was hurrying from the doorway, eyes gleaming above the edge of the white mask. Oakley faced the man, braced himself; and a sob broke through his lips.

The black form paused. He spoke quickly: "It's too late! You will die with her!"

Oakley straightened, his eyes narrowed, gleaming. "Not quite," he said quietly. "Neither of us is going to die. I've just dumped a pound of cyanide into the tank and the pool. Your *Piranha* are dead."

A THROATY curse came from the white-masked man. He bounded toward the pool, peered into it. On the black surface of the water silver things were floating—*Piranha*—killed by the powerful poison in the water. The silver cloud was scattering, rising.

Oakley poised, and leaped.

The white-masked man whirled at the same instant. Oakley's automatic was in his hand. As Oakley sprang toward him, the gun spat fire. A bullet clicked against the tiles; another splashed into the pool as Oakley flung himself desperately and grappled. The gun flew into the pool.

For one brief moment the two men struggled silently on the brink of the pool. Oakley struck out recklessly, and felt his knuckles crash into his antagonist's face. The white-masked man jolted back, twisted, and broke into a crazy run. He sprang into the shadows beyond the corner of the house.

Oakley tottered as he followed. He was dashing past the corner when he sensed a movement in the darkness. The next instant he collided with a dark form that sprang away from the side of the house. Oakley flung out his arms, and gripped a man's body. The man wrenched away, desperately, and struck out.

In a flash, before the hard knuckles smashed into his eyes, Oakley glimpsed a terrified face. The face of Josef Hirsch!

The power of the blow jarred Oakley against the side of the house. He sagged and hung to the wall. As he straightened, he heard swift footfalls through the grass. It was the thought of Cherry Morris that kept him from giving chase. He hurried back to the swimming pool, to the brass ladder to which the girl was lashed.

He loosened the rope around her head and removed the gag. "Cherry! Are you hurt?"

"No, Oke—no." She was breathless.

Swiftly Oakley worked at Cherry Morris' bonds. As he pulled at the knots, he heard the sound of a car grinding up the driveway from the public road. Its lights swung toward the pool; it stopped as Oakley pulled the last rope free.

He lifted Cherry from the water, supported her as two men came running.

"I say!" blurted Archibald Brixey.

McClane lumbered to a stop. "What the devil? We heard shots!"

Oakley stepped grimly into the house and sought a telephone. Of the operator he demanded the number of Josef Hirsch, and got it. When a maid answered he snapped: "I've got to see Mr. Hirsch immediately. Where is he?"

"He went to the studio early this evening, and said he'd be busy there almost all night."

Oakley tramped out again. "Cherry, my dear," he said, "a hot bath and bed for you. McClane, be a good scout and drive her home. Archie—you're coming with me. Make it snappy!"

CHAPTER FIVE

A MATTER OF RECORD

OAKLEY said nothing as he drove swiftly to the big Associated Studios lot. He made his way past gatekeeper and cops, strode to the door of Sound Stage Five, and shouldered in to find the place humming with activity. On the set, facing them, was Josef Hirsch, again in shirt-sleeves. He was talking to Carlotta Vine with offensive bluntness.

Oakley walked quietly to a spot beside the director. When Hirsch glanced at him, he said affably: "Good evening, Hirsch. You made the trip fast."

"The trip? What trip?"

Hirsch hesitated, his eyes jerking nervously. He snapped orders that sent the players and technicians scurrying away. Oakley led him aside; he followed defiantly. "I don't know what you're—"

"Don't pull that," Oakley interrupted. "You were at Carmore's place a few minutes ago. I saw you. In fact, you pushed a fist into my face. Open up."

Hirsch paled. His voice dropped. "God, Oakley—I can't give you any explanation now. All right—I was there. I did hit you because—because I knew it might look bad for me to be caught there." He blustered. "You refused to handle my case. I had to do my own detective work."

"Hirsch."

The director looked around at Ernst Stengel, who had just come through the door. The latter seemed annoyed.

"The lab is waiting. You've given them no films to develop tonight. Will this picture ever be finished?"

"Keep Oakley away from me and I'll finish it!"

Oakley nodded. "Go ahead. But when you're through, Hirsch—"

Hirsch stamped off. Stengel, preoccupied, sank into a chair beside the set. Oakley and Brixey shifted to a position from which they could view the stage.

The huge, hideous face of the Taoistic God of Anger leered out of the temple as before. Now Hirsch called Carlotta Vine to the center of the temple floor. As another player followed, an actor made-up as a Chinese, Brixey's aristocratic eyebrows arched.

"I say, Oke—that's not Dwyer, is it?"

"Dwyer is still being held at headquarters, but it looks very much like him."

Hirsch finished his directions, and strode back of the ring of cameras and spotlights. Oakley stepped close to him. "Who's playing the Chinaman now?"

"John Sandler," Hirsch answered shortly. "We had to pick a man that looks as much like Dwyer as possible— Let me alone, Oakley!"

Hirsch shouted for silence. "Lights!" and the flat glare disappeared. Semi-darkness filled the sound stage, except for the fantastic face of the God of Anger. Circled with a spotlight, it stared with its one popping eye out into the darkness. Facing it, on the set, back to the cameras, stood Carlotta Vine. The actor who looked like Dwyer disappeared behind the huge head.

SILENCE fell as the taking of the scene began. For a long moment Carlotta Vine stood motionless, facing the hideous idol. Then she began to move forward, her small feet lagging, as if drawn by hypnotic power.

Oakley glanced about swiftly. He moved through the gloom noiselessly, toward the side of the set. He passed behind the sidewall, into the passageway running alongside the temple. Beyond, the darkness was deeper. He kept moving cautiously, until a glow of light was visible through an opening in the rear.

There Oakley paused, watching. He could see the inside of the great shell which formed the idol's head. Light was shining through the twisted, open mouth. In the glow, the actor, John Sandler, was crouching out of sight of the cameras.

Suddenly Oakley tensed. He detected a furtive movement in the darkness behind the set. He could not place it; he could see nothing. After a moment of silent search, he glanced back.

Behind Sandler, now, a dark form was hovering. It seemed shapeless; yet its arm was upraised, its shoulders hunched. Even as Oakley glimpsed it, he realized that this figure had stolen out of the darkness into the space behind the idol, unseen by the cameras, unsuspected by Sandler. And suddenly the arm fell swiftly.

Sandler collapsed with scarcely a sound. The dark figure bent as

Oakley started forward. He stepped to the opening which gave into the space behind the idol, while the dark figure made strange movements. Then the figure raised, its shape different somehow. Evidently the man had shed a coat; he was stepping toward the open mouth of the image, and in one hand he was gripping a blow-gun. As he raised it, Oakley glimpsed his face.

It was the made-up face of Sandler; yet Sandler was lying unconscious!

"Drop that!" Oakley snapped and Hirsch's voice called: "Cut! Cut!"

The man with the blow-gun raised the weapon suddenly. A sharp intake of breath sounded as the tube turned full upon Oakley. He leaped on the instant. His one hand knocked the blow-pipe downward; his other went hard to the yellow face. There was a crunching sound, a muffled cry. The man with the blow-gun wrenched away desperately, stumbling into the dim light.

Startling, grotesque, he seemed—a yellow-faced man garbed in Occidental clothing, queer pupilless eyes staring, mouth gaping stiffly open. Oakley sprang again.

Another muffled cry sounded as the man with the blow-gun whirled. He leaped into the open, and stopped short. Hirsch was hurrying onto the set; Archibald Brixey was behind him. The man with the blow-gun poised; he swung, desperately seeking a way off the set.

Oakley's voice came sharply. "Easy. You're cornered."

The saffron face turned expressionlessly to Oakley. The blow-gun glinted in the light again. Oakley started forward frantically. He heard a sucking-in of breath—a resonant puff of wind—and seized the arms of the yellow-faced man.

He looked down, and his eyes widened. One of the man's hands was extended stiffly; his vacuous eyes were staring at it. On the flesh above the wrist a tiny tuft of feathers was quivering. Over the skin ran a single drop of blood. Oakley stared, realizing that this man had shot the dart deliberately into his own skin. Almost instantly his body toppled.

Oakley caught him, lowered him. In the light the yellow face kept its implacable expression.

"Sandler!" came from Hirsch.

"No, not Sandler," Oakley said softly. "Sandler's behind the idol, unconscious from a blow on the head. It isn't Dwyer, either, of course. What you're looking at is not a face at all. It's a mask.

"Nothing else. A mask duplicating Dwyer's face, made up as a Chinese. *Papier-mâché*, like the idol."

"But—who is it?"

Oakley stooped. His fingertips lifted the light shell from the face it covered. The Oriental features came away in his hands— "Stengel," Oakley said.

THE EVERLASTING bright sunshine of Southern California was beaming through the windows of the inner sanctum of Secrets, Incorporated, next morning. At the desk was Archibald Brixey. Oakley and Cherry Morris entered. "Here is the typed transcription of the report you dictated, Oke. Want to look it over?" Archie asked.

"Right now, Archie," Oakley said. He read passages of it rapidly.

Horrible as the means of murder was, Ernst Stengel's motive was in itself praiseworthy. His first wife, now ill in New York and under the care of a specialist, had stood by him during the heartbreaking period when Stengel was striving to win a place for himself in American films. Those were days of poverty and struggle for them. Once Stengel began to succeed, he fell prey to the Hollywood manner of living. It was not long before he had divorced his first wife and married again, this time to the sister of Josef Hirsch.

Mrs. Stengel the second was selfish, vain, pampered; she set about getting everything possible from Stengel. Her brother, thoroughly grasping, instigated and furthered her selfish plans. Early in their married life, she induced Stengel to have drawn up by her brother's lawyer, and signed, a legal disposition which left all Stengel's property to her and Karl, omitting completely any benefits for the first wife. It was an ironclad document. The Stengels then owned and were living in the house which they later sold to Carmore in order to provide for Mrs. Stengel a more sumptuous home.

Stengel soon realized the selfishness of his second wife. When he learned that his first wife was suffering and alone, that his daughter was succeeding in films on her own, he became remorseful, realizing that he had committed a great injustice to them.

Stengel was a man only too human, yet half mad. His situation was made worse by the fact that the temperamental Hirsch was prejudiced against Carlotta Vine and unreasonably fighting her attempts to succeed in films. He was the greatest single danger threatening her career. Stengel planned death for Hirsch, not only because of Hirsch's enmity for Carlotta, but because Stengel knew he had instigated the second Mrs. Stengel to demand the legal disposition. He planned death also for the woman and young man who stood between him and justice for his first wife and daughter.

Stengel took over the effects of the sound engineer who died on the boat returning from South America after the filming of *Hell on Earth*, and he brought the *Piranha* into the country. Among the engineer's effects also was a blow-gun and a supply of *thara*. He planned the hidden tank connected with the swimming pool of his house. The workmen who did the job have been located. He was forced to wait until the *Piranha* became mature; and in the meantime Mrs. Stengel had nagged him into selling the place in favor of a grander establishment. Though he complied, he did not abandon his plan.

He engaged my services as a blind to cover himself, but also to protect Carmore, his friend, and Dwyer. His first two attempts to kill Hirsch having failed, he made use of the blow-gun and *thara*. He paid a workman at the studio to make a mask duplicating Dwyer's made-up features—the man has confessed receiving hush-money. Once having made it seem that Dwyer was guilty, Stengel sincerely determined to clear the man, but his concern for Dwyer was quickly overshadowed by his anxiety for Carmore when Carmore was suspected.

The night Stengel abducted Karl, he took the risk of exposing himself, deliberately, to help prove Carmore's innocence and, incidentally, Dwyer's. He may have planned to allow the Chinese mask to be found, later, in a further attempt to clear them without incriminating himself. His professed fear of the "curse" on the *Hell on Earth* company was only to fog the issue while he could achieve his ends with safety to himself.

His final attempt to kill Hirsch failed and exposed him. Regardless of his motives or his acts, he did succeed in his aim doing the justice he had committed against his daughter and his first wife. Carlotta Vine and her mother will share his estate, as is right. It is to be hoped that her career will continue to the heights of stardom.

DEATH LIGHTS THE CANDLE

IN THE CREDULOUS HOLLYWOOD MOVIE COLONY A WEIRD NEW SECT HAD SPRUNG UP— THE CHILDREN OF THE MONAD. AND IN ITS WAKE A GHASTLY FEVER WHICH TURNED YOUNG MEN TO WITHERED GAFFERS OVERNIGHT. WHAT WAS THIS GRIM DEATH—LIT BY THE FLAME OF A CANDLE— THAT BURNED MEN UP BEFORE THEIR TIME? HOW COULD ONE MAN, AND ONE ALONE, SNUFF OUT THE SEARING BLAZE OF THE GIANT TERROR TAPER?

CHAPTER ONE

THE MUMMY AND THE FLAME

CLAY OAKLEY of Secrets, Incorporated, Hollywood's ace private investigator, knocked at the heavy door. No immediate answer came from inside the sumptuous neo-Spanish villa, though lights were shining through heavily curtained windows, filtering dimly across the gardened grounds. A brooding silence shrouded the place, a murky quiet quite out of keeping with the garishness and hustle of the nearby film capital.

Oakley remarked to the elegantly attired Archibald Brixey, his assistant: "After a call as urgent as this one, I should expect a quicker answer to my ring."

"In Hollywood it is futile to expect anything logical, Oke," Brixey observed gloomily, fingering his monocle.

Oakley smiled. He knew that his companion was nobody's fool; that behind his foppish exterior mannerisms lay a keen intelligence backed by a well trained pair of fists. Two good reasons why he had annexed him as an associate.

A soft footfall sounded behind the door; it inched open and a slanted eye looked out.

"To see Mr. Rystrom, please," Oakley announced, and extended his card toward the saffron hand which reached for it.

THE JAPANESE servant mouthed something unintelligible, then led the way with evident unwillingness into a large, dimly lighted, antique-furnished living room, and disappeared behind thick portieres. Oakley and Brixey waited in silence even heavier than the isolated quiet outside.

"Something about this place," Brixey remarked, "is strange."

The portieres swung again.

She peeled the curtains
apart and peered through.

The young woman who came into the room, anxiously and quickly, was beautiful. It was Oakley's business to know Hollywood inside and out, and he recognized her at once. Estelle LaSalle was a popular and talented young actress whose face was known to millions. She was also the niece of the man whose home this was—Robert Rystrom,

a producer in the Greater Classics Studios. She studied Oakley with troubled eyes.

"You say you came to see Mr. Rystrom?" she asked quickly, without preliminary formality.

"Yes." Oakley introduced himself and Brixey. "Mr. Rystrom telephoned me at my office half an hour ago and urged me to come—on, he said, a highly important matter."

The sartorially perfect Brixey's gallant bow to the lady went unnoticed by her. She looked startled, bewildered, then said in a rush: "But there must be some mistake."

"Mistake?"

"My uncle is ill—seriously ill. He has been confined to his bed for weeks. He couldn't possibly have called you."

Oakley's eyebrows arched. "The man who called me declared he was Mr. Rystrom. He spoke in a husky, weak voice, like that of a sick man. He begged me to come—begged desperately. Are you sure—"

"I'm positive he didn't call you," Estelle LaSalle broke in. "There is no telephone in his room. He couldn't have left his bed. A nurse is with him almost constantly, and she wouldn't have permitted it if he had tried it."

"Perhaps," Oakley said quietly, "I had better speak to Mr. Rystrom."

"But you can't!" The actress's protest was almost frantic. "No one can see him. The doctor forbids it."

Oakley sensed deep turmoil in the girl whose face he studied silently for a moment. He asked with surprising, disarming candor: "Isn't it just possible that Mr. Rystrom has a reason for wanting to consult a detective—secretly?"

The girl's breath caught and she exclaimed: "Of course not! I assure you it is a mistake. Someone played a practical joke on you—pretended to be my uncle. It's the only possible explanation."

Oakley almost asked, "Is it?" but didn't. He bowed. "I'm sorry to have disturbed you, then, Miss LaSalle," he answered. "Very sorry."

At a clap of the girl's hands, the Japanese servant appeared suddenly from behind the portieres. Oakley got the impression that he had been waiting anxiously to show them out. The girl hurried from the room as Oakley and Brixey were escorted to the entrance, and for a moment her slender, supple body was silhouetted enchantingly against a brighter light beyond.

Oakley and Brixey paused in the gloom of the grounds as the latch clicked behind them. "Strange," the latter remarked, "and I don't like it."

"Very strange. Even if Rystrom didn't call me," Oakley declared, "I never heard a more desperate voice in my life than the one I listened to over the phone. It might very well have been that of a dying man." He shrugged, started off toward where he had left his roadster in the winding road, near the gate.

THE GRAVEL path led around a corner of the villa and Oakley was at the bend, with Brixey beside him, when his hand shot out suddenly, signaling a stop. In the darkness Oakley stepped aside to the corner, and peered past. Brixey leaned over his shoulder, looking along the stucco side of the house. Oakley had glimpsed a furtive movement in the gloom; and now, as they watched, it came again.

A few yards away a window was raised; the heavy curtains were moving. Through them a white hand came—the slender, well kept hand of a girl. Next, a trim oxford appeared and, following it, a beautifully curved, sheerly stockinged leg.

Brixey breathed: "Not bad. Not bad at all."

The girl brought herself to a sitting position on the windowsill, legs braced beneath her. She leaned out, balancing with some difficulty, for with both arms she was clasping close, two large gilt picture frames, covered backs outward. She hopped down quickly and, without turning her face toward Oakley and Brixey, hurried away.

She hastened along the path, keeping to the grass. The gloom wrapped her, faded her from sight. Oakley, as she vanished, stepped to the window, peered in, and saw an elaborate study. On the opposite wall two patented picture hangers supported nothing.

He turned down the path just as the sound of a motor came from the road. The car was already moving away when Oakley and Brixey reached the gate; its red tail-light blinked out around a bend. Promptly Oakley slipped under the low-slung wheel of his roadster.

"Can this be burglary, Oke?" Brixey asked as he settled to the seat and the motor hummed. "If it is, she has quite the most bewitching legs of any burglar I ever saw."

The roadster whirred around the bend. "It wasn't Estelle LaSalle," Oakley remarked. "Though to judge from several of her movies, she's not so bad as far as legs go, either."

The winding road led down a slope toward the center of Beverly Hills, and Oakley covered it swiftly; but, by the time he reached Wilshire Boulevard, the mysterious girl's car was out of sight. He chanced the jumping of a red light, turned east, and wound his way ahead of the swiftly flowing traffic. He was rolling over the car tracks into Los Angeles when he eased up on the accelerator.

"The young lady," he said, "has slipped us." Then he exclaimed suddenly: "It *was* Rystrom who called me! The man was desperate—frantic. He was begging for help. I was a fool not to insist on seeing him."

"But what can the beautiful burglaress have to do with the call from Rystrom, Oke?" Brixey inquired. "What were those things she was carrying away? And if Rystrom is actually desperate to see you, why did Miss LaSalle stand you off?"

Oakley's foot pushed the brake as a red light gleamed. Suddenly he twisted at the wheel and sent the car shooting off to the left. Brixey sat up very straight. "Where to?" he asked.

"Back to Rystrom's."

"But we couldn't get in last time and—"

"This time," Oakley promised grimly, "we're going to get in."

THE ROADSTER purred past the gate of the spreading Rystrom estate, and Oakley swung off the road near the corner of the spiked fence. With Brixey following he walked up the slope. The gate, Oakley guessed from vast previous experience with Hollywood exclusiveness, would be locked, but the fence was not high. He poised, swung over it, and bade Brixey follow. Then, side by side, they walked on toward the sprawling villa. Quietly they shifted away from the entrance toward the side flanked by the gravel path.

Near the front corner of the building the curtains at the open window were still wafting. Oakley went to it, peered again into the study, swung a leg over the sill. He climbed on through, crossed the room and had paused beside a carved desk as Brixey joined him.

"It's my opinion, Oke, that this manner of entering a house is illegal."

"Illegal," Oakley agreed, "but in this case highly effective."

He crossed to the door of the study and looked out into a broad, dark hallway. Silence lay within the house, and that certain stifled atmosphere created by illness or tragedy. Quick steps took Oakley toward a heavily carpeted staircase. Brixey followed as he ascended.

They were halfway up when a sound startled them. Footfalls in the hall above came steadily closer while Oakley poised. He turned, with a quick gesture to Brixey, and descended swiftly. They reached the foot of the stairs, whirled, and pressed themselves through a dark doorway as a figure appeared above.

Estelle LaSalle, clothed now in the lace and silk film of a negligee, dainty satin mules on her feet, came down slowly. She paused within a few feet of where Oakley and Brixey hid in the blackness, then turned to the door of the study, and stepped in, reaching for the light switch. Suddenly there was a half-choked exclamation from her. "Oh!—they're gone!"

She stood a moment in consternation. As though unable to believe her eyes, she hastened into the room, staring at the blank wall where the two empty picture hangers were exposed. Her face grew pale, her body rigid, her white hands formed into fists.

Oakley moved. He glided into the hallway and past the lighted door, still unseen by the amazed girl who continued staring at the blank wall. Brixey followed him to the stairs and up them silently. They paused in a gloomy, empty hallway.

"Now where," mused Oakley softly, "is Rystrom?"

Quick footfalls sounded again below. Oakley and Brixey stepped aside as Estelle LaSalle hurried from the study, her negligee snaking across the floor behind her. Oakley looked thoughtful and began to drift down the hall.

The girl's strained voice sounded faintly—"Police headquarters! Give me police headquarters!"

Brixey paused abruptly. "I say!" he murmured.

"We," said Oakley grimly, "will have to move fast."

Long strides took him along the thickly carpeted hallway to where, in a recess, he spied a telephone on a stand. He picked it up. The girl's voice came clearly over the extension wire. Brixey fidgeted while Oakley listened.

Estelle LaSalle was saying: "They're priceless—priceless! You've got—"

"All right, lady. There's a squad car heading for your place right now. When did you discover—"

Oakley waited to hear no more.

"In a few moments, Archie," he said, turning down the hall again, "we're going to have a very efficient radio car on our tails if we don't watch out!"

On the last word the sound of a rattling doorknob came suddenly. Oakley took a quick step back to the recess, and with a whirl turned into it. Brixey squeezed against him, startled.

A **DOOR** in the upper hallway opened. The rustling sound of stiff garments followed as someone came toward the recess. Oakley saw a woman, wearing a nurse's starched uniform, go past. She glanced neither right nor left, but advanced to a door in the rear of the hall and went through it.

"Now!" said Oakley. Rapid steps took him along the hall with

Brixey at his heels. The nurse had left ajar the door through which she had come. Oakley pushed it wider, stepped through, and paused.

One dim light was burning under a shade at a corner table on which an opened magazine lay. Evidently the nurse had just left the chair beside it. The faint glow shone over an immaculate white bed at the farther side of the room, and in the bed a form was lying, motionless.

Oakley moved toward the bed, saw a face—turned upward in complete repose—a horrible face. The skin was shrunken, dried, yellowed, as if by age. The cheeks were hollow, the closed eyes bulging. Thin hair topped the face, straggling brown and gray. One scrawny hand lay outside the covers, a thing of parched skin and bone.

Oakley said: "God!"

"My word!" Brixey breathed. "He's little more than a living mummy!"

Oakley bent closer. His fingertips touched gently the lax wrist, and the skin felt scaly and surprisingly hot. He studied the gaunt face, his eyebrows drawing together, then rose. From the foot of the bed he lifted the nurse's record.

The temperature chart showed a red line straight across the graph— an unwavering fever of 105. The pulse rate was indicated as 110, the respiration as 48. More than six degrees of fever, the pulse thirty beats above normal per minute, and the respiration also thirty above normal. Oakley frowningly replaced the chart.

He bent again over the emaciated form on the bed and once more his fingertips touched the thin wrist. Suddenly he jerked, and Brixey, bending over, exclaimed, "Oke!"

The eyelids of the man on the bed were twitching. They opened quickly—from protruding, exhausted eyes that turned to Oakley's lowered face. The dried lips parted. Rystrom breathed heavily, staring as though at an image in a dream.

"I'm Oakley," the private investigator said quietly.

"Oakley!" It was a gasping whisper.

Rystrom moved quickly, frantically. He raised, and the hot bony fingers of his hand gripped Oakley's wrist. His tongue crossed his parched lips.

"Oakley—thank God—thank God!"

"Easy, Rystrom," Oakley said. "I came right away, but I was kept from you. Did anyone know you phoned me?"

"No—no one knew!" The man was gripping Oakley's wrist as

though holding to life itself. "Oakley—they're killing me—killing me!"

"Easy," Oakley cautioned again.

"It's burning me up—the flame! The flame inside me! I didn't know until today what it was, but I know now—I know! It's the candle—the candle—"

"The candle?" Oakley repeated quietly.

Rystrom's thin hand flew to his chest, pounding hollowly. "It's in here—the flame—burning—burning my heart out! Oakley, for God's sake—drive them out—drive them out!"

"Tell me," Oakley said quietly, "about the candle."

Rystrom could not have heard. A frenzy was gripping him. He spoke in quick, cracked tones. "They're killing Jaeger, too! Stop them! Destroy it—destroy it! The Monad—"

"The what?"

"The—Monad!"

SUDDENLY Rystrom sagged back. His head melted into the pillow; his jaw sank; his lids drooped partly over those ghastly protruding eyes.

Oakley's fingertips pressed the thin wrist and he stood a moment unmoving. At last he straightened and said: "Not a living mummy, Archie. A dead one."

Brixey swallowed. "Dead?"

"Dead."

Brixey took a quick step toward the door. "We've got to get out of here—we really have!"

"Oke," said Oakley succinctly. But he paused by the bed-stand. On it was an array of medicine bottles. He was removing the cork from one of them when a new sound stiffened him. A latch had clicked down the hall.

Brixey exclaimed: "The nurse is coming back!"

A swift glance showed Oakley no other door leading from the room. The window was far above the ground. He strode quickly to Brixey's side; and Brixey gasped as he opened the door and stepped out.

Oakley walked directly toward the nurse—and past. She stopped short in the middle of the hall; her mouth opened and a squeak issued from it. Brixey swung along beside Oakley fumbling for his monocle. "Good night," he said affably.

A shriller noise squeezed from the nurse's throat as they hurried by. Once at the head of the stairway, Oakley bounded. He went down the flight in three leaps. At the bottom he paused an instant, hearing a rustling noise beyond.

In the living room Estelle LaSalle had been moving toward the entrance foyer. The cry from the nurse had stopped her short. As Oakley slid out of sight she called: "Miss Benson! What's wrong?"

"Two men!" shrilled from above. "Two strange men!"

Oakley stepped into the study, tugging Brixey after him. As he moved he heard the sharp rasp of a door buzzer. Estelle LaSalle did not appear from the living room, but the quick sound of her mules slipping across the floor told Oakley that she was answering the summons.

"Let us," said Oakley quietly, "depart."

A spread of the legs and a duck of the head took Oakley through the open window of the study. Brixey melted out behind him. They paused, hearing gruff voices. Oakley risked a second to step to the corner of the house and peer past. He turned back to say, "The police have arrived, Archie," and at that they ran.

When they had leaped the fence, they darted along the outside of it, noting with satisfaction that no squad-car patrolmen were hovering about the roadster. Evidently it had not been spotted. Oakley was behind the wheel and starting up when Brixey slid his long length over the opposite door.

And as the roadster slinked lightless around a bend in the road, Oakley spoke one word—"Murdered."

CHAPTER TWO

WARNING IN RED

OAKLEY drove past the banner-flung facade of the celebrated Grauman's Chinese Theatre, swung into the parking space, left the car there, and entered an office building.

Behind a door labeled simply *Secrets, Inc.*, he found Miss Charmaine Morris—his other assistant—pert, blue-eyed, with hair of a blonde redness which wreathed softly about a beautiful face. She sat with sleek pumps tucked contentedly beneath her chair and answered, to Oakley's, "Cherry, darling, Oke greets you"—"I thank you very much."

She followed into the inner sanctum; watched Oakley throw off topcoat and hat and stride into the adjoining record room while Brixey sprawled horizontally in a modernistic easy chair. When Oakley reappeared her rich red lips bunched in a pout.

"From the expressions on your faces, gentlemen," she said, "I see very little chance of my getting treated to a hamburger sandwich tonight."

Oakley had a photograph in his hand. He flipped it before Brixey's eyes, and Brixey gazed upon the likeness of a healthy, stalwart man of forty-odd.

"Who's that?" Oakley asked.

"I haven't the foggiest," said Brixey.

"That's the gentleman you saw die in bed tonight. This photograph was taken only a year ago."

"Rystrom?" Brixey sat up. "Impossible!"

"Rystrom," Oakley affirmed, seating himself behind the desk. "Something devilish happened to that man. God, what a change!"

Cherry Morris nodded despondently. "No hamburger sandwich tonight."

"But what can it be, Oke?" Brixey inquired. "What got him?"

"Suppose we check back on what happened to us," Oakley suggested. "A little more than an hour ago I got the call from Rystrom begging me to come. We went. We met Miss Estelle LaSalle, Rystrom's niece, and she gave us pause—plenty of pause. Did she know Rystrom had phoned me?

"Perhaps not. If not, she acted in good faith. If not, Rystrom had managed to get out of bed and to the telephone in the upper hall secretly, as he told me. But perhaps he only thought he'd done it secretly. Perhaps Miss LaSalle saw him. If she knew of the call, she had some deliberate reason for keeping us away from Rystrom. Right?"

"Very right," said Brixey.

"We come now to the interesting phenomenon of a young lady with beautiful legs crawling out a window carrying what seemed to be two gilt picture frames. We didn't see her face, but we can be sure she is no common crook. Who was she, and why did she, and what were they? Ideas, Archie?"

"No ideas," said Archie.

"Rystrom was desperate, certainly. He spoke of a candle. He spoke of a flame inside burning him up—that may have been figurative. The man's mind may have been affected, yet it seemed clear. Then he spoke of the Monad. What, Archie, is a Monad?"

Brixey brightened. "At last my education becomes of some practical use! I can tell you exactly what the Monad is—more properly, the great Chinese Monad. It is a diagram of the Great Extreme. It was evolved in the Eleventh Century by the philosopher Chou Lien-hsi. He used it to illustrate a philosophy, a dualistic system, involving the great extremes of Yang, or Light, and Yin, or Darkness. There's a lot more to it, but it had to do originally, of course, with eternity."

Oakley sighed. "I shouldn't have asked you," he said.

Suddenly from the outer office came the click of a latch and the slam of a door. Cherry whisked into the reception room, closing the door after her. Oakley sat in thought as a booming voice penetrated.

"Oh, yes, I'm going to see him, all right!"

"Oh, no," came Cherry's firm answer, "you're not!"

THERE was a clatter of the knob, and the door swung open, disclosing Cherry backed to the sill. Facing her was a huge mass of brawn, bull-necked, bulldog-shoed, impressively gruff—Detective-Lieutenant McClane from police headquarters.

"Observe, Archie," said Oakley quietly, "what happens when an irresistible force meets an immovable object. Cherry! There's blood in his eye. Stop risking your precious life and let him in."

Cherry stepped aside with an indignant toss of her head, began powdering her patrician nose. McClane laid heavy feet on the floor on the way to Oakley's desk. He leaned across and glared. "How would you like," he asked, "to get pinched?"

"I shouldn't care for it," Oakley confessed.

"Too bad. Because it's due to happen—and damn soon, too!"

Oakley looked startled. "Not really! What for?"

"For burglary, technically known as illegal breaking and entering. To make it more impressive, we'll add grand larceny. What did you do with 'em?"

Cherry Morris stopped rouging her luscious lips. Archibald Brixey sat up very straight. Oakley took a breath.

"McClane, are you serious?"

"No—it's only a joke. Like hell! What did you do with 'em?"

"With what?"

"With the couple of old manuscript pages you stole from Rystrom's house tonight?"

Oakley sat back and teetered. Archibald Brixey rose. "Please excuse me," he said, moving toward the door. "I've got to see a dog about a man."

McClane's huge hand clamped on Brixey's arm. "No, you don't. Both of you are in on this and I wouldn't be surprised if your dazzling red-head is an accessory. You crazy shamuses go too far!"

Brixey's muscles tightened. He detached himself from McClane's clutch so deftly that the big detective jerked a hand toward his holstered service gat.

"Don't," said Brixey, coldly, "do that again."

Oakley snapped out: "What the devil are you talking about, McClane?"

McClane thrust out a belligerent jaw. "Burglary, I told you! I don't know what the hell you're up to, Oakley, but the goods are on you."

"Explain," Oakley suggested.

"You tried to get into Rystrom's place with a fake story about a telephone call. Failing that, you opened a window. Estelle LaSalle saw you the first time, and the nurse saw you the second. The description she gave fits you perfectly. What's more, one of the squad-car men saw your roadster and was going toward it when you hopped in and sneaked away. Is that evidence or is that evidence?"

"It's mock-turtle soup," Oakley answered.

"It's evidence," McClane insisted literally. "You were in that place illegally. At the same time a couple of framed what-you-call-'ems disappear. Two and two make four. Suppose you tell it to the skipper."

Oakley smiled. "I thought," he said, "we were friends."

"Your mistake. I'm a dick and you're a shamus. Dicks and shamuses are never really buddies."

"I've helped you crack half a dozen tough cases," Oakley retorted with an impatient gesture, "and now you come in and try to pinch me on an absurd charge. Be yourself. Look here. I went to Rystrom's place because he called me and asked desperately for help. I was not permitted to see him. If I did go back later for the purpose of seeing him—"

"You admit it, then!"

"I admit nothing except that I'm wasting time talking sense to you.

If I did go back, any illegal entry I committed might be excused in the light of the fact that Rystrom is now dead—and murdered."

McClane's cigar dangled. "Murdered?"

"You get it," Oakley remarked wryly. "Why the hell aren't you working on that angle instead of puttering around here? Get Rystrom's medicine bottles and have the stuff in them analyzed. Fog the medical examiner into making an autopsy. Take your brains out of the frigidaire and thaw 'em."

McCLANE gulped. "Is that straight?" Then, "No, you don't. I'll look into that, but you can't throw me off the track that easy. You snitched those framed dinguses out of Rystrom's place tonight and you're trying to pull the wool over my eyes by springing this—"

"I did nothing of the sort!"

McClane shrugged, slipped a document from his pocket, and laid it on the desk.

"John Doe warrants," he said.

Cherry Morris looked dismayed and said, "Oh, Oke!" Archibald Brixey lowered one eyebrow threateningly. Oakley did not move.

"Ever hear," he asked McClane, "of false arrest?"

"This is no—"

"I've got a reputation to protect, McClane. One pinch would ruin it. If you want to go through with it, Oke—but I hope you've got plenty of money in the bank, because you're going to need it."

"Money in the bank?"

"To pay for heavy damages for false arrest and defamation of character. I'll do it, McClane—I promise you. I'll sue you for everything you own, down to your last shirt, and get it. Maybe you'd like to think it over."

McClane's teeth dug into his cigar. "It's a bluff," he declared.

"Is it? Want to find out? It might be expensive."

McClane growled, picked up the warrant, and slipped it into his pocket. He tramped toward the reception-room door and paused, glaring back.

"Smart guy," he said, leveling a blunt forefinger, "this time I'll take a chance and let you off, but I'm warning you. You can't trifle with the law. You can't break into houses and—"

"I know, I know," Oakley interrupted wearily. "One slip and you'll have the pleasure of heaving me into the jug. Skip it."

"Hrrr!" said McClane.

He tramped out. When the outer latch clicked, Cherry Morris guided her shapely feet toward Oakley's desk.

"Oh, Oke, he meant that! You've got to be careful!"

Oakley shrugged. "The case is McClane's now. Rystrom—my only connection with it—has died. We might," he suggested, eyeing Cherry, "go out and get that hamburger sandwich."

"Swell!"

"So—"

The telephone clattered. Oakley answered—and the voice that came over the wire was husky and strained.

"Yes, Oakley speaking," the investigator said. "Who's calling?"

"Jules Jaeger. Mr. Oakley, I've got to see you—at once—urgently!"

Jules Jaeger.

Oakley knew the name as that of one of the most successful directors on the Greater Classics lot. Of French extraction, he had achieved a few outstanding pictures since his appearance in Hollywood. Oakley remembered him as a dynamic, nervous man; but his voice seemed tired and worn.

"See me?" Oakley asked. "Why?"

"I can't tell you over the phone," Jaeger said hastily. "I am a friend of Robert Rystrom's. Tonight he telephoned me—"

Oakley sat up. "Telephoned you—Rystrom—tonight?"

"Yes! He was like a crazy man. He told me he was dying. Urged me to engage you—said you can be trusted completely—that you're the best private detective in Hollywood and—"

"Engage me—why?"

"I—Mr. Oakley, I am an ill man. I am suffering from the same fever. I—I'm afraid—"

"What?" Oakley's hand tightened on the phone. "How long have you had it? What do your doctors say?"

"Weeks—long weeks. I am confined to my bed now. The doctors cannot help. I have things to tell you which I cannot mention over the phone. Robert Rystrom—he has made me afraid for my life!"

"I'll come, Mr. Jaeger," Oakley said firmly. "I'll come right away. Expect me."

"Yes—yes!"

Oakley frowned and rose. "No hamburgers now, Cherry—sorry," he said. "Archie, you're coming with me."

CHERRY MORRIS, wrinkling her nose with disappointment, turned away as a sound came from the outer office. Oakley pulled into his topcoat and yanked on his hat.

"Something," he said, "damn strange has—"

Cherry Morris interrupted, looking in through the partly opened door. "My hamburger recedes still farther into cosmic space," she declared. "There are two people to see you, Oke, dear. Monica Currin is one, and a Mr. Frank Gifford the other. They *must* see you and"— Cherry added it archly—"I do believe they're in love."

"No," Oakley said.

"They're not in love?"

"No, I can't see 'em. Send 'em away. I'm off."

Cherry turned back, and the result was an argument in the outer office. Oakley heard a girl's voice raised anxiously, a man's protesting one intermingling. Cherry was coolly adamant, but the altercation continued until Oakley strode impatiently toward the door.

"I'll tell 'em myself," he decided. "Come on, Archie. We've got a case connecting with Rystrom, and nothing's going to stop me—"

He opened the door, and gazed out at the couple in the reception room. The girl, Monica Currin, possessed a beauty of personality rather than facial prettiness; she was a promising young actress in the Greater Classics Studios, with stardom a certainty. The young man beside her, a stranger to Oakley, was handsome, brisk-mannered, clear-eyed and obviously angry. As Oakley opened the door they were saying together, "We've *got* to see Mr. Oakley!" and, "It's terribly important!" They broke off when he appeared on the sill, eying him expectantly.

His eyes flickered down, then up. He said over his shoulder, "We're not going just now, after all, Archie," and stepped back. "Please," he invited the couple, "come in."

His gaze dropped again for an instant as Monica Currin walked toward the desk in the inner sanctum. She was wearing trim, shapely oxfords. Her ankles were slender, carved, smooth beneath gossamer silk. Oakley had seen both shoes and ankles before—had seen them, in fact, issuing from the window of Robert Rystrom's villa.

Monica Currin, potential film star, was, Oakley felt positive as he settled behind his desk, the mysterious girl who had crawled out that window carrying two gilt picture frames.

"What," asked Oakley, "can I do for you?"

Frank Gifford leaned across the desk. "We can speak to you in complete confidence?"

"You may."

Brixey promptly retired.

"We—we want you to understand that we're here for a rather odd purpose. I hardly know how to begin, or how to put it. We scarcely know what you might do to help us but—it's been so strange—"

"What's been so strange?"

"Robert Rystrom—"

Oakley sat straight as Gifford paused.

"Yes?" he asked.

"Perhaps, Monica," the young man said, "you'd better."

THE GIRL fingered her purse with a hand on which gleamed the stone of an engagement ring. "Robert Rystrom," she began, "is my oldest and dearest friend. He gave me my start in pictures. If I ever amount to anything in films, I will owe everything to him."

"You already amount to a great deal in films, Miss Currin," Oakley said gallantly.

"Thank you, but—you must understand how much I admire and love him. He's been kind and sweet and unselfish—almost a father to me. He's utterly unlike most of the executives here in Hollywood, and I—I frankly worship him. I'm here now because I'm so worried about him."

"Why worried?"

"Months ago he became ill. At first it was thought to be overwork, but resting didn't help him. His health has failed—quickly. Lately he's been confined to his bed, and he has grown steadily weaker. He has failed so alarmingly that I'm afraid now he's—he's dying."

"What," asked Oakley, "is his ailment?"

"That's the strange part of it. It's a fever—a fever that hasn't responded to treatment. He has had it for months—it has been literally consuming him, burning him up. Doctors haven't been able to help him, for no one has been able to diagnose the disease."

"Rystrom has had competent medical advice, of course?" Oakley asked.

"The best—but he has been withering away in spite of everything done to stop the fever. Frank—Doctor Gifford—can tell you—"

"You're a physician?" Oakley asked.

"Yes," Gifford answered. "I was called on the case early, because Monica asked Rystrom to see me. His temperature was a hundred and five, had been for weeks, and wouldn't come down. His pulse and respiration were far above normal. He had lost weight at the rate of three to five pounds a week.

"I made blood tests, and found nothing wrong. I don't think this thing which has him is a disease at all. A fever, but—" Gifford shrugged. "I couldn't do anything to help. It was the most baffling case I ever tackled. I tried my best, but I was dismissed—"

"Dismissed by whom?"

"Miss LaSalle."

Monica Currin resumed. "The situation has become so strange. Estelle, you see, is Bob's—Mr. Rystrom's—niece, and lives with him. She has cared for him constantly, taken complete charge of him. She is a very strange girl and—recently she began acting in a most peculiar way. She dismissed Doctor Brice—the last specialist—and refused to let even me see Mr. Rystrom. Then she called in a certain Doctor Kox."

"Who," asked Oakley, "is Doctor Kox?"

"No one seems to know, and Estelle will not explain. I have never seen him. He is some kind of a faith healer or mesmerist or—I don't know what. But Estelle called him in as a last resort—ridiculous! While Mr. Rystrom lays so gravely ill she—" Miss Currin broke off in exasperation.

Oakley's fingertips drummed. "Well?" he asked. "You've come to me—why?"

Monica Currin opened her purse. She withdrew a folded paper from it, and held it in trembling fingers. Before she passed it to Oakley she spoke quietly.

"I found this quite by accident. It was crumpled up—had been thrown into a corner of the room, the last time I saw Mr. Rystrom. He saw me pick it up—and all at once he became frantic. He told me not to touch it—to get rid of it—and became almost hysterical. Estelle rushed in and ordered me out, blaming me for upsetting him.

I took the paper with me. I don't know what it means. Here!" she passed over the paper.

OAKLEY peered at words lettered in red on the wrinkled sheet. The strokes were tapering; each looked like a tongue of flame. It was a short message—

> There is yet time to fill your heart with faith, to achieve the glory of everlasting life, before
> ### THE CANDLE KILLS

"The candle?" Oakley asked.

"I don't know what it means," Monica Currin exclaimed. "But it's a threat—I know it is! I—I think that someone is trying to kill Bob Rystrom!"

"Kill him?" Oakley echoed quietly. "Why?"

"I don't know!"

"Who would gain by it?"

"Only Estelle, but—that doesn't make sense. Estelle has plenty of money of her own, besides her big salary from the studio. She couldn't be capable of such a thing, anyway. But I know—I know someone is trying to kill Bob Rystrom!"

"See here," Oakley said impatiently. "The only person who would gain by Rystrom's death doesn't need to—yet you suspect the man is being murdered. That doesn't tie up. Doctors haven't been able to help him, but you expect me to, somehow. What is this?"

Doctor Gifford leaned forward again. "We want you to investigate that threatening note," he declared. "We want you to investigate this Doctor Kox. Something damnably strange is going on, and we've got to know what it is. Our one concern is to save Bob Rystrom."

Oakley fingered the red-lettered note, his gaze shifting from the physician to the girl. He asked, at last, quietly: "Are you willing to let me handle this case in exactly my own way, without interference—with the understanding that it will cost you a sizable fee?"

"Certainly!"

Doctor Gifford's further answer was the quick removal of a check-book from his pocket, the scratching of his pen as he wrote. He handed over the slip and Oakley glimpsed the figures, *$1,000.*

"You are," he asked softly, peering intently at the girl, "genuinely concerned for Rystrom? You want to save his life?"

Tears came into Monica Currin's eyes. "Must I tell you again—" she began.

"No," Oakley answered, "you need not. Very well—I'm on the case. I'll report to you, so give your addresses to Miss Morris as you leave. But mind you"—he leveled a finger as the pair rose—"I handle this in exactly my own way."

"You have *carte blanche,* Oakley," Gifford declared.

Oakley nodded. "Good night," he said. He watched them as they rose uncertainly and went toward the door, Gifford's hand closing snugly about the girl's.

She was about to step out when Oakley asked so sharply that she brought up short: "Miss Currin—when were you last at Rystrom's place?"

She answered without turning. "Weeks ago."

"You mean minutes ago, don't you?" Oakley asked. "You were there tonight."

The girl turned and startled light burst in her eyes. "No! No, I wasn't."

Oakley leaned back, lips pursed. "Good night," he said again.

The girl's eyes lingered on his frightenedly until the piercing sagacity of Oakley's gaze forced them away. She caught at Doctor Gifford's sleeve, turned quickly, and hurried through the door. Oakley sat unmoving, eyebrows curving high.

Brixey came in quickly. "I say, Oke!" he exclaimed. "She lied to you about that!"

"Yes, Archie—she lied."

"Why," Brixey inquired with a frown, "did she? Why should a beautiful young movie actress sneak out of the house of the man to whom she owes her career, taking a couple of framed manuscript pages with her? What has that got to do with high fever and threatening notes? Does it make sense?"

"It does not." Oakley rose briskly as Cherry entered. "Darling, there's work for you. Get the names of all the doctors called into the Rystrom case, and go to see them. Look your most alluring, and learn all you can. I'm particularly interested in a certain Doctor Kox. Now do your stuff—and file that check, don't cash it."

Brixey was blinking. "But—Monica Currin doesn't know that Rystrom is already dead—and you didn't tell her. You know she's the girl who sneaked out of Rystrom's house with those framed things—and you didn't spring it on her."

"For reasons," said Oakley, "of my own. Come on, Archie."

Brixey hurried with him down the stairs, over to the parking space beside Grauman's, and into the roadster. The engine purred contentedly as Oakley sent the car along Hollywood Boulevard. He angled off toward Wilshire, turned west, and as he drove his eyelids drooped and his lips moved unconsciously.

"I wonder what it means."

"What what means, Oke?"

"The candle," he said. " 'The candle kills.'"

CHAPTER THREE

PAGES MISSING

THE HOME of Jules Jaeger was, like most of Hollywood, Spanish in its tendencies. It sat on a quiet street in the borderland between Los Angeles and Beverly Hills, far less ostentatious than most homes of those in the movie big-money. Oakley braked, went to the door with Brixey, and knocked.

A French maid took his card and said: "Mr. Jaeger is waiting to see you, *m'sieu.*"

They followed her up iron-railed steps, entered a front room where a man lay in bed. He had a high, bulging forehead; his face tapered, and his eyes shone unnaturally bright. At his impatient gesture a uniformed nurse retired as Oakley and Brixey took chairs. Then he strained up, his gaze beseeching.

"Mr. Oakley? This man with you?"

Oakley gestured the introduction. "He can be trusted implicitly. Now—"

Jules Jaeger leaned on one elbow, breathing rapidly. His skin was flushed and fever-dried. In his eyes a fearful light was shining.

"You must help me!"

"I'll try."

"You must help *aussi* Robert Rystrom!"

"I am afraid," Oakley said quietly, "that is impossible now. He is dead."

Jules Jaeger's breath caught. "Dead! Of the fever?"

"Of the fever—yes!"

"Mon Dieu!"

Jaeger sank back. His eyes clung to Oakley's. Oakley pulled a chair close.

"It—it is happening to me as it happened to Rystrom!" Jaeger gasped. "He withered—he aged day by day. Look!" He held up one thin, parchment-skinned hand. "It is old—horribly old. My face, my whole body—it's as though the years fly past like days!"

"Steady," Oakley cautioned.

"I am not old—not old!" Jaeger protested huskily. "I am only forty—young. But look at me—look at my eyes. My hair is turning gray, my body wasting. I am a young man—yet I am old—I am dying!"

"Certainly you're not. Rystrom was ill much longer than you have been. Perhaps, some way, we'll be able to stop this fever—"

"But the doctors—they can do nothing!"

"It is not a case for doctors, I'm afraid," Oakley reminded Jaeger. "You have had the best physicians, I suppose?"

Jaeger's dried, peeling lips formed a "Yes."

"Have you by any chance consulted a Doctor Kox?"

"No."

"Do you know anything about him?"

"No."

"What do you know about a candle—a candle that kills?"

Jaeger's eyelids fluttered. "A candle that— Nothing! What do you mean?"

"I'm not sure myself," Oakley said with a wag of his head. "Have you received any messages threatening your life?"

"No."

"Had you and Robert Rystrom anything closely in common? I mean, can you account for the fact that both you and he contracted this same strange fever?"

Jaeger breathed hard, as though gathering strength, then sighed. "We saw little of each other. The last time was in the studio dining room. He was mentally upset—I happened to be too."

"By what?"

"By this thing—this cult—called the Children of the Monad."

Oakley sat straight. "What in the world are the Children of the Monad?" he asked.

JAEGER waved a thin hand. "The picture colony—Hollywood—
it is strange. Rife with peculiar beliefs, cults, religious brotherhoods,
odd sects. The people here flock after new spiritual leaders—new-
thought addicts—rejuvenators—adherents to the power of the sub-
conscious mind. The people here are childlike—credulous."

"In such things," Oakley opined, "there may be something."

"Yes, of course. I have no quarrel with the beliefs of others, though
I myself am a sceptic. My only interest is in making good pictures—
perhaps, some day, great pictures—if I live. When interference comes
I grow impatient. Rystrom was even more impatient with upsets than
I. He was disturbed by this cult called the Children of the Monad."

"Why?"

"Just what the cult is, or how it functions, I don't know. The members
evidently meet in secret. Everything about it is secret, strange. All
that is known, to those outside, is that there is such a cult. It has a
strong fascination for some minds, for it absorbs them completely."

"Yes?"

"I am necessarily vague," Jaeger went on rapidly. "Several of my
players belong, I know—they are so absorbed that their work has
suffered. Rystrom found such to be the case, too. We were working
with actors and actresses who are semi-fanatics, full of a strange self-
absorption. It grew so bad that Rystrom had demanded of them that
they—"

"Yes?" Oakley urged.

"He learned enough, by questioning them, to be sure they are
members of the Children of the Monad. He demanded that they cut
loose from it. They refused. Instead, they tried to convert him to the
creed, talking vaguely of it, promising him new life—something of
the sort. They spoke of abundant health, unlimited energy, everlasting
youth—"

The re-lettered message found by Monica Currin flashed into
Oakley's mind. "Everlasting youth?" he inquired.

"Yes. The keynote of the belief seems to be that the Children of
the Monad live forever, and forever stay young. You can imagine how
deeply that appeals to actors and actresses who dread age and the loss
of their screen attraction. There are apparently scores of men and
women in the studios who hope to stay youthful forever by steeping
themselves in the philosophy of this cult of the Monad."

"Absurd."

"Absurd, of course—but the belief holds them so strongly that they scarcely think of anything else—they offer gifts to the priest of the cult—"

"Gifts?"

"Money is never accepted, I know that much. Only offerings of other kinds. An actress I know, for instance, presented to the cult a valuable Ming vase. I noticed one night it was gone from her home, and by questioning her I gathered that she had offered it. Things that are old seem especially desirable—"

"Old things? Why?"

"They give them up, and it becomes a sort of denial of age. Bestowing old things on the cult tends to wipe out the concept of passing time—something like that. I can't tell you more about it—I am only inferring. Robert Rystrom was angered by the whole thing. He was so impatient with the effects of the influence of the cult that he threatened to investigate it and wipe it out of existence."

"He threatened that?"

"Yes—threatened to destroy it. It was shortly after that he was taken ill." Jaeger was talking rapidly, breathlessly now. "I came to feel the same about it, just before the fever took me. I broke contracts with two actresses whom I suspected of being in the cult. I warned all others that I would do the same to them unless they abandoned the absurd worship. *Mon Dieu*—I defied the cult of the Monad as Rystrom did, and now I am burning up—as he burned—"

"Easy!" Oakley studied the dried, hot face of the director. "No need to—"

"Rystrom died because he opposed the cult!" Jaeger exclaimed fearfully. "I am afraid! They have some strange power that destroys men—ages them before their time—because of their refusal to believe—"

"Would such a thing," Oakley interrupted, leaning forward, "as old pages of manuscript make a desirable gift to the cult of the Monad?"

Jaeger's eyes flashed. "Old manuscripts! Yes! What do you know about them? What—"

"Rystrom had several pages, and they disappeared before he died."

"Yes—yes, he did!" Jaeger's parched lips worked. "I—I own several pages of manuscript like them! I have them now—ancient sheets of vellum written in Greek. *Mon Dieu!* I have defied the cult! Does it mean—does it mean I'll die as Rystrom died? This fever—is it their way of—destroying me?"

Oakley frowned impatiently. "Believe me," he said, "I'm as anxious as you are that you go on living. I'm as anxious as you are to get to the bottom of this case. Where are your manuscript pages? May I see them?"

JAEGER elbowed higher, jerked open a drawer of a bureau sitting near the bed, fumbled out a ring of keys. He tendered them to Oakley with a hand that shook.

"They are in the library, in a drawer of my desk—the only drawer that is locked. Take them, Oakley—take them away!"

Oakley rose with the keys. "Stay here, Archie," he said, and turned toward the door.

His hand was on the knob when he stopped short. From below, shrill, ear-piercing, startling in the quiet of the house, sounded a shriek. It was a scream of fear, uttered by a woman.

Oakley snapped into the hallway and bounded to the stairs. His hand swung toward the automatic holstered under his arm as he spun about to see the French maid backing out of a dark doorway down the hall.

One hand was at her lips; she was staring wild-eyed into the gloom of the room beyond; her face was white as death.

"What's wrong?" Oakley demanded.

The maid's hand fluttered toward the door. "In there—the library— a burglar!"

Oakley's gun came into his hand as he eased toward the door, peered into the darkness. Somewhere beyond, a quick movement sounded.

Two swift steps took Oakley through the door and pressed him against the wall. He felt a draft that meant an open window.

He slid his fingers across the wall, searching for a light switch, and as he did so, called sharply: "Stay where you are!"

The crash of a gun answered him. Crimson fire darted from the darkness and a thud shook the wall beside Oakley's head. In the lightning-fast gleam he glimpsed a face—a square, tight-lipped, brutal face, framing low-lidded eyes. It was gone in an instant as Oakley side-stepped and tripped against an unseen chair.

The curtains at the windows flipped. A dark form materialized on the sill and as quickly melted away. Oakley raised swiftly, his eyes accustomed to the gloom now, and pushed at the switch he saw near the door. A warm glow filled the room.

Outside, heels were clicking swiftly over the cement pavement of the driveway.

Oakley whirled, taking in the room at a quick glance. Against one wall sat a plain desk, with one drawer wide open, and on the floor before it lay a tire-iron, abandoned. Marks on the lip of the open desk drawer told him the burglar had pried the iron into a crack to force it. The maid had evidently surprised him rifling it.

Oakley turned and was out the door as Archibald Brixey sprang to the bottom of the stairs.

"Come, Archie!" he snapped, then gasped, "Watch Jaeger!" to the maid, as he eased the entrance open and peered out.

From the street came the snarl of a starting car.

Oakley bounded to the sidewalk. Halfway down the block a light coupé was starting up swiftly. That it contained the escaping prowler seemed a certainty. Oakley's car was facing in the same direction. He wriggled behind the wheel as Brixey spilled in.

"Look!" Brixey gasped.

Near the far corner a heavy sedan was spurting from the curb, swinging toward the center of the street, almost directly in front of the speeding coupé. The lighter car jerked away to avoid the imminent collision, then sped alongside, horn blaring. Oakley's starter was growling as the crash of gun-fire sounded along the street.

"God's sake!" Oakley blurted.

Flame licked from the muzzles of guns thrust through the windows of the black sedan. The smack of lead on the coupé's shatter-proof glass mixed with the blasting of the shots. Seven crashed in swift succession. The coupé swayed crazily as it plunged ahead.

At the end of the street loomed a concrete-enforced embankment flanking car-tracks. The coupé lurched, but did not turn; it nosed suddenly into the wall with a resounding crash, a tearing of wrenched metal—and jarred to a standstill.

The black sedan darted toward it, stopped. A black figure leaped out, opened the coupé, leaned in, whirled, and raced back. Oakley was just swinging away from the curb as the black car swung around the corner and vanished with the shadow-man climbing in from the running-board.

"My word!" Brixey gasped.

OAKLEY'S foot shifted to the brake as he reached the corner. He hung to the wheel an instant, then twisted to the curb, left the motor running, while he hopped out. He sprinted to the wrecked coupé. Its left door had burst open; it was hanging wide and disclosed the driver sagging across the wheel. Oakley gripped the man's shoulders, raised him. He peered into the square, brutal face of the man who had fired at him in Jaeger's library. Red was dripping across it, from a gash in the forehead that revealed the splintered edges of torn bone.

"Nasty!" Brixey said, peering over Oakley's shoulder.

Oakley saw something glitter on the floor. He reached in, felt of it, then let it go. Evidently an automatic that had dropped from the driver's hand. The man was breathing in quick gulps. One broken headlight of the coupé was shooting skyward, and the gleam of the other against the concrete shone in the driver's rolling eyes as they opened.

"Who is he, Oke?"

Oakley's hand thrust into the inner coat pocket of the man at the wheel and withdrew a wallet. He flipped it, saw a few small banknotes, a pocket stuffed with what seemed to be folded newspaper clippings.

"Lecrone!" the man mumbled. "Lecrone!"

Oakley straightened, glancing about, his face grimly hard. Along the street, windows had lighted and doors were opening. People were looking out; some were coming out to the sidewalk; several were hurrying toward the intersection. One of them called: "Anybody killed?"

"In a moment," Brixey said, "we will be engulfed in the midst of a mob."

Oakley retorted with a snap: "We will not!" He stuffed the wallet in a pocket, ran for the roadster. Brixey, startled, swung lean legs after him. Oakley eased behind the wheel and threw off the brake as someone called: "Hey! Where're you going? Come back here!"

"Hit and run driver!" another screeched.

The roadster's motor whined. Brixey looked back as wind tore past. Oakley swung sharply into the next street, crossed back, lurched around a corner. The shouts from the wrecked coupé were repeated. Brixey settled, peering at Oakley wonderingly. "Most unpleasant," he said. "Our precipitous departure might make trouble for us, Oke, really."

"No more trouble than having to stick around answering the questions of a horde of dim-witted cops! I'm mad as hell!"

"In case you're chasing that black sedan," Brixey remarked, "it's gone in the opposite direction."

"We're not chasing any black sedans. We couldn't spot it now if we wanted to." Wilshire was looming close, and Oakley used the brake again. "I'm not so interested in finding out who killed that mug as I am in learning who's trying to make a fool of me!"

The car hesitated, swung, and dove into the traffic on the boulevard, turning toward Los Angeles.

"I'm going to corner Monica Currin," Oakley declared coldly, "and call her hand."

CHAPTER FOUR

DANGER IN VELLUM

ON VINE STREET, Oakley drew to the curb, left Brixey gaping in the car and hurried into a drug store. From the pay telephone he called the office of Secrets, Incorporated. The voice of Charmaine Morris answered almost immediately.

"Cherry, darling," Oakley said without preamble, "I want you to beat it out to Rystrom's place and keep an eye on it. Especially keep an eye on Estelle LaSalle. That woman's up to something and I want to know what it is."

"Your merest whim—"

"Any dope," Oakley interrupted, "on Doctor Kox?"

"Cherry has been trying, Oke," the girl answered, "but she must confess defeat."

"The address," Oakley demanded, "of Monica Currin?"

Cherry gave it, and he jotted it down. "Hop onto the Rystrom job right away, precious. I'll try to relieve you there later," he concluded. "On your way."

"My relief will come," answered Cherry as she hung up. "When you can take time out to buy me that hamburger."

Oakley returned hastily to the car. He swung it into Beverly Boulevard, turned west again, and drove through a residential district spotted with apartment houses. He didn't speak until he drew up before a palm-decorated doorway. "Prepare to be ungallant," he said as they climbed out.

They rode in the elevator to the seventh floor of the building, and found the door of Monica Currin's apartment. It was locked. Oakley was prepared for such things. He slipped a leather case from his pocket, a steel pick from the case, and inserted the angled implement into the key-hole while Brixey eyed the corridor anxiously.

"Burglariousness," he commented, "seems to be the fashion."

Oakley straightened, turned the knob and stepped in. He clicked on the lights and found a modernistically furnished feminine room, tables littered with movie magazines. A bedroom connected, and Oakley went into that. The air was scented, the lights soft, the bed satin-spread.

Brixey fidgeted. "May I ask your purpose, Oke?"

"Information," Oakley answered shortly as he looked around the apartment.

He opened doors, found closets and a bath, learned that only two rooms comprised the apartment. He pulled open the drawers of a dresser, found numberless pairs of silk stockings, gossamer underthings, filmy pajamas. Brixey's interest in the search deepened. "Lovely!" he declared.

Oakley pushed hands deeper into the foamy garments. "Ah!" he said, and straightened.

He brought out a brown, wide-necked bottle which bore no label. It contained scores of capsules filled with yellow powder.

Brixey looked uncomfortable. "Ladies," he said, "have some secrets gentlemen shouldn't know about."

Oakley's head wagged. "If this were medicine Monica Currin was taking," he said, "it wouldn't be hidden in the rear corner of a bottom drawer."

"What else could it be?"

Oakley didn't answer, but removed an envelope from his pocket and dumped a dozen of the capsules into it. He slipped the envelope into his pocket, corked the bottle, and returned it to its hiding-place. Then he closed the drawers and looked about.

"We'll have it analyzed," he said.

HE STEPPED back to the closets. On the high shelf of one of them suitcases were sitting—lightly constructed airplane baggage. Oakley lifted one, shook it, found it empty, shook another, and heard a sliding, rattling noise.

He brought the case down, opened it on the bed, and straightened with satisfaction. "That," he said, "removes some doubt."

In the suitcase were two gilt picture frames. Beneath their glasses lay time-stained parchment-like paper covered with symbols unintelligible to Oakley. He studied them, noted their apparent age, and glanced at Brixey.

"Greek," said Brixey. "Written in ancient Greek."

"How about a translation?"

Brixey smiled. "The King James version is an excellent one," he answered.

"The King James—" Oakley broke off in amazement.

"It's a page from the New Testament, Oke."

"My God! Isn't there any sense to this thing at all? We started out with a Chinese symbol and now we're in the middle of a Greek version of the Bible!"

"It's a muddle," Brixey said. "But, still, these manuscript pages must be very valuable, because they're very old."

"That doesn't explain," Oakley declared, "why a promising young actress stole them out of the home of her best friend and benefactor. It might explain why that crook broke into Jaeger's house after Jaeger's pages, but—"

Oakley paused abruptly and Brixey gasped: "We're caught!"

A key was clicking in the lock of the living room. Someone was in the hall, about to enter. Oakley moved quickly to the communicating door as the outer one opened.

A girl came in first—Monica Currin. She paused suddenly, eyes widened at Oakley. Behind her appeared Doctor Frank Gifford. He, too, brought up short, staring. Oakley smiled and Brixey nodded gravely.

"Good evening," he said.

"How did you get in here?" the girl blurted.

"I picked the lock," Oakley confessed. "If a certain police detective I knew were here, he would say that I committed illegal breaking and entering."

Frank Gifford stepped past the girl quickly. "What's the idea?" he demanded. "We retained you on an important case and next we find you prowling about Miss Currin's apartment! Are these your methods?"

"These," Oakley agreed wryly, "are my methods, depending on circumstances. I came here to learn things, and I have. I want to learn more."

Monica Currin was still wide-eyed, frightened. Doctor Gifford advanced to Oakley pugnaciously. "Miss Currin didn't retain you for any such purpose as this. You're off the case. I'll stop payment on the check."

"The check," Oakley answered, "will be returned to you promptly. I'm glad you said that. It opens the way for me. I want to know why Miss Currin turned burglar tonight."

"I didn't," the girl gasped.

Oakley gestured. "I saw you. You carried two old manuscript pages from Rystrom's home tonight, and you hid them in your closet. Then you came to me with a bedtime story about being worried about the man you'd just robbed and—"

"It's true!" the girl protested. "I'm frightfully worried! I'm terribly distracted because—"

"You don't know yet," Oakley interrupted, "that Robert Rystrom is dead?"

Monica Currin recoiled, one white hand flying to her red lips. She uttered a breathy "Oh!"—an exclamation of genuine anguish. Doctor Gifford turned pale and stared.

"Dead," Oakley repeated, "and murdered?"

"For God's sake!" Gifford blurted. "What the hell are you trying to do to her, Oakley?"

MONICA CURRIN sank into a chair, eyes brimming with tears. "It—it's all right, Frank," she whispered. "After all, we—we expected it." Her hands formed into fists as she strove to control herself. "What is it," she asked Oakley quietly, "that you want to know?"

"Are you ill, Miss Currin?"

"Ill?" she repeated. "No."

"You're not taking any medicine? Haven't you any in this apartment?"

"No."

Oakley's face tightened. "I'll let that go," he said. "But I'm going to find out right here and now why you stole those manuscript pages from Rystrom tonight, then came to me and lied about not having been at his house."

The girl said quickly: "I'll tell you."

Doctor Gifford still faced Oakley belligerently, and Brixey kept a wary eye on him. Oakley went to the girl.

"See here—I don't want to be hard on you, but you've placed me in a damned unpleasant situation. It appears to me that you've tricked me, and the consequences have not been happy. Well?"

"I did go to Bob's house tonight," Monica Currin admitted, her chin firm and high. "Estelle had refused to let me see him—and I couldn't be put off any longer. I had to get in without her knowing it, and I was desperate enough to—to go in through a window."

"Yes?"

"I went to Bob Rystrom's room. It was horrible to see him like that. It was tonight I found the paper on the floor—the one I gave you saying, 'The candle kills.' He became so upset that Estelle heard us. She came in—she ordered me out—forced me to leave."

"But you went back?"

"Yes. I went back to the window, after she thought I had gone—I was so anxious about Bob. Estelle was in the library—with a man— the man I told you about—Doctor Kox. I heard her call him by name. Then I caught a glimpse of him. He is a large man, partly bald, with a full face and piercing black eyes. There is something terrible in those eyes—almost hypnotic. He was peering at Estelle and she looked terribly frightened—her face was flushed, and she was trembling. Doctor Kox was saying, 'The end is coming—because he will not believe.'"

"Yes?"

"She said, 'He can't die—he can't. You've got to save him!' Doctor Kox said to her, 'The life-force has become the death-force for him because he has defied it. We can only hope.' Estelle was pleading. She said, 'What can we do—what can we do?' and he answered, 'Perhaps a gift—'"

"Yes?"

"Then she turned and looked at the framed manuscript pages hanging on the wall. Doctor Kox said, 'Let him deny the illusion of Time by offering those symbols of age to the flame of the candle.'"

"The candle!" Oakley exclaimed.

"Yes. They began to take them from the wall and just then the Japanese servant came. He handed Estelle a card. Doctor Kox saw it, too. Estelle went into the living room. Doctor Kox took the framed pages off the walls, put them under his arm, and began to leave the room—but he turned back, suddenly, and replaced them. He listened to the voices in the living room, Mr. Oakley—and one of them was yours. The idea that a detective was in the house must have upset Doctor Kox for I heard quick steps and saw his shadow cross the wall and vanish through a door which led to the rear of the house. It seemed as though he wanted to leave without being seen. I—I was so worried. I knew that Bob Rystrom had paid a large sum of money for those two pages of old manuscript—they were precious to him. My only thought was to save them for him. I went back into the room, and took them."

"And brought them here—to save them for him? Don't you know that technically that was a crime?"

"I didn't think—"

Oakley leaned closer. "Are you," he asked quietly, "a Child of the Monad?"

The girl looked startled. "What? No, of course not!"

"Is Estelle LaSalle?"

"I don't know. She is so strange. It is possible that she is, but—"

"Do you think she killed Bob Rystrom?"

"No, no—I couldn't accuse Estelle of that! She loved Bob Rystrom dearly, was deeply concerned for him. She spent days and nights on end, caring for him. Why—why would she do such a horrible thing?"

Oakley straightened. "I don't know," he said. "But I'm positive that Rystrom was murdered—and behind that murder, somehow, is this cult called the Children of the Monad."

IN THE BEDROOM the telephone rang. Oakley turned as Doctor Gifford moved toward the door. He touched the doctor's arm quickly and said: "I'll take it."

The instrument sat on a table beside the bed. Oakley lifted the receiver. "Yes?"

"Oke!" came over the wire.

"Cherry! What in the world—"

"I thought I'd find you there. Listen, Oke! I've been watching the

Rystrom place the last few minutes. Estelle LaSalle is there. A man just went into the place—a large, fattish-faced, bald gent."

"Good work! That was Doctor Kox! I've just had his description from Monica Currin. It seems she has seen him. Keep your eyes on things there a while longer. I'm coming right out."

He left the telephone quickly and in the next room paused, eyeing Doctor Gifford and Monica Currin speculatively. "Against my better judgment," he said, "I'm inclined to trust you two. But you've got to be careful. The police are looking for those two stolen manuscript pages. It wouldn't be so pleasant for you if they found them in your possession. It would be still less pleasant if they found them in mine. Better get them out of sight."

The girl rose quickly, stepped into the bedroom, and took up the framed pages. She returned them to the suitcase, replaced the case on the closet shelf. All the while Oakley eyed Doctor Gifford.

"As a medical man," he suggested, "you might know of some poison which would kill a man as Rystrom was killed."

"No!" Gifford exclaimed. "I know of nothing of the sort. I've done research on it, trying to match Rystrom's symptoms with those produced by known poisons. None tally exactly. I know nothing—"

"Let it go," Oakley interrupted. He moved to the door. He grasped the knob and was just about to turn it, when a knock sounded on the panels. Oakley paused, frowning; then he swung the door wide.

"Hell!" he said.

Just beyond the sill loomed the great hulk and scowling face of Detective-Lieutenant McClane.

"I thought so!" McClane growled.

"Do come in," Oakley remarked, "and have a cup of tea."

The big detective stepped in. He closed the door and stood backed against it. His gaze shifted suspiciously, came back to Oakley, and sharpened.

"I was a damn fool to let you off the first time," he asserted. "This time I won't."

Brixey stepped forward frowning. "See here—"

McClane grunted. "You two make an easy pair to spot. You were seen beating it away from the auto wreck on San Vicente. Beating it away from a guy who'd been shot in the head—murdered."

Oakley's eyebrows leveled. "All right. So what?"

"I put a squad call out, and one of the radio cars spotted your roadster outside here. The elevator man told me the rest. You've got some telling to do—to the skipper."

"Don't be a damn fool all your life, McClane!"

"I was a damn fool before, for letting you go, but not this time. I can still add two and two. Maybe Grubby Grube wasn't working with you, but anyhow you collected the two manuscript pages he stole out of Jaeger's, didn't you?"

"Grubby Grube? Talk sense!"

"I'm talking sense! Grubby Grube is the dead crook you left in that car, the guy who broke into Jaeger's place and grabbed the two manuscript pages out of the desk. Whether you had Grubby working for you or not, you collected those two pages belonging to Jaeger just as you grabbed the pair belonging to Rystrom. I've got it all, Oakley."

Out of the corner of his eye, Oakley saw Monica Currin's hand raise to her throat. She started to say, "He didn't—"

OAKLEY cut her off. "Just what," he asked, "about those manuscript pages? What are they? What'll you do about 'em?"

"They're plenty valuable—plenty—and you know all about it. You know the stake's at least half a million, Oakley—otherwise why would you go about busting into people's houses and stealing 'em? You must've got the lead on 'em soon after Gentleman Gus Geist bumped himself off when we cornered him—"

"Gentleman Gus Geist?" Oakley repeated. "You're talking in riddles. I still want to know what you're going to do about 'em?"

"I'm going to heave into the jug," McClane answered grimly, "the party that stole 'em."

Another sidewise glance and Oakley saw Monica Currin standing pale and frightened.

"Look here, McClane," he said. "I've got no time to waste with you, but I want to get this straight. Who in hell is Gentleman Gus Geist? And where does he fit into all this?"

"One of the slickest international thieves in the business, as you well know, Oakley. He's the bird who stole the Codex in the first place—"

"Codex?"

"And having stolen it," McClane went on heavily, "found himself with a white elephant on his hands. Worth more than half a million, and he couldn't do anything with it. So he worked his way here to Hollywood, split the Codex up and peddled it around page by page to thirty or more people, in order to scatter it, so it wouldn't be located—"

"You mean Gentleman Gus Geist is the one who sold these manuscript pages to Rystrom and Jaeger in the first place?"

"Why ask me when you know already?" McClane demanded. "What you probably don't know, though, is that Geist couldn't keep his fingers still, and we got a blackmailing angle on him, ran him down, and cornered him, and he upped and shot himself through the bean. Which left Grubby Grube, his partner, the only one knowing where the pieces of the Codex were scattered. Right, Oakley?"

"If you say so, McClane. This is all news to me, you know."

"Like hell! So you must have connected somehow with Grubby Grube—or maybe you didn't. Anyway, you found out about the Codex and your fingers began to itch. You couldn't buy the pieces up, and so you planned twenty or thirty robberies in order to get hold of 'em. Being a shamus, you would work it neatly—like going to Rystrom's tonight on a fake call."

"It wasn't a fake, McClane."

"A fake call, meaning to grab the two manuscript pages while you were there. If you weren't actually working with Grubby Grube later tonight, you had him spotted, and you followed him while he led you to another place and where more pieces of the Codex were. Jaeger played into your hand unconsciously tonight by calling you to his house, and when you spotted Grube getting away with a couple more of the pages, you beat it after him, and plugged him through the head, grabbed the pages—"

"Plugged him!" Oakley gasped. "McClane, you're crazy!"

"So you don't know anything about it?" McClane inquired. "Maybe you weren't even anywhere around that car of Grube's when it crashed a little while ago?"

"Maybe not."

"Aw, well," McClane said. "We'll soon have it all settled. Because I found Grube's gun in his car, see. And I saw a couple of fingerprints on it that don't look like Grube's. Those prints're being brought out now. We work fast, Oakley. Let's go down to headquarters and see if those prints match up with yours."

A CHILL passed through Oakley. He remembered that he had seen Grube's gun on the floor of the coupé and had touched it. Fingerprints! They would match up with his, certainly.

"And just to make it regular," McClane declared, "I'll take your rod and search you before we leave."

The chill in Oakley's body grew sharper. He had in his inside pocket the wallet belonging to Grubby Grube. He felt its weight against his body all at once, as though it had suddenly become a thing of lead. Once it got into McClane's beefy fingers—

McClane reached. He took hold of Oakley's coat and his hand slid toward the inner pocket.

"Don't!" Oakley snapped.

McClane paused. "I remind you, shamus, that the charge is no longer burglary. It is now—murder."

His hand reached deeper.

Oakley stepped back quickly. His lips were thin-pinched, his eyes narrowed. He gave McClane a shove that heaved the big dick toward the bedroom door. Archibald Brixey went into action at the same instant—a sharp, breath-taking tackle that propelled McClane through the door.

Monica Currin cried out faintly as Oakley grabbed the door shut. The key creaked in the lock. McClane's fists hammered on the other side.

"Let me out of here!"

"We're very sorry," Brixey said, "that we must decline."

Oakley turned quickly to Monica Currin. "Don't tell him you've got those two pages of Rystrom's!" he whispered. "If you do, he'll drag you to headquarters and grill hell out of you—he's like that. Let him stay in there a while. I'm taking the key!"

McClane was still hammering.

Oakley looked grimly at Brixey, hurried from the apartment. Past the elevator shaft, he began running down carpeted flights. Brixey legged beside him breathlessly.

"Oke, the telephone's in that bedroom! He'll have every radio car in town looking for us within a minute!"

"You're telling me!"

Oakley raced through the foyer of the building into the street. Brixey scrambled into the roadster beside him as he slipped under the wheel. The motor rushed, the wheels spun. They swerved past a corner, and headed west on Wilshire.

"After all," Oakley said, "Cherry's expecting me, and I couldn't disappoint *her.*"

CHAPTER FIVE

THE TRAIL LEADS HOME

OAKLEY angled off Wilshire almost at once, shifted to Santa Monica Boulevard, and presently was following a one-lane road through Beverly Hills. His wary glances about disclosed no radio cars on his trail so far. Suddenly he turned again, winding up a hill toward the Rystrom estate.

"Oke," said Brixey plaintively, "am I stupid, or don't you know what this is all about, either? Of course, it's obvious that some other crooks have learned all about this Codex and are trying to get hold of it, and we have made ourselves the goats. But this Doctor Kox and the Children of the Monad are behind it. Though that doesn't account for the name Grube uttered in the car, which was, as I remember it, Lecrone."

"Doctor Kox," nodded Oakley, "is our man."

As Oakley turned around the next bend, a heavy black sedan shot past. He gave it a glance—and his foot shot to the brake pedal. He was slowing when the sedan swerved out of sight. Then, almost at once, a light roadster appeared ahead of Oakley's, its headlights shafting. It slammed to a stop and from its open window a head appeared.

"Oke!" a girl's voice called.

"Cherry!"

She rolled her roadster closer. "That's Doctor Kox in the sedan— he just left!"

"Go after him, Cherry! Stick close!"

Promptly the girl's roadster spurted. It swerved away around the bend behind Oakley. He stepped on the accelerator and climbed the slope, searching for a chance to turn the long car end for end. "Now, we'll join the parade," he said as he swung into sight of the Rystrom villa.

He was twisting the wheel to nose into the driveway, in order to turn around, when a pair of bright headlights appeared beside the villa. A car was coming toward the gate. Oakley promptly straightened the wheels and shot ahead. Brixey twisted back, peering, as the other car, an expensive coupé, trawled into the road.

"In that car," he announced, "is the alluring Miss Estelle LaSalle."

"We'll leave the other car to Cherry," Oakley decided, "and watch the girl."

Estelle LaSalle's car was rolling down the slope; it passed out of sight. Swiftly Oakley backed into the driveway, turned and eased after it. He gave the girl a long lead.

The sedan and Cherry Morris's roadster were both out of sight. Estelle LaSalle's coupé turned at Santa Monica Boulevard, heading toward Los Angeles. Then it turned again, this time swinging into Hollywood. Presently they passed the Roosevelt Hotel on the right, and Grauman's on the left.

Suddenly Miss LaSalle's car swung to the curb. "My word!" said Brixey.

The girl had slipped from the wheel; she was hurrying into the entrance of the building which housed Oakley's office. Oakley promptly parked behind the coupé. He strode swiftly into the lobby, heard an elevator grinding in its shaft, and bounded up the stairs. On the third landing he came to a stop, facing the door lettered simply, *Secrets, Inc.*

Estelle LaSalle was knocking on it.

HE UNLOCKED the door. Light switches snapped as he led the way into the inner sanctum. He settled into his chair at the desk, waved Miss LaSalle to another, and suggested to Brixey: "The outer door."

"I'll jolly well watch it!" Brixey exclaimed.

Estelle LaSalle's beautiful face was turned full to Oakley's; her luminous eyes were wide with fear. Oakley studied her intently. "Now," he asked, "why are you here?"

She sat straight, pale, trembling a little. "I hardly know where to begin. It's so horrible—the police—asking me questions—investigating. They've taken Robert's body away—insisting on an autopsy—it's so horrible—"

"Murder," said Oakley, "is frequently horrible."

The girl went breathless. "Then you believe it, too!"

"It's a certainty."

She sat erect, silent for a moment. Then, "If—if it's true—we must do everything possible—to learn who—"

Oakley's fingers drummed. "See here. I'm sorry to press you, but"—he smiled tartly—"it's necessary. Minutes are precious. So far as investigating the Rystrom case is concerned, I'm already in it—above my head. Now you've come here to ask me to look into it—is that true?"

"Yes!"

"Why?" Oakley demanded. "What are you afraid of?"

"I—afraid?"

"Aren't you?"

"Ye-es," she confessed reluctantly.

"Afraid that you'll be involved—that the publicity will ruin your screen career?"

"Partly, but—"

"What else?"

Estelle LaSalle sat forward tensely. "Whoever is guilty of the horrible thing must be found and punished. I will go to any extreme to learn the truth and punish the guilty one. You must help me! Help me save the innocent—"

Oakley's eyes narrowed. "Who," he asked bluntly, "sent you here?"

"Who sent me?" she asked in surprise.

"Just that! You're not here of your own accord. You're not worried about yourself. It's fear for someone else that's got you by the throat. Who sent you here—Doctor Kox?"

The girl stiffened. "You know of him!"

Oakley's knuckles rapped. "Did Doctor Kox send you here?" he demanded.

"Yes," she whispered.

"Why?"

"You must understand!" she blurted. "It was I who urged Doctor Kox to try to help Robert. He did everything to try to save Robert from the fever. I believe in him—implicitly."

"Well?"

"The police would not understand. Doctor Kox is a strange man—a man of extraordinary powers—a man who has steeped himself in philosophy and knowledge beyond the grasp of ordinary minds. He must not be molested by the police—he must not! You—you must prove that he has no connection with the horrible thing that has happened!"

Oakley's forehead furrowed. "It's my opinion," he declared, "that Doctor Kox has a very direct connection with the horrible thing that has happened."

The girl half rose, her breath catching. "You can't—you can't believe that."

OAKLEY looked up suddenly as the connecting door opened. Archibald Brixey stared in, pale as his spotless stiff collar. "Oke! There's a squad car outside! They've spotted your roadster!"

Oakley waved a hand swiftly. "Keep that outer door locked!" Brixey disappeared swiftly as Oakley turned to face Estelle LaSalle again. "Look here!" he exclaimed, his eyes kindling. "I don't share your confidence in this mysterious Doctor Kox—far from it. In plain words, I think he's a crook."

"Oh, no!" the girl exclaimed.

"No?" Oakley echoed. "All right. But—what connection has he with the Children of the Monad?"

Estelle LaSalle came swiftly to her feet. "The Monad!" she breathed.

"What connection have *you* with the Children of the Monad?" Oakley persisted. "Are you one of them?" As the girl stared at him speechless he repeated it grimly. "Are you?"

The moment of silence that followed was broken by another click of the connecting door latch. Archibald Brixey's pale face again looked through.

"Oke! Another squad car's joined the first—and McClane's getting out of it!"

Oakley's lips tucked in tartly at the corners. He bowed to the wide-eyed actress. "I'm afraid," he said, "I must bid you a hasty good night. Come, Archie."

The girl's startled eyes followed him as he opened a door in the side wall. He clicked a switch that brought a glare down upon rows of green filing cabinets lining the walls, cabinets packed so closely that even the single window in the rear was blocked.

Brixey was hesitating in the reception room, but he hurried into the record room as Oakley turned away. Oakley closed the door and shot a thick bolt into its socket. He moved to the cabinet which sat in front of the window, and slid it away. At the same moment the sound of a heavy knock penetrated to the inner sanctum from the outer door.

"Oakley!" boomed the voice of McClane. "Open up!"

Oakley slid open the bottom drawer of the cabinet. From it he removed a small coil of rope. Uncurling it, he said: "I thought I might have use for this!"

As he slid up the rear window and hooked an end of the rope about a stout fastening screwed to the frame of the window, there was another loud knock from the outer door, and McClane's voice boomed again.

"Break the glass! He's in there, all right! We've got him!"

"Not quite, I hope," said Oakley.

A crash of a shattering pane, sharp and sudden, followed. Heavy footfalls tramped into the office. They came toward the door of the record room as Oakley flung one leg over the sill.

"Oakley!" McClane's voice bawled.

"Follow me, Archie," Oakley said.

He slid off the sill, went hand over hand down the rope into the court behind the building. At the whipping lower end of it he paused while Brixey descended. Side by side they crossed toward the rear of a building in which lights were shining, from which the odors of cooking emanated. It was the back of a restaurant facing on the next street.

Unconcernedly, but hastily, Oakley opened the kitchen door. Brixey followed him through while a white-aproned chef stared startled. They entered the restaurant proper, strode past a soda fountain, and stepped into the street.

"Now," said Oakley briskly, "a taxi for you, Archie." He slipped from an inner pocket the envelope containing the capsules he had found in Monica Currin's bedroom. "To Donaldson, the analytic chemist, and get him out of bed if necessary. I want a full report on this stuff, whatever it is. Also, I'll need you, Archie. Both, as soon as possible, at the Oriental Hotel. On your way!"

He stepped to the curb, flagged a passing taxi. He got in, said, "Step on it!" and as the cab spurted off, he looked through the rear window. Brixey had signaled another cab and was ducking in.

THE ORIENTAL was an unsavory hotel in the Lankershim district, but it offered Oakley reasonably secure safety from the police.

The taxi had carried him to it by a circuitous route. Now, in a shabby room, he paced the worn carpet, muttering comments of an unflattering nature about McClane.

No word had come yet from Brixey. Oakley ceased his nervous pacing and turned to the telephone. He called the number of Secrets, Incorporated, without much hope, and was pleasantly surprised to hear Cherry's voice answer.

"McClane still there?" he asked cautiously.

"Oke! It's all right! Where are you?"

"Down the rabbit's hole," he answered wryly. "What happened to you and your friend Kox?"

"Oh, Oke! He slipped me!"

"Better and better!" sourly.

"I came here right away, hoping to find you, and instead found the place full of McClane. He was raging. He grabbed me and started to take me to headquarters, talking about murder and things. He was very difficult."

"But you handled him, darling—I can tell that!"

"McClane," said Cherry pertly, "thinks I have pretty legs. And pretty hair. He began by threatening me with the electric chair and ended by trying to date me up."

"Is he still hollering for my hide?"

"Very much so. Oke, darling, I was never so worried in my life. McClane's got squad cars looking for you. He telephoned headquarters while he was here. I heard things. An autopsy has been performed on Rystrom. The verdict is—natural death, evidently due to nothing more heinous than old age."

"Old age, my hat!" Oakley snapped. "Men don't die of old age at forty."

"Nevertheless, that's the verdict. Rystrom's medicine has been analyzed and is entirely innocent. Estelle LaSalle was found here, I understand. She was questioned, and released—went home. Anything else?"

"Plenty else!" Oakley answered. "Archie and I have got to stay under cover. The rest is up to you. Most important of all I want to know about something called the Codex…. No—C-O-D-E-X. Find out what you can, then beat it back to Rystrom's and resume keeping an eye on Estelle LaSalle. Stay on that job—it's important. And call me when you get a chance. You sure nobody's listening in?"

"I don't think so."

"Don't let McClane fool you. He'll keep an eye on you, all right—for more reasons than the pretty legs and hair. Look in Number Ten File, the fifth name on the list. I'm at that place, and I'll stay here."

"All right, but Oke—I'm worried about you!"

"That," sighed Oakley, as he hung up, "is pleasant to know."

He paced the floor again. Suddenly he fished into his inner pocket and withdrew the wallet which had so nearly clinched McClane's case against him—Grube's. He unfolded two newspaper clippings and studied them. One was tattered from much carrying about, the other was newer. The first read—

CODEX DISPLAY POSTPONED

London, Eng.—The advertised addition of the Codex Sinaiticus to the British Museum's display of rare old manuscripts has been postponed.

No information as to the reason has been announced. Rumors that the precious manuscript disappeared enroute from Moscow to London have been denied.

—that and nothing more.

Oakley perused the other. In its headlines figured the name of Gentleman Gus Geist. In substance it repeated what Oakley had already learned from McClane. Geist, attempting to extort blackmail from Miss Wanda Ellis, movie star, has been sought by the police, cornered in his hotel room, and removed dead after having shot himself in the head. There was a short biography of Geist.

—international thief, extortionist, and forger wanted in half a dozen European countries. He once forged notes on the Bank of England, but escaped. At the time of the theft of da Vinci's *Mona Lisa* from the Louvre in Paris, rumor connected him with the daring crime. His presence in this country was not known prior to his unmasking by the police today, following his suicide.

The police, the item added, were looking for one Grubby Grube, known to be Gentleman Gus Geist's right-hand man. Oakley probed deeper into the wallet and found another dog-eared clipping.

Los Angeles police have been warned to watch for two crooks known as Hugo Lecrone and Wally Kohler who are thought to be hiding in the city. Lecrone and Kohler are on record as having worked a fortune-telling racket in eastern cities.

A soft knock on the door brought Oakley to his feet. He called through the panels, "Who is it?", heard Brixey's voice mumble, and opened the way. Brixey entered quickly as Oakley locked the door. "An odorous place," Brixey said.

"What about the analysis on that stuff, Archie?"

"It's in Donaldson's hands now. It'll take time. We'll have to wait. In the meantime, must we hide ourselves in this vile hole?"

"In the meantime," Oakley answered sourly, "we can't do anything else. Pause and reflect, Archie, and you will reach the inevitable conclusion that you and I are in one hell of a mess!"

AT MID-MORNING, after a restless night on a lumpy bed, Oakley was pacing the floor again. Brixey perched on a chair, fidgeting, smoking endless cigarettes. There had been no telephone call from Cherry Morris. The newspapers for which Oakley had sent out told the story of Grube's death, but there was no satisfaction in them for Oakley except that his name was not mentioned.

When the telephone clanged he leaped at it.

"I've got most of the dope you want," came Cherry Morris' voice.

"Where're you calling from?" Oakley demanded. "Sure McClane's not—"

"I am calling from what is politely called a ladies' retiring room, and I'm positive McClane isn't within earshot. He's had me followed, though, damn him. I must be losing my sex-appeal—"

"To the point, Cherry!"

"About the Codex. Here goes clear back to Eighteen Forty-four. It seems that a German scholar named Constantine Tischendorf traveled at that time through the Sinai Peninsula to a Greek monastery atop Mount St. Catherine, which is thought by many to be the place where the burning bush business happened to Moses. The Smithsonian Institute now has an observatory there.

"At the monastery, Tischendorf discovered in a wastebasket forty-three vellum leaves—pages of a manuscript. The monks had apparently tossed them aside for the purpose of lighting fires. He recognized them as fragments of an ancient Greek Biblical text."

"Is this getting us anywhere?"

"Be patient. He induced the monks to give the manuscript to the

Czar in return for thirty-five hundred dollars. It was a bargain, because the Codex Sinaiticus, which is what we're talking about, is the oldest known copy of parts of the Holy Bible and was recently bought by the British Museum from the Soviet Government for one hundred thousand pounds."

"McClane was right!" Oakley said bitterly.

"It is, you see, something. It vies in antiquity with the Codex Vaticanus. I've found that S.W. Rosenbach, the book collector, says that the price was the highest ever paid for a book or manuscript. The Soviet Government offered it to him last year for a million and a quarter. The purchase by the British Government was important enough to be announced in the House of Commons by Prime Minister McDonald. There's more to it, but that's the gist."

"Cherry," said Oakley, "I thank you. Now on to your next job— watching Estelle LaSalle. If anything funny happens—let me know."

"O.K."

Oakley hung up and peered at Brixey.

"It seems, Archie," he said solemnly, "that we are indeed into something. Those manuscript pages were destined for the British Museum, but instead got to Hollywood, of all places."

He tackled the telephone. In a moment he had connection with Donaldson, the analytic chemist. When Oakley asked, "Got that stuff figured out yet?" the drawling answer came, "Yes—just finished."

"What is it?"

"Alpha-dinitrophenol."

"Tell me," pled Oakley, "in words of one syllable."

Brixey perched anxiously on the chair as Oakley listened at the phone, mumbling while he made rapid notes. When Oakley hung up he turned and peered at Brixey wearily.

"Does it mean anything?" Brixey inquired.

"Plenty! The stuff we found in Monica Currin's room is a chemical which produces in the human body exactly the effects that killed Rystrom and are now killing Jaeger."

"Then she was tricking you? That beautiful little minx is a murderess?"

"I'm not sure of that—but listen. Dinitrophenol is a yellow crystalline powder, easily obtainable, costing about sixty cents an ounce—a blessing and a curse. A doctor and a professor at the Stanford University School of Medicine have been experimenting with it, and the results of their experiments have been published. This stuff is not generally known, but here's the dope.

"A dose of the variant alpha-dinitrophenol equal to five one-millionths of a person's weight—that would be about seven grains for a two-hundred-pounder—steps up a person's metabolism instantly to fifty percent above normal—metabolism being the process of the body of building itself up from food and eliminating waste products."

"I know—go ahead!"

"It increases energy in small doses. It also causes loss of weight at the rate of about two pounds a week without diet or exercise. It's used in some patented dopes taken by women to reduce. Larger doses—ten grains—cause profuse sweating. Fourteen grains cause a high fever, step up the pulse twenty to thirty beats a minute, the respiration up fifteen to thirty. That checks with Rystrom's chart!

"Bigger doses," Oakley continued, reading from his notes, "raise the metabolic rate so high that the victim soon dies of simply having lived too fast! And that's what happened to Rystrom. He was killed by being given heavy doses of alpha-dinitrophenol!" Oakley flung himself into a chair.

"My God!" Brixey exclaimed. And then, anxiously, "What do we do next?"

"We do the only thing we can do, Archie," Oakley answered with a sigh. "We wait—wait here in this hole while McClane does his damnedest to hook us both for murder. God help Cherry—alone on the job!"

CHAPTER SIX

THE CHILDREN OF THE MONAD

MISS CHARMAINE MORRIS, as capable as she was beautiful, had kept herself busy following Oakley's urgent orders. Succeeding, at last, in throwing off the plainclothesmen put on her trail by the tenacious McClane, she had begun the vigil of watching the Rystrom villa. During the daylight hours she had observed it from a distance; and now, as darkness closed down after an uneventful day, she approached it cautiously.

Leaving her little roadster parked out of sight around the bend, she walked to the side fence and followed it up the slope. The Rystrom villa lay enveloped in quiet gloom, its windows dimly glowing. Except for the shaded lights, there was no sign of life about it. Cherry Morris' prolonged observation, however, had assured her that Estelle LaSalle was inside.

For two hours she sat on the grassy slope before a movement near the house surprised her.

A side door opened and a girl's figure was silhouetted against the light shining from inside—Estelle LaSalle. The actress hurried along the gravel path toward the rear, and stepped into the garage. Presently the sound of a motor carried to Cherry Morris, and headlights shafted across the grounds.

Cherry sprang up and ran to her roadster. She started it, and drove carefully around the bend toward the Rystrom place. In a moment she glimpsed the expensive coupé crawling into the road. It turned east, picked up speed.

Cherry spent a moment making sure none of McClane's men had her spotted before she took up the chase in earnest. At Santa Monica Boulevard she saw Estelle LaSalle's car turn east again. It led the way into Hollywood, on through into Los Angeles. Presently another turn took the actress's car toward open country, and Cherry followed it cautiously.

The narrow paved road which Estelle LaSalle selected led through orange groves and truck farms. Soon, Cherry knew, it would climb toward Arrowhead Lake.

Presently the road became wider, the going faster. Estelle LaSalle was wasting no time. She maintained a steady, fast pace which Cherry Morris matched to the fraction of a mile. Soon the coupé took a turn that brought it onto a secluded, tree-lined side road.

In the shafting light of the coupé's headlamps other cars appeared, parked beside the road. Cherry saw Estelle LaSalle's ease off the pavement into a large parking area crowded with all manner of motor vehicles, most of them noticeably expensive. They were, Cherry saw, all grouped around a small gray-stone building which looked like a church or chapel.

Estelle LaSalle was slipping out of her coupé as Cherry prudently rolled on past. Cherry stepped on the gas, found a driveway a bit farther on, turned about, and retraced the way. Again she passed the little chapel. Estelle LaSalle was not in sight; she had evidently gone inside. Cherry drove on and a moment later pulled to a stop near a filling station on the main route. She went in, found a telephone and called the Oriental Hotel.

Oakley answered. "What news, Cherry?"

"Listen, Oke! Remember the little place that used to be known as the Cloisters Inn?"

"Do I remember it! We dined handsomely there a number of times!"

She did not, therefore, need to explain the nature of the quaint place once called the Cloisters Inn. During the post-frontier days of California it had been a small church. The amazing influx of settlers to the district had soon necessitated a larger church, which had been built. The abandoned one had been deconsecrated, and converted into a tearoom and restaurant.

SOME time ago the restaurant had failed, and the little chapel had remained closed. Cherry and Oakley, driving from Hollywood one evening for dinner, had found it boarded up tight. It had sat bleakly moldering for months in its remote location.

"It is now in use again, Oke," Cherry declared. "For what purpose I'm not sure. I just followed Estelle LaSalle to it. There are a lot of cars parked around it and there must be a hundred people inside. I'm going to try to get in and find out what's what. I've got a feeling I'm close to something important."

"For God's sake be careful, Cherry—"

She hung up, hurried back out to her roadster. She started up quickly, swung into the side road, and proceeded with heavily beating heart toward the gloomy spot where the chapel lay.

Darkness cloaked the chapel and the clearing in which it sat. No lights gleamed through its stained-glass windows; no sound came from within its time-worn walls, yet about it hung an atmosphere of secretive activity.

Another car was rolling slowly along the road ahead of Cherry Morris as she came opposite the little building. Its headlamps blinked off as it turned into the parking space. Cherry promptly switched out her own lights, twisted the wheel, and braked to a stop beside it. From the other car a woman alighted.

Cherry left the wheel and followed quietly. At a worm-eaten, oaken door in the side of the chapel the dark figure of the woman paused. There was the click of a rusty latch as the door inched open on darkness. From the lightless interior came a whispering voice.

"Who calls?"

"Eternal life beckons," the woman said.

The door opened wide; the woman vanished through it; then the latch creaked again as it closed. Cherry Morris stepped closer. Her knuckles tapped faintly—

The latch scratched again; the door inched; and the voice whispered once more: "Who calls?"

"Eternal life beckons."

The dark way opened and Cherry Morris stepped through. The musty air smelled of age and heavy incense. There was no light at all, until the unseen guardian of the door pulled aside a heavy black curtain. Then deep blue light shone through. In the space beyond, Cherry saw the woman who had just entered. She stepped past the curtains and they rustled back into place. The glowing blue light hurt her eyes, but within the curtained space she was able to see many hooks on the walls, and clothing hanging from them—women's dresses. She was alone in the blue glow with the woman who had preceded her.

That woman Cherry recognized as a middle-aged actress who had appeared often in pictures, playing society parts. She was removing her dress quickly. She glanced at Cherry Morris curiously, and Cherry, to avoid suspicion, unsnapped the fastenings of her own dress.

Cherry Morris concealed her astonishment as the actress stripped off every stitch of clothing. Stark nude, the woman hung her clothing on a hook and then, from another, took a long, white, filmy gown, resembling a toga. She slipped it on; the outlines of her body were dimly visible through it. In bare feet, erect, her face glowing, she moved past Cherry Morris, pulled aside another curtain, and stepped through. Cherry hesitated.

From beyond the curtains through which the woman had passed, now came the low, throaty tones of an organ.

Cherry Morris, clad now only in a silken slip, looked about quickly, searching for another garment such as the actress had donned; but there was none—on any of the hooks! Troubled, she hung up her dress, got her revolver, moved to the curtains, peeled them apart, and peered through.

THE CHAPEL lay beyond, its old walls illumined by a flickering yellow light. Its source was a huge flame burning in the apse—a saffron flame writhing from the wick of a gigantic crimson candle. The huge taper stood at least six feet tall against the dim windows beyond, a thing of red wax, as thick as a human body. And in its light stood a strange congregation.

They were facing the candle in the apse, fully a hundred men and women, all wearing those filmy toga-like costumes. Their heads were raised, as the organ pealed; and they gazed at the bright flame of the tremendous taper. The lilting, yet solemn strain of the music was causing them to sway from side to side, slowly; and the flame of the candle, weaving in unfelt winds, seemed to weave from side to side in rhythm with them.

Just beyond the black curtains the actress who had preceded Cherry Morris came to a pause. On a table a steaming samovar was sitting, its bowl full of a gleaming yellow liquid from which vapor rose. An attendant behind it had filled a small silver cup with the fluid and had passed it to the actress; she was drinking of it. Emptying the cup, she left the samovar, and took her place in the congregation, facing the great red candle.

Beside the apse, two black curtains were hanging and on each was a design in silver—glittering brightly in the candle light.

Cherry Morris drew back. Without one of the filmy gowns in which the strange assemblage was clothed, she dared not enter the chapel. Turning quickly, she searched again; but there was no gown. Cautiously she moved to the other curtains, peeled one back, and peered into a long, dark corridor.

At the other end of it a curtain moved. A figure appeared—a huge man clad in a flowing white robe similar to the garments worn by the congregation; differing only in that on the front of his toga was embroidered in silver thread the same circular symbol which appeared on the curtains.

His was a benign, though heavy face; his bald head was framed by tufting dark hair. He came with folded hands from the space behind the far curtains, and moved to enter the body of the chapel. His hands parted the drapes and he disappeared, while Cherry Morris stared.

Doctor Kox!

Cherry moved quickly. Noiseless steps took her along the curtained passage, toward the space from which he had emerged. She paused, listened, and peered into a room lighted by a single candle burning on an antique table. She stepped through.

From the chapel came the sound of singing voices.

Cherry looked around quickly. This curtained space was evidently some kind of an office; the table served as a desk. On the table lay a sheet of paper on which a column of figures was written. Cherry laid down her gun, picked it up, peered at it, saw that the numerals began with *1* and continued through *43*—the number of pages in the Codex Sinaiticus! Check marks stood against most of the numbers.

Cherry straightened as soft footfalls sounded behind the curtains through which she had come. The steps were coming toward her. She glanced about wildly as she saw the drapes move. Swiftly she stepped back, reached to other black drapes in the rear of the space and, finding an opening behind, moved through.

Here another candle was burning, casting its light upon myriad objects arranged on shelves. Cherry glanced at them quickly, and caught her breath. She saw old vases, pieces of antique furniture, ancient articles of silver, a worm-eaten chest. Everything visible seemed old and precious; this corner of the chapel was a veritable storehouse of priceless things. The sight held her fascinated until a voice sounded from the little office from which she had stepped.

A low voice asked: "Someone here—who does not belong?"

"Yes! One too many came in—one more than the number of gowns!"

"A convert?"

"Not without our knowing it, Hugo!"

The low voice growled. "Don't call me that here! By God, this is getting dangerous! We've got to let the rest go—and get out of here!"

"The missing pages—"

"Never mind the missing pages! We've got enough! Who's the extra one? A man—a woman?"

"A woman! She's not in the changing room now—she's not in the chapel! She's sneaked off somewhere. God, Hugo, I warned you you were going too far—"

The low voice growled again. "Shut up! Go in there! Tell them the service is concluded! Tell them the life-force is threatened—any kind of bunk you want to—but get 'em out! We're clearing out of here tonight!"

"But the woman—the extra—"

"We'll be clear of her before she can make any trouble, whoever she is!"

FOOTFALLS sounded again as the second man withdrew through the farther curtains. Cherry Morris heard a sound of breathing from close at hand. Then, abruptly, even as she recoiled, the curtains moved.

Suddenly there appeared through the drapes a huge, white hand; after it the square-chinned, bald, tufted head of Doctor Kox! And as he came into view Cherry realized with a pang of dismay that she had left her gun back on the table in the other room.

He stopped short, staring, as Cherry Morris recoiled. Her eyes widened wildly; she started to rush past him. Suddenly he lunged at her, his loose-sleeved arms groping. He enveloped her in thick arms, pressed her close to him as she struggled to free herself. One heavy hand clamped across her mouth as he pinioned her motionless; his labored breath beat into her ears. His grip crushed Cherry Morris helpless.

In the chapel the organ was still pealing. Through its trembling voice came the sound of shuffling bare feet. A man was speaking sonorously. There came a metallic sound like the sliding of curtain rings on a rod.

Thick lips muttered into the girl's ears.

"You little fool—you know the candle kills!"

Cherry Morris' slender body tensed. She opened her mouth quickly, drove her teeth hard against one thick finger of the man who held her. A gasp of pain followed, and the arms around the girl loosened. Wildly she tore away. She whirled, slapped twice, stingingly, at the cruel, fattish face. Desperately she sprang away, tearing through the curtains.

Doctor Kox shouted hoarsely.

Cherry Morris jerked to a stop. Just beyond the curtains a man was moving—a short, stocky, reckless man also garbed in a flowing circle-embroidered robe. His teeth bared when he saw her and he sprang, groping. The girl whirled desperately, half fell through the black drapes.

She found herself in an enclosed space before the apse. The black curtains bearing the silver symbols had been drawn close in front of the gigantic, flaming candle. The space in which the strange congregation had stood was blanketed away. Cherry reached for those curtains.

A quick scramble sounded behind her. Hard hands gripped her shoulders, closed around her again. A hot hand clamped over her mouth. She felt herself dragged backward. For a moment she was blinded, helpless.

Then she felt herself thrust against something, felt a thick rope whipping around her wrists. As her hands were fastened behind her, the strands were wrapped about her body. Again a rope rasped against her, binding her ankles to the thing against which she was pushed.

The two men drew away. She saw their hard faces gleaming in bright yellow light. She tried to tear herself free, and could not. She flung her head backward, peering up at the blinding light behind her. Within a foot of her eyes a gigantic flame was leaping, writhing. As though it were a thing alive, it was swinging hotly to touch her.

She was bound helpless to the shank of the huge red candle!

CHAPTER SEVEN

THE CANDLE KILLS

OKE OAKLEY, in the evil-smelling quarters in the Oriental Hotel, clamped the telephone receiver to his ear and heard the voice of Cherry Morris.

"I'm going to try to get in and find out what's what. I've got a feeling I'm close to something important."

Oakley blurted: "For God's sake be careful, Cherry—" The line went dead.

He turned to stare at Archibald Brixey. "Damn it to hell, she is onto something. Abandoned chapel in use again. It can't be anything but the headquarters of the cult of the Children of the Monad. And she's gone in!"

Brixey rose with alacrity. "I don't like this!"

"Nor I!" Oakley snatched up his coat and slipped into it. "We're not letting her tackle that alone!" He pulled on his hat. "Come, Archie!"

Oakley snapped open the door and Brixey hurried with him down the stairs into the shabby lobby. They stepped into the dark street together, peered along it. There was not a moving car in sight; no taxi was near. Oakley moved fast, toward a sedan standing a few yards away.

He opened the door, slid beneath the wheel, gestured Brixey in beside him.

The ignition key was in the lock.

"To our crimes," Brixey sighed as the car started from the curb, "we now add automobile stealing."

Oakley stepped on it. He headed from the Lankershim district through Los Angeles. He hopped red lights, swerved around corners. Finally he sped onto the highway which led, he knew, to the building which had once been the Cloisters Inn. The speedometer flickered high.

Miles clicked past. Presently Oakley's toe touched the brake pedal and the sedan creaked and bucked. A quick twist sent it shooting into a dark side road. Oakley eased the accelerator back and peered ahead. Shortly his hand touched the switch that blinked the headlamps out. "There it is!"

A car swung out of the parking space as Oakley turned into it. He stopped, sprang out, gave a glance at the departing vehicle, and decided to let it go. All around lay black, empty space. Cherry had spoken of many cars, and now there was none in sight.

With Brixey at his side, Oakley trod to the worm-eaten door at the rear of the chapel. He knocked. No answer came from inside. He pressed the latch; it was firm. Suddenly he stiffened.

From the interior of the chapel came a muffled, far-away sounding cry.

"Cherry!" Oakley blurted.

Quickly he raised the latch and flung his weight against the door. There was a thump and a creak—nothing else. Brixey seconded him; they hurled themselves together against the old wood. Again there was no headway. And again they drew themselves back, gathering all their strength, poising. They charged.

EVEN as they moved they heard the latch click as a hand inside loosened it. It was too late to stop themselves. They slammed hard against the wood, and it gave before them. Flung off balance, they spilled through the doorway, into darkness.

Instantly, out of the gloom, came a rush. Oakley's hand snatched at his armpit holster as he sprawled to the floor. A weighty body crushed down on him. Hard fingers gripped his wrist. He wrenched away, and felt his automatic torn from his fingers.

Nearby Brixey was gasping, struggling with another unseen antagonist. Oakley brought his knees up sharply, and squirmed. Hands gripped his clothing, tugging at the neck of his coat. He flung his arms back and heard a ripping of cloth as he tore away. The coat came off. He rolled, trying to rise, as the heavy figure leaped on him again.

He struck sharply, swiftly, at a dim face from which hot breath beat. A groan answered and the gripping arms loosened. Oakley's shirt ripped as fingernails tore into it. He thrust away and sprang to his feet. Out of the gloom rose a huge form loosely enveloped in white. Oakley drove fists at it savagely.

Brixey was still writhing on the floor, battling the other man.

In the ghostly blue light the white-clad figure before Oakley whirled and melted away. Dark curtains jerked aside. Oakley sprang after. He brought up with a jerk, staring at more black curtains ahead, on which silver designs were traced. Through the drapes the bulky white figure was springing.

Oakley snapped aside the figured curtains. Again he brought up short. Yellow light gleamed in the apse of the chapel—the flickering glare from the gigantic red candle. Bound to it by thick ropes, stood Cherry Morris. Terrified, she was recoiling from the swirling flame that seemed to be reaching for her with a hot embrace. The fire swung close to her glistening hair as Oakley sped ahead.

From the dark corner of the apse the white-clad figure whirled. The bald, tufted head of Doctor Kox shone in the glimmering light as he rushed; and the flame was reflected from the blade of an ancient broad-sword that swung high. The keen edge slashed down as Oakley sprang.

One of Doctor Kox's huge fists gripped at Oakley's throat as a scream tore from the lips of the girl bound to the candle. Oakley flung up an arm to ward off the blow of the sword; he caught at the thick wrist. His left hand drove savagely into the full face of Doctor Kox; he advanced, striking again—again. The leering face went lax; the white-robed form recoiled.

Oakley snatched at the hilt of the broad-sword and tore it away. He whirled toward Cherry Morris, slashed swiftly at the ropes that bound her. Her ankles came free and she sagged to the floor, calling, "Oke!"

Oakley spun. The furious face of Doctor Kox loomed like a twisted mask in the flare of candle light. Oakley raised the glittering blade. "Back up!"

He flung the weapon. It whirled as Doctor Kox cringed low, clattered ringingly against the stone wall. The white-garbed man straightened swiftly. Oakley cursed himself for having relinquished the weapon. Now he poised to leap as Doctor Kox snatched it up. Again the blade swung high as the big man leaned, his eyes glittering with a murderous light—leaned to slash.

The candle was tottering on its base as Cherry Morris shrank from it. Oakley's arm curled about the thick red shank. He swung it low, heaved its great weight into his arms, and leveled it like a battering ram as black smoke writhed from the dancing flame. Great red gobs of wax dripped from it as Oakley sprang.

The flame licked up across the terrorized face of Doctor Kox. The weight of the tremendous candle crushed hard against the thick, white-robed body. A crunching of broken bones sounded as Cherry Morris cried out sharply. Doctor Kox straightened revulsively, pinioned against the wall, as hot red wax flowed across his gown—as the candle winked out, filling the apse with thick darkness.

Oakley stepped back, lowering the candle to the floor. He heard the thud of Doctor Kox's falling body as from beyond the curtains came a call from Brixey. "This chap," cried Archie, "has ceased to fight."

Smooth, slender arms closed about Oakley's shoulders. He breathed the perfume of Cherry Morris' hair as she clung to him. Her voice was a broken sob. "Oke! You're all right, aren't you, Oke?"

Oakley pressed her close and breathed deeply. "Everything," he said, "is all right now."

IN THE LIVING ROOM of the Rystrom villa in Beverly Hills, Oke Oakley faced the unkindly McClane. In the room also were Cherry Morris and Archibald Brixey; with them were Estelle LaSalle, Monica Currin, and Doctor Frank Gifford. It was Oakley who was doing the talking.

For an hour he had directed his discourse at McClane, while McClane sat with implacable glumness and listened.

"Now," Oakley said, "you realize why I telephoned you to come here and, in a way, gave myself up to you, McClane. You know now why I wanted to talk with these two young ladies first. Do you get it?"

"I suppose so," McClane said.

"Checking back, as a summary, this is it," Oakley declared. "The two crooks we cornered tonight in what was once the Cloisters Inn were Hugo Lecrone, otherwise known as Doctor Kox, and his sidekick, Wally Kohler. Lecrone's specialty was fortune-telling rackets and the like. But his masterpiece of crookedness was the cult known as the Children of the Monad. He doped it out very neatly to appeal to the credulous movie people. The cult promised eternal youth and beauty, and they fell for it hard.

"Lecrone's way of cashing in was to accept gifts of valuable antiques from devotees as a sort of denial of age and the passing of time. Then he'd sell them, of course, and rake in plenty.

"Gus Geist and Grubby were two gentlemen of crime of another feather. You already know it was Gentleman Gus Geist who contrived to steal the Codex Sinaiticus while it was on its way from Moscow to London following its purchase by the British Museum. But he couldn't dispose of it intact so he worked his way to Hollywood and sold the separate Codex sheets, merely as old manuscripts, in order to get a little cash out of it and get rid of the thing. Men like Rystrom and Jaeger bought the pages in good faith, not knowing their real nature. In this way the Codex became scattered in the homes of movie people.

"Lecrone's dead, but you have Kohler's confession, so you know how Lecrone learned about the Codex when one of his devotees gave him several pages. He wanted to get the others, and did get most of them as gifts. But he had to have the whole thing, in order to preserve its full value. The British Museum has tried to keep the theft of the Codex secret, but there must be a reward offered for it. Maybe Lecrone was after that.

"But trouble developed. Men like Rystrom and Jaeger began to fight the cult. That upset Lecrone's plans, especially since Rystrom and Jaeger owned parts of the Codex. Lecrone found it necessary to eliminate the danger threatened by Rystrom and Jaeger.

"He took various steps. Part of the ceremony of his cult was the drinking of a certain tea before the service. This tea was merely a solution of alpha-dinitrophenol, which Lecrone, being a smart guy, used after reading about the stuff in the journal of the American Medical Association. The small doses he gave his adherents at each meeting pepped them up, made them feel swell, and deluded them into thinking they were regaining their youth. It could also be a powerful weapon.

"First he tried to induce Rystrom and Jaeger, through his adherents, to join the cult. They refused. Desperate, obsessed with the desire to reassemble the Codex, Lecrone took the next step. He stole into this house at night, unseen, and mixed dinitrophenol into opened packages of brown sugar. You have Kohler's confession explaining that. He chose the brown sugar because he learned, through Estelle LaSalle, who was unaware of his plans, that Rystrom used it on his morning cereal, and no one else in the house did. Rystrom began to develop a fever."

QUICKLY he went on. "It wasn't Lecrone's intention then to kill Rystrom, but to make him believe that the fever was due to his opposition to the cult—the life-force turning into the death-force. Age creeping up swiftly when he might have eternal youth. He came to the house, brought by Estelle LaSalle, as Doctor Kox and tried again to influence Rystrom to join. Again he failed. The only alternative then was to eliminate Rystrom altogether.

"He gave Estelle LaSalle capsules to give to Rystrom as medicine, saying they would cure the fever in time. Miss LaSalle did not know that the stuff in the capsules was maintaining the fever, not curing it. She continued to give Rystrom the stuff, desperately trying to help him. Lecrone's note—'The Candle Kills'—was a last desperate attempt to influence Rystrom and avoid the necessity of a murder—but that, too, failed.

"Rystrom's death meant danger to the cult would be eliminated, and that two pages of the Codex would come to Lecrone. Because, you know, on Rystrom's death, Miss LaSalle inherited all Rystrom's estate and it was a certainty she would turn the pages over to Lecrone as a gift, since she was under his influence."

Estelle LaSalle shuddered

"As far as Jaeger goes," Oakley continued, "you know from Lecrone's confession that he did almost the same thing—doped a white wine that Jaeger drank regularly, instead of brown sugar. The man is safe now, since he'll take no more of the dinitrophenol.

"It was Miss Currin, of course, who suspected something wrong first. She held out on me, not telling me everything, because she was unwilling to accuse Miss LaSalle without certain evidence. It was she who found in Miss LaSalle's room, upstairs, the bottle of capsules which were being given to Rystrom. She took them home, and was having some analyzed even as I was. Her chemist was slower than mine, and she was waiting for his report before making another move.

"There you have, McClane, a picture of two women both apparently guilty and neither really so. Miss LaSalle was entirely unaware of what she was doing. Miss Currin's supposed theft of the pages of the Codex was a move to protect Rystrom's property, and the presence of the dinitrophenol in her room I've explained."

"But Grubby Grube," McClane put in.

"You know that," Oakley answered. "Hard-pressed for money, it was his idea, too, to reassemble the Codex from those to whom the pages had been sold. Lacking the finesse of Lecrone, he chose burglary as his means. Lecrone got onto Grube, and knew that Grube was getting away with a few of the pages. It was Lecrone who followed Grube to Jaeger's last night, shot him, and got away with the two pages of the Codex that Grube had stolen from Jaeger's desk."

"Maybe," McClane declared.

"Go on being a damned fool, then, McClane!" Oakley snapped. "You've got it all, and you know it. Miss LaSalle must be let alone. She is suffering enough now without your getting nasty to her about it. The same goes for Miss Currin."

McClane rose and sauntered to the door. "They're all right," he said. He opened the door, started out, paused, and looked back at Oakley. "Shamus," he said, "I hand it to you!"

Oakley smiled and rose. He said goodbye to Estelle LaSalle and Monica Currin. Archibald Brixey bowed elegantly. When they left the house Cherry Morris was between the two.

"Oke," she said.

He paused and looked down into her bright blue eyes, and smiled. "Yes?"

"Let us," she said softly, "drop in somewhere and get that hamburger."